When Blood Drops Fall

When Blood Drops Fall

Kevin Patrick Smith

The Redemption Series

† Redemption lies on many paths †

Sometimes the blood of the innocent
is shed to redeem the guilty

ISBN: 978-0-9961286-0-5   Softcover
ISBN: 978-0-9961286-1-2   Ebook

www.kevinpatricksmith.com

www.whenblooddropsfall.com

To all who have ever felt
they've gone too far

To . . .

My beautiful wife Karen, your hand in mine, walking through all of life, this man could not ask for a stronger friendship or greater love.

And for my children

Always believe, imagine, create

Thank You

Karen Kollasch, Greg Gill, Paul Strahan, Cindy Covalt, Kaleah Plain, for first opening the pages, your insight, advice, and confidence.

Julene Smith, for your masterful eye and encouraging little side notes.

Kevin Patrick Smith

When Blood Drops Fall

Kevin Patrick Smith

1

And darkness fell . . .

Blood trickled down her tiny fingers and beaded into droplets, each one losing its battle with gravity as it fell from the metal table to the pool of glistening red on the floor.

A deafening sound rushed into Cain's ears. The heat was intense. A shadowy figure reached toward him, wrapping itself around him. The figure tugged at Cain's body. Cain gasped for air, wanting desperately to pull away. He couldn't move. He couldn't breathe. *No, no, leave me alone!* A flash of light fluttered across Cain's mind, then, darkness.

He awakened, startled, and lunged forward in terror, his chest slamming into the steering wheel. He felt trapped, flung the car door open quickly and jumped into the street. The humid summer air hit his body. He was drenched with sweat, his face tender, stinging. A sharp, piercing headache centered itself on the right side of his head. He hurt, all over. He slumped forward, leaning against his knees. *Another crazy nightmare*, he thought. *When will this end?* He turned his hand palm up to look at it, spreading his fingers apart, the skin tacky and fused together between them. He couldn't get the image of the little girl out of his mind.

Cain parked parallel to the cars along the street in front of Ray's house, blocking the school bus behind him. Ray yelled from the porch. "Kenny, you're gonna miss the bus! Come on!"

Cain watched as Kenny ran across the lawn toward him. *Don't worry. That bus doesn't go anywhere until I move my car.*

He stuck his head out the window, smiling back at the driver. It wasn't the first time.

Kenny ran over and opened the passenger door.

"Hi, Cain."

"Hey, buddy! You better get on that bus."

"She can wait."

"You're gonna make the lady mad."

"She's alright. I'll see ya later."

"Have fun at school!" Cain yelled as he ran off.

He watched as Kenny jumped up into the bus.

People were jockeying their cars for positions in the stop and go traffic in a slow motion race. The prize was to get to work early. It was total gridlock, car grills threw frustrated glances as taillights growled back in fiery anger.

"Be nice to live on the north side. Break free of all this craziness, retire, get an acreage, maybe something along the river," Cain said.

"Yeah? Most you're gonna afford on this pension is a travel trailer. Suppose your acreage could be the campground at the lake. You could take showers in the bathroom sink like that public intox Si picked up last week."

"I'm done with this, the traffic, the people, tired of the drive."

"Well, if you don't stop buying fine wines and those little toys of yours, you won't have a retirement. What'd you say the last one cost you?"

"They're not toys, Ray, they're collector's items. They don't lose value."

"So you're gonna part with them when you retire?"

"Eventually, if I have to."

"Uh-huh. I know you better than that."

"I've got other ideas."

"Hey, turn in here. I didn't get a chance to eat this morning."

Cain cut hard through the traffic and turned into the drive of a severely run-down fast-food restaurant, coming to an abrupt stop as a young girl scurried across in front of them. She stopped mid-driveway and piercingly gazed at Cain, then darted down the sidewalk.

"Haven't seen her for a while," Ray said.

"Heard things didn't go well with her parents after we took her in wasted that weekend."

"Shouldn't be running the streets. Guess you can't really blame the parents, though"

"I'll take two breakfast burritos," Ray told Cain. "You want something?"

"Four breakfast burritos and a coffee, black," Cain spoke into the air toward the menu sign. "You want anything to drink?" he asked Ray.

"I still got half my cup from home."

⬦

Cain examined the picture laying before him on his desk. It was a crime scene photograph of a man who had been killed two weeks earlier. He looked as if he'd been torn apart by some beast, some mechanical demon. The killing was violent, the method cruel and awful. He was found at home, had been stabbed in the back of his head, a hole gouged out and his brain matter pulled onto the floor. His torso was torn open at the lower abdomen and the number one deeply carved into his chest. The victim's left leg was completely severed at the knee joint, his head partially ripped away near the neck and four fingers detached from his right hand. A foot was pulled free at the ankle. The killer, in some deranged mindset, had neatly placed the detached body parts back together where they belonged, pushed into the places they'd once been: the leg, the foot piece, and the four fingers.

There were no fingerprints. The killer left them little to work with. It was as though he planned the layout of the entire scene.

The victim was a prodigy in the field of genetics, and having made significant discoveries in botanical engineering, had recently won a world renowned award for his efforts.

There was one perplexing piece of evidence found at the scene. In the victim's clenched hand was a Medal of Honor. The name inscription on the back of the medal bar was faded beyond recognition. It was determined he had no direct relationship to anyone in the military.

The other significant evidence was that the victim's mother received a phone call just a few days before his death. The caller had told her it was important that he contact her son. She thought it was something to do with his work so she gave the person his phone number. Within forty-eight hours of the call her son was dead. Another call had been made to the victim's home from the same secluded payphone near the riverfront. She had put her son right into the hands of the killer.

"Where's the case paperwork I had on my desk?"

Ray tossed a folder across his desk onto Cain's as Cain stood and made his way toward the coffee pot and an irresistible chocolate cake left over from days before. He rubbed his hand across his eyes trying to wake up.

"How old's this coffee?"

"Julie ran this weekend's through some fresh grounds this morning," an officer at a desk across from the coffee pot said.

Cain gave him a strange look. "That's disgusting, Si. Have you tried it yet?"

"Worked for me, but I mixed it with my energy drink."

"What's with all the good stuff being here on my days off? Ray and I are stuck eating scraps."

"You missed the captain's enchiladas yesterday," Si said.

"What? Those are the best enchiladas I've ever had."

Ray spoke. "Better not let Holly hear you say that!"

Cain returned to his desk, began eating his cake and watched two officers talk with a mother and father about their runaway child. He took a sip of his coffee, then winced at the bitter taste, glancing over at Si and shaking his head in disgust.

A supervisor stepped out from one of the offices nearest Cain's desk.

"Guys, got a dead prostitute in an alley off First Street Northeast. Trash men found her when they rolled a dumpster to lift it. Tech team's headed that way."

"So much for a day at the office!" Cain said, tossing his fork down at the plate of cake.

                              ▲

A light, cold rain began to fall over the city as they left the building.

"I hate rain like this. It's just enough to irritate me" Cain said.

"Wasn't supposed to hit till tonight."

As they walked up to the car Ray's phone rang.

"Hello." Ray paused. "By all means. Go ahead. If you think that's best. Alright, yeah, see you in a little bit."

"What's up?"

"Ana said they need to process the scene immediately because of the rain. They're setting up. She's concerned about some evidence issues."

"Any tracings of our killer?"

"Too many variations, the body's intact, no signatures."

                              ▲

Cain turned into the alley that spanned the distance of a city block behind a row of two-story brick buildings. Rusted metal fire escapes led to second story apartments on three of the buildings. At the base of one of the stairs, just to the side of it, was a dumpster area with a chain linked fence. Its gates were in the open position, swung outward and away from the container area. The dumpster sat in the middle of the alleyway. A trash truck was parked about twenty feet away on the other side of the alley. Nearby, two men stood talking to an officer by a police car. A white partition was erected across the west side of the dumpster area blocking the view from the sidewalk where a crowd had gathered.

He brought the car to a stop in an open blacktop area behind one of the buildings, the tires rolling across broken glass. An officer motioned for them as they left the vehicle. They walked toward the officer.

"Kollasch, what do we got?"

"Witnesses say they watched her and the boyfriend walk into the alley last night. They were just talking, then started arguing."

"Do we have statements?"

"We've got guys working on it."

"Any names?

"Not yet. Areas not uncommon for this. A lot of the women aren't from around here. They just come for the work. Neighbors say the boyfriend lives just around the corner on First Street. That's about all we've got. Washington's questioning a few more people.

Cain and Ray walked to the dumpster area. Toward the back side lie the body of a young woman, probably in her early twenties. She had been dragged around the edge of the dumpster. Her body was pushed as far into the corner as possible, her legs and arms twisted and contorted in unnatural positions. Bruising covered the entire side of her left cheek from the middle of her face and across her temple to her ear. Blood was crusted on her swollen nose. It was obvious from the asphalt embedded in her face that her head had been slammed into the pavement several times. Pieces of her teeth were stuck in her lower lip. Her hair was matted in front from lying against a garbage bag and blood had fused it to her forehead. The misting rain now blended with the blood and trailed across her face in several diluted lines. There was garbage on top of her lower legs and garbage rested between her back and a cinderblock wall section of the dumpster area.

"She was covered in trash, papers," Kollasch said. "The techs moved most of it. The trashmen noticed her after moving a piece of cardboard while cleaning up around the bin."

"Trash in the trash, huh?" an officer nearby said, smirking a little.

"What?" Ray bit at him.

"Nothing."

"This is somebody's little girl!"

Cain looked at the officer, speaking to him sharply. "Go do some perimeter control. You shouldn't be this close anyhow."

The officer gave him a disgruntled look and walked toward a police cruiser, saying something to another uniformed officer. Cain and Ray looked at each other and shook their heads, then began to meticulously examine the scene. After carefully going over the dumpster area Ray turned and talked to a technician near a white paneled truck.

"Ana, is your team just about done?"

"Yeah, pretty much. We got everything we needed from her when it started raining, so as soon as your done I'll call for body removal."

"Let's get the rest of the trash off this gal and get her bagged up. This looks cut and dry."

"Should be," Ana said. "Head, face and neck were covered with fingerprints, some impressed right into the blood. We got flesh out from underneath three of her nails and I've got her hands bagged. She got some good swipes at 'em. Guess we'll see if the boyfriend's missing some flesh."

Cain reached down with his gloved hand and carefully moved the trash away from her head as Ray pushed loose trash from around her legs and feet.

"We'll get him, girl. Don't you worry." Ray paused. "One way or another, he'll get his due." He tapped his pen against his notepad.

The front door of the apartment was open as Ray, Cain and three uniformed officers approached. A man sat on a couch in the middle of the living room, a cigarette in his mouth and an ashtray full of spent ones setting next to a bottle of liquor and half empty glass on the coffee table. Smoke rose into the air around him. He leaned backward, stretching his arms above and behind him and taking another long drag on the cigarette.

"What do you want?"

"We need to talk to you about your lady friend. What do you say?"

Cain carefully looked at the coffee table and couch near the man. He didn't appear to be armed.

"I say that whore should've made more money last night. She was out for six hours. This is all she gets?" He threw a wad of cash onto the table in front of him. The wad broke apart as it hit the table, some bills landing on the table and some on the floor. "She's a worthless piece of trash."

This guys not hiding anything, Ray thought.

"Looks like we've got a real winner," Si whispered.

"Why don't you stand up real slow and put your hands on top of your head, alright? We'll keep this simple, okay? No problems?" Ray said.

The man rose and stood to his feet.

"Move to your right."

The man complied with his orders.

"Turn around. Now get down on your knees and cross your feet."

Ray opened the door wider as Cain entered slowly, his revolver pointed at the man. Si moved in behind him.

"Bring back your arms to me, further, further."

Si grabbed the man's left hand.

"Ouch! Hey, take it easy, my hand."

Si pushed the man's hand into a cuff and then applied the cuffs to his other hand.

"Stand him up," Ray said.

As Si lifted him up Cain and Ray noticed the blood on his t-shirt. In the light of the room, his face was clear, and visibly swollen. There was blood crusted around his enlarged nose and one eye was puffy with a hue of purple at its lower edge. A strong smell of alcohol filled the room.

"That's a pretty nasty scrape on your neck," Cain said mockingly. "Looks like she broke your nose."

Ray lifted up his hands slightly. "Little blood on your hands?" The man's hands were badly scraped, missing large patches of skin near the knuckles. Bigger chunks of skin were hanging off his fingers and there was asphalt in some of the wounds. Ray threw a question at him, just to solidify what the man had already said, knowing their suspect would probably be stupid enough in his current state to give them the answer they needed.

"Why'd you do it man? Was she really that bad?"

"I got what I wanted out of her."

Ray pulled Washington aside and spoke to him as they lead the suspect out. "Call Ana and tell her to take his clothing straight into evidence when he's processed. Also, get a tech down here before you leave with him and have his hands bagged."

Cain sat at his desk, debating whether or not to finish the chocolate cake that had now crusted over with a hardened layer of frosting. He poked at it with the plastic fork as he looked over their documentation on the prostitute-bashing boyfriend, then reached across and tossed the paperwork into the cart by a supervisor's office.

"Well, that one should be easy," Cain said.

"Yeah, clearly guilty, said Ray.

"Today went by fast once things got moving. It was an alright Friday."

"I needed a day stuck inside."

Cain eyed the second half of Ray's sandwich they'd picked up on the way back to the precinct.

"Do you want it?" Ray asked.

"It's just sitting there."

"Go ahead, gonna give me heartburn anyhow. Hollys probably got dinner ready by now."

Cain grabbed the sandwich, unwrapped and ate it as he surveyed the large room. Along one side, farthest from the front door, supervisor's offices ran the length of the room in an L-shape from one corner to the next. Blinds were drawn shut on several offices, while others sat in full view, inviting everyone to judge unkempt or meticulously OCD inspired desktops. Shelves stood in the offices holding binders, files and books. Pictures or certificates lined the walls of most. Small tables sat outside the offices with in-baskets on each one.

Pearl, a sergeant in her late sixties who refused to retire, sat at her desk flipping through policy manuals and tapping on the computer keyboard in front of her. She stood, frustrated, and walked across the room to a shelf along the wall and pulled several large three-ringed binders from it. Two phones rang into eternity, their lights flashing as they were endlessly ignored.

"Who's got Policy Manual Five?" Pearl asked.

"Chris had it yesterday." Si pointed toward a desk.

"Chris?" Pearl yelled across the room.

"He's not here today."

Pearl walked over to Chris's desk and after shuffling through several items in the cluttered mess held the folder up in triumph. "Alright, you guys know the rules. Use a manual, put it back!"

Si mockingly mumbled from his desk on the other side of the room, saying her next sentence for her. "I've spent the last three years re-writing these."

"I heard that!" Pearl said, giving him a stern look.

"Sorry, Momma."

"If I was your momma you wouldn't have come out looking like that!"

Another officer piped in. "Hey, Si, you better back down while you're ahead. You'll be pushing pencils for the next ten years."

"What do you mean? I am pushing pencils."

"Yeah," Pearl said. "And you could use some spelling lessons."

Cain laughed inside at the two of them bickering until a commotion at the stairs drew his attention.

The front door slammed against the inside wall as two officers struggled with a woman in the entryway. "Whoa, whoa, whoa," one yelled. Cain jumped from his desk and bounded down the steps, grabbing the woman's head from behind and pushing her downward. An officer popped his knee into the her calf. Her legs gave out from under her. Two more officers joined in grabbing her legs and rendering her motionless.

"Can we get some more help down here?" one yelled as he held her arm in a tight grip. "Get her right leg!"

She struggled against them, kicking, cursing, trying to pull her arms away to fight more and squirming under the weight of several officers and a patrol supervisor who had come down to help.

"You gonna stay put or you gonna fight? This can be easy or hard, whichever you choose!" said the supervisor.

"Washington!" an officer yelled to the sergeant as he handed him leg irons.

"Man, Heiden, you need to get off that stuff. You're a mess."

"You ready to stop fighting? We'll get you to your feet."

"Alright, yeah, fine!"

"What happened to you getting help? Weren't you just in treatment?" Washington asked.

"She just punched her parole officer in the face."

"What about your kid? Boy can't raise himself alone while you sit in lock-up somewhere tweaked out on some poison." Washington said.

Three of the officers led the woman to the ramp and into the downstairs booking area. Cain made his way back to the main room.

"Hey, let's get outta here," he said to Ray. "I'm done with this day."

"Sounds like a plan."

Ray pushed the papers on his desk into a pile as Cain pulled his jacket from the back of his chair.

"So, when are you dropping Kenny off in the morning?"

"Probably between eight and nine. Holly's appointment is at 9:15. That should give us plenty of time."

"I'll be ready for him."

"You better. He's looking forward to hanging out with you."

2

"That looks pretty good, don't you think?" Cain set down the little jar of paint and the airbrush sprayer.

"Yeah, that's a awesome hotrod," said Kenny.

"It's my favorite. One of the finest looking machines ever built. A 1953 Corvette. First ever made. It took me forever to find a model of it."

"Why's that?"

"There were only three hundred of the 1953 ever produced. I guess the models must be as hard to find as the car itself."

"I like it red."

There was a knock on the door and it opened.

"Daddy!" Kenny jumped up and ran toward Ray.

"Well, what's the verdict?" Cain asked.

"Still one hundred percent pregnant! Baby's doing just fine."

"I'm getting a little brother," Kenny said to Cain.

"Well, we'll see," Ray said. "Maybe the baby will be a little girl. You'd like that also, wouldn't you?"

"Noooo," Kenny said, stretching his 'o'. "Baby brothers are cooler."

"I guess we'll just have to wait and see."

"Daddy, look at the car we painted."

"That looks great. Is Cain going to give it to you, you know, when he outgrows it?" Ray smiled.

"Funny," Cain said.

Ray settled into the softness of the brown faded leather couch as Kenny made his way along the built-in bookshelf in Cain's living room, running his fingers over the paint jobs of several car models resting on the counter connected to the shelf.

"Someday when Cain gets a job, he's going to buy a real Corvette," Ray said from across the room. "He's wanted one since we were kids."

"Really?"

Cain shrugged his shoulders. "Well, you never know now, do you?"

"What's this one?" Kenny asked.

"That's a 1969 Ford Mustang. Now, your dad probably hasn't told you, but that's the car he drools over! Someday I'm gonna own one just in spite of him."

"Oh, I know!" Kenny giggled, rolling his eyes. "Daddy was driving and saw one and almost crashed our car. Mom was mad!"

"I'll have to remember that next time he's teasing me."

Kenny had made his way to the end of the counter and was rubbing his little hands around in the dust that had collected on several bottles laying flat on top of each other near the bottom shelf.

"What are these, Cain?"

Ray teasingly answered for Cain. "Those are something else Cain can't afford on his salary."

"Those are drinks, but only for big people. Sometimes I like to have a drink of one when I eat."

18

"Oh, I get it, it's alcohol. What are these, Cain?" Kenny asked while pointing at several books.

Cain kind of laughed inside, knowing full well that Kenny was more than likely going to ask him about every last item on the shelf. "Those are books about the kind of work your dad does. I bought them for him at Christmas and he made me read them also. Actually, I don't think your dad's read any of them yet. And above that are some pictures and old stuff."

"Who's that?" Kenny asked, pointing to a picture of a younger Cain and a woman.

"Hey, Kenny, why don't you come over here and hang out with your daddy?" Ray said.

"Well, I will, but..."

Cain answered his question. "That's my wife Del and I on our honeymoon."

Ray and Cain's eyes met each other. "She died a few years ago when you were just a baby. You came to the funeral with your mommy and daddy. Your daddy thinks I don't like to talk about it, which is true, but I can handle it sometimes."

"How'd she die?" Kenny asked.

"She died of cancer."

"I heard that's bad."

"Yes it is. It really is bad, Kenny."

Ray interjected. "I know you're not into girls yet, but don't take any pointers from Cain. It took him forever to ask her out."

As he looked at the picture Cain remembered the conversation he'd had with Ray years earlier.

"Okay, I don't understand you sometimes, man. Why don't you just ask her out?" the younger Ray said. "You don't have any problem asking other gals out."

"Those girls are different. Delores is not going to go out with me. I'd like to think that I've got a certain element of class about me, but I know I just don't sit at those levels."

"Oh, come on! It's not the class. It's who she is! She's tough. She's strong. She's one of the most confident women we've ever met, and that's why you're scared."

"She's an amazing woman, you have to admit it, maybe a little too amazing."

"There goes your mind wandering again. I can see it in your eyes. You should just ask her out and get it over with. If she rejects you, you just go on with life. There are other women."

"She rejects me, I don't think I could go on with life."

Cain thought about Delores. He'd met her in college. The first time he saw her was when she adamantly stood up in a classroom and argued a point with a professor. The professor had refuted her theory only to be equally challenged in his thinking by Delores, her foot staunchly planted as she stood declaring her argument against his relentless spewing of supposed knowledge. She was a brilliant, beautiful, fascinating woman. Everything about her had wrapped itself around his heart in that very moment and taken him captive. Cain was smitten, soon realizing his only escape was to fall madly in love with her and relentlessly surrender.

Ray could see that Cain had wandered in his mind to some far off place. "Holly was wondering if we're still getting together tomorrow."

Cain surfaced from his daydream, wanting to go back and stay there forever. "Yeah. I don't see any reason why not. Should be nice to get out in the air a little."

The doorbell rang and Kenny jumped up. "Pizza!"

"Pizza? How do you rate to get pizza? Cain never buys me pizza."

"He said if we finished painting the Corvette he'd buy pizza."

Cain handed Kenny some bills. "Just hand him the money and tell him to keep the change."

"So, yes for tomorrow?" Cain asked Ray.

"Yeah, we think it'll be good for Patricia to get outside. Hopefully our favorite spot will be available."

"I can get there a little early and grab up the table we like. Can't seem to sleep past six lately anyhow."

Kenny opened the door, gave the deliveryman the money, then staggered back into the living room with two large pizzas he could barely carry stacked on his arms. He stretched his head upward to see over the boxes.

"Man, those are huge," Ray said. "Is that one pizza for each of you? You were planning on eating all that by yourselves?"

"No, silly," Kenny said. "Cain got some for you, too. Cain, what game did you say us men were going to watch?"

Cain's mind wandered to a day he'd spent with his father years before in this same place by the pond.

"Do you see them go?" his father had asked, pointing to a small group of ducklings following their mother off the edge of the pond, flapping their wings and pushing themselves along in the water with their webbed feet, trying to catch up to her.

Cain, eight years old at the time, had just finished feeding them broken pieces from a loaf of bread. The duckling's mother had tired of the situation and waddled toward the edge of the small pond, her brace of young ducklings following her lead and taking tow behind her.

"Why do we have to feed them?" Cain asked his father.

"We don't have to feed them. Their mommy will take care of them and teach them how to feed on little fish and insects. She'll stay with them until they're old enough to take care of themselves. We just like to see them up close so we give them something to eat."

"Wow, watch them gobble it all up!" Kenny's voice shook Cain from his thoughts. Kenny reached into the bag, grabbing another handful of breadcrumbs and flinging them across the water at the edge of the pond.

"They're pretty hungry, huh?" Cain said.

"Yep!"

"Kenny, come get a sandwich!" Ray yelled. He stood next to a picnic table with a butter knife in one hand and jar of mustard in the other. An old metal blue and white cooler sat on the edge of the table. Paper plates were weighed down with a ketchup bottle and various picnic items were spread across the rest of the table. A few plastic cups that had played victim to the light breeze now lay on the grass in the shade of the picnic table. Holly's dad Herb sat at the table, rambling on about how the food was going to spoil if it wasn't put back in the cooler soon and how someone should have weighed down the plates and cups better. Kenny ran towards Ray.

"Cain, are you going to have a sandwich?" Holly asked as she walked up and sat next to him on the little wooden bench. Her belly now showed a pronounced and visible bump through her t-shirt.

"Maybe in a little bit."

"Are you having fun?"

"Oh, yeah. Kenny sure has a lot of energy, doesn't he?"

"That little boy knows how to keep me moving all day."

"Maybe you'll get a little girl next time."

"You men all think little girls are supposed to be easier to handle. Ray said the same thing. Girls can be tough too."

"Whoa, I didn't mean it like that. I meant, well, you know. Sometimes girls are more gentle and calm spirited, like you." Cain tried desperately to fish up from the hole the conversation had just fallen into.

"I know what you meant, Cain." Holly smiled.

"Are you ready to have that baby?"

"Baby can wait. I'm in no hurry. I've got two months left and that's just fine with me."

Cain watched the ducklings paddle across the water in front of them again. "You know, my father used to bring us right here to this spot. Seemed like we were feeding the ducks at this pond every couple days, or looking back now, maybe even more. He really enjoyed life. He was always pointing out the simple things to us, a momma duck and her ducklings, a fawn deer in the tree line near the house nursing off its mother, and rabbits, oh the rabbits! Dad used to plant a little garden just for the rabbits right next to the big garden."

"Your dad was a good man."

"Yes, he was."

Holly's mom re-iterated the call for food. "Are we feeding people or feeding the bugs, cause the bugs seem to be eating more then you guys are! Cold cuts are getting hot!"

"We're coming, Patricia," Cain said.

3

Cain watched, terrified, as the maniacal killer thrust the stainless steel blade into the head of the little girl. An utterly useless struggle ensued, the child writhing in pain, flailing her arms and kicking her little feet, tiny toes curled tightly, trying relentlessly to break free of his grasp. He was too strong for her. His choice of victim sickened Cain. Cain felt a deep disgust in his mind as the man turned and he saw his face. The killer had no visible emotion. His eyes were a blank stare. There was something about him that resonated deep within Cain. *I know this man*, Cain thought. *Who is he?* He was methodic in what he did. He seemed unscathed by his actions. It was then Cain realized. He knew. Deep inside, Cain knew the killer had done this before. He was no strange madman though. He seemed normal in the full sense of the word, nearly business-like. He wore rubber gloves, as if they would protect him from the child, from what he had done to her. There was blood and bits of flesh on the front of his body. His clothes were covered with some sort of fabric. He peeled it away, and little bits of the child's flesh fell to the floor. He walked from the room, leaving her lifeless body to lie on the table. The little girl didn't even get a chance to cry.

Cain felt himself pushing forward, accelerating, as if coming upward out of the ground. There was a rush of adrenaline. He wanted to scream, but couldn't. He tried to pull away from his bed, but was unable to. He was pinned, trapped, his arms held by some invisible force, restraining him, holding him down. He was shoved up against a wall, waiting to break through into his reality. Then the wall shattered. He awakened, his sweat drenched hair splattering against the side of his face. His sheets were soaked with perspiration. His heart pounded hard inside his chest. He was scared, yet found comfort in the feel of his bed beneath him. It had all been another terrible dream, a horrid nightmare. He'd been having these repetitive dreams for months now, sometimes the same victim, sometimes a different one, a little boy, a little girl; always grisly and horrifying, always bloody. *Oh God, I can't let my job affect me like this. I have to keep this in check. I have to keep focused on what matters. We've got to stop this killer.*

The sound of the rush hour traffic filled the air and echoed through the canyons of buildings. Cain had his normal routine, stopping by Ray's house, blocking the bus, smiling at the lady driver, the usual perfect timing. It had been several weeks since the Food Prize winner had been killed. Now they were whizzing along through traffic responding to a call from the university's police. There had been a murder. From the initial information it was apparent their killer had taken another victim.

The rustic institution appeared through a scattering of ancient pine trees surrounding its outer grounds. Ray turned onto the main street of the campus, then made an immediate left onto the next street. He then turned right.

"Do you have any idea where you're going?" Cain asked.

Ray pulled the car over to the curb near a group of college students. "Yeah, I'm going to ask these kids where the building is."

"Hey, can you tell me where the Virchow Lecture Hall is?" Ray yelled out the window.

A short young girl strained under the weight of a load of books and a violin case as she juggled them from arm to arm while trying to answer them.

"Yeah, you're pretty far off. It's in the old section of the campus. Go up here and take a right at this corner and then just drive. It's on the far south end of the university. You'll see a bunch of older brick buildings. The lecture hall sits right next to the Karkinos Research Institute. When you hit the t-intersection, turn right and it's about two blocks down on your right, no, no, on your left. The names are on the buildings. If it's the crime scene you're looking for there's a bunch of students out in front of it across the street. I just talked to a friend of mine who's standing there."

"Thanks," Ray said. "Amazing! Talk about interconnectivity."

They pulled into the drive in front of the Virchow Lecture Hall. The building stood on an older section of the campus, its red brick facia contrasting with the thick, white painted window frames. Its location had conveniently allowed campus authorities to seal off the scene. Two uniformed campus police officers stood blocking the entrance. A group of college students curiously gathered across the street. Others went about their business, walking quickly from one place to the next, armfuls of books in hand and headphones plugged in. They were oblivious, their minds consciously subdued in some electronic realm.

Around the back side of the building Ray pulled the car into an old unused concrete drive where two university vehicles sat, along with city police vehicles. A crime scene investigator opened the door on the back of a white van.

"Good morning, boys."

"Morning, Kayla. What's going on inside?" Ray asked.

"Scene was cleared by Greg for initial processing. Chelsea's inside waiting for your walkthrough. I'll be in there in a minute. I had to go to the lab and grab a few things we were out of."

The brick pillared, concrete step entrance was marked off with crime scene tape. Cain stepped over the tape. Ray lifted it and went under. Along the outside edge of the building were offices. The lecture hall was in the middle. It could be accessed from three different sides. Their feet echoed as they made their way down the long hallway that wound alongside the offices in a horseshoe pattern. At the south end of the hallway there was an office taped off. By the door, university police stood in the hallway talking to Si about some game they had gone to recently.

"Si, what's going on?" Cain asked.

Si was ready with all the information. He was the kind of young officer that got into every intricate detail of the job. He had interviewed for a detective position and was one of the top picks until he blew out his knee playing football and was out for six months after surgery.

"Female victim, thirty seven years old. Looks like this is your killer again. I told them to get you guys right away. It's the same layout, same everything, sharp instrument shoved into the back of the head, brains scrambled and spilled out all over the place, empty cranium. But get this: The number *three* carved into her abdomen."

"That's not good. She's got a number three? If this guy's going in order, then there's another body out there somewhere, one we haven't found yet!" Ray blurted out.

"We've either got something nearby that he just did, or somewhere else. God only knows how long. Maybe there's one that's been sitting for a few weeks."

Cain turned to the other officer in the hallway who had just arrived. "Chris, call in some more officers and get with campus police. I want a thorough search of the grounds. Tell them to pay attention to secluded areas where people may not have been today."

"At least he didn't rip apart the torso like the last one, huh?" Si said.

"Yeah, made for a heck of a mess to work the scene. Anything else significant?" Ray turned, asking the university police officer. "What was her position here at the university?"

"She was a researcher specializing in cellular biology."

"When was the last time she was seen alive?"

"Last night by a co-professor after giving a lecture. He said he left here around 9:15."

"Maybe someone didn't like what she was talking about," Ray said.

"The lecture was on some kind of breakthrough in cancer research. Hard to believe anybody would have a problem with something like that."

Ray's eyes met Cain's.

Cain shook his head, then pulled a notepad from his pocket. Ray began to make simple sketches of the crime scene on a clipboard. "Thirty-seven years old, great," Cain said. "Clear connection to our other victim, but why?"

"Did anybody else enter the room?" Ray asked.

"A colleague found her," Kayla said. "He'd come in to pick up some printouts he left here last night. He believed she was dead, so he didn't touch anything. Paramedics determined she was dead. She was already pooling."

Si spoke. "I've got their names for you. Campus police stayed out and I've been on the door since the paramedics left."

Cain and Ray slowly made their way further into the room. Kayla stood by with the video camera. Once their initial walk through of the room was done, they concentrated on the center of the crime scene. The victim's body lay contorted and twisted, her eyes in a blank stare toward the ceiling, glazed over. Her left arm was turned down to her side, the right up toward her head. Her right hand was gripped into a fist, tightly clutching something, a slight shimmer glowing from inside her folded knuckles.

"It looks like we've got something here," Cain said.

"Chelsea, can you get this out, please?"

Cain moved back so Chelsea could work on opening the woman's hand.

"Come on girl, give it up. Yeah, the paramedics were right. She's pretty rigor, probably seven or eight hours in. She was most likely killed last night right after her lecture." Chelsea worked at opening her fingers.

"What is it?" Ray asked.

She carefully pulled a shimmering bracelet from the victim's hand. The bracelet had several stones in mounts separated by short links of chains. In the middle of the bracelet was the largest stone and hanging from its own separate chain link was a small medallion. Chelsea held it in her hand for Ray and Cain to view. "That is one beautiful bracelet," Chelsea said as she laid it on an evidence bag on the desk.

"Yeah it is," said Ray.

"We really need to know if this was the victim's, which it seems like it probably wouldn't have been, or if this was placed by the killer," Cain said.

"Well, the killer placed something at the last scene. Why wouldn't it be?" Ray asked.

"Take a close look at this thing." Cain pointed at one of the stones.

Ray viewed the bracelet closer as Chelsea moved it around in her fingers.

"It's got an inscription on this piece here," Chelsea said as she flipped over the small medallion to reveal the writing on it. "It says, 'This will not conquer me.'"

Ray focused on the words. "This will not conquer me? So is

it a cancer bracelet?"

"Seems like that," said Chelsea.

Ray looked at Cain, wondering where his mind might be.

"Okay, so it's a cancer bracelet that's a little different. It definitely looks different," Chelsea said.

"It's not just different, it's extremely different. This chain looks like platinum," said Cain.

"Really?" Ray leaned in for a closer look.

"Yeah, and check this out. Chelsea, turn that encasement over."

Chelsea rolled the chain with her gloved hand until one platinum encasement mount stood out. It had a different kind of gem in it than the other mounts.

"That's a pink sapphire!" Cain pointed. "And it's big, at least three carats. All these link pieces here, those look like pink diamonds. They're real diamonds, but they're flawed. They turn pink when they're heated to take out the flaws. This piece was probably special ordered and custom made."

"Maybe our biologist professor had cancer and was real passionate about beating it," Ray said.

"Could be, but we're talking about, well, I'd say roughly a six to eight thousand dollar bracelet, maybe more. So if it was placed by the killer, he feels like he has something important to say and he's not afraid of spending some money to do it."

"Yeah. He's saying something here. We just have to figure out what," Ray considered out loud.

"How does a Medal of Honor connect to a cancer bracelet and who knows what piece of evidence was left on victim number two?" Cain said.

"If there *is* a victim two."

"Whoa, right here," Ray said. The little white house with the wrap-around porch sat in an older neighborhood on the south side of town. Square pillars accented the porch on each side. A flower bed spanned across the front of the porch from one side to the other with steps rising from the center. A vehicle that didn't seem to show enough wear for its years sat in the driveway. It was apparent that an older person had taken good care of it.

They pulled into the drive to avoid parking underneath the trees on the street, the kind that dropped berries on cars all day long in the summertime, spilling their guts as they hit. Cain and Ray made their way up the drive. It was badly worn, cracks causing it to be uneven in spots. Resilient weeds appeared to push the cement apart as they rose up out of the darkness chasing the sunshine above. Petunias spilled out of planters, cascading over the edge of the porch. The porch creaked as they stepped onto it. Ray rang the doorbell, which like many doorbells had some of its plastic chipping away from wear and a brownish circular stain from too much heat. As they waited for somebody to come to the door Cain watched a small spider jaunt out from behind one of the address numbers and pounce on a helpless little bug that had landed there seconds earlier.

They heard somebody fiddling with the locks on the inside of the door. The door opened only a little, stopped by a chain slider lock. An elderly woman asked if they were from the police department and Ray told her yes. The door shut again and she re-opened it after removing the chain from its slider.

"I was expecting my son. Come in. I hope you don't mind the mess."

Cain looked around the front living room as they walked in and saw nothing more than a few newspapers that looked like they might not belong on the coffee table. The house was well kept. He got a picture in his mind of his widower's apartment and shook his head.

There was a faint smell of tea in the air, the smell you get when you brew it in a kettle. The front room was inviting. It was the kind of place you'd want to bring your kids to visit grandma.

The victim's mother was in her late seventies, a head of thinning white hair covering a strongly wrinkled face. She was adorned by a simple set of earrings and mauve colored plastic rimmed bifocals. The glasses seemed to match the silky purplish colored dress that swayed back and forth near her knees as she walked. A large silver colored butterfly with sparkling purple and pink enlaced jewels was pinned to the front of her dress.

"It's important we look into as many leads as possible in immediately after . . ." Cain stopped himself from finishing the sentence.

"She was our late flower. I always called her that. We had nearly raised all of our children when she came along. I thought my well had dried up. My husband and I weren't expecting that surprise! I was forty-five years old. My husband was fifty. He's gone now. Anyhow, for years we figured we were finished, then, well, one thing lead to another and oh, you don't need to hear that."

Cain had been thinking the same thing. No, he didn't need to hear that. He'd already had enough random thoughts about her and an elderly husband dance across his mind and quickly took advantage of the opportunity to change the topic.

"Ma'am, is there anybody who was upset with your daughter, maybe an old boyfriend, a colleague, anybody she was afraid of? Did she recently talk to you about feeling apprehensive or threatened by anybody?"

"I can't think of anyone. People liked her. She was doing cancer research. She'd found a way to isolate the cells during treatment that wouldn't weaken the patients as much. She also told me that she had made advances toward a possible cure.

You know, her father died of cancer. She was very passionate about her work. That girl would update me on every little thing she did."

"Did anybody else know about what she was working on?"

"She was getting ready to give the information to a panel of research scientists at the university. There are grants, you know, funding available. That's what she was trying to accomplish with her lectures. She knew there was money to be made in any cure, so she kept a lot of key information right here." The mother pointed to her head. "She felt that if the information got into the hands of some big pharmaceutical company they would keep it from the public and restrict access. She didn't want it to get tied up in testing and red tape for years by the government. She wanted to make sure it would be hard for the anyone to hold it back from immediate public use, even if just for trials."

"Did she ever talk about being threatened or feeling that her life was in danger because of her work?"

"No, and I don't think she would have worried me with something like that."

"Do you know if she owned a bracelet with pink diamonds and a pink sapphire in it? It had a medallion with the words, 'This will not conquer me' on it," asked Ray.

"My daughter rarely wore any kind of jewelry. She's never really liked bracelets. They used to irritate her skin when she was a child."

"Okay, if you think of anything else just . . ."

She interrupted Ray's sentence. "There is one more thing. I got a call last week from a man who was looking to meet with her. It wasn't unusual to get calls here at the house for her. Sometimes she sets her phone to forward to this number when she's here. I figured she'd just forgot to switch it back over. I told him she would be giving the lecture yesterday at the research institute at the university and that he should be able to find her there. I really thought it was something to do with funding or grants for her research."

Cain and Ray looked at each other, now realizing they were dealing with someone who had a precise plan, and a method for accomplishing it. Their killer was following a specific process for each murder.

"He said something strange right before he hung up. It didn't seem odd at first, but the more I've thought about it, it's kind of bothered me. He said, 'Thank you, I couldn't have done this without you. I wondered what he meant by that. At the time I didn't give it much thought, but since this happened, his words just keep coming back to me."

Ray turned the key in the ignition and the car started. It struggled to idle as he leaned forward, resting his arms on the steering wheel.

"It's okay, Ray. I'll be okay."

Ray's phone rang.

"Hey, this is Chelsea. I did some initial testing on the bracelet. I got some of her palm print patterns on just a few of those diamonds and the casing. I didn't see a single finger print of our victim's or any other print for that matter, anywhere on the thing. It was perfectly clean except for her palm ridges. It definitely looks like our killer planted it. There's no way she wouldn't have touched the thing in some way when she grabbed it to put it on."

"Okay, thanks, Chelsea."

"What's up?" Cain asked.

"From what she's seeing, the bracelet was probably placed by the killer."

"Alright, he's given us our second mystery clue. Have to wonder what he'll do for the next one."

"Unfortunately, I have a feeling we'll eventually know the answer to that question."

"God, I can't believe the garbage this world dishes out," Cain said.

"Have you ever thought some things are so far outside our control that we're just not meant to figure it out?"

"Where are you going with this?" Cain asked.

"You know where I'm going with it. Look at this case. What are the chances that you ended up on a case with that last victim?"

"Coincidence, not a big deal, Ray."

"Hmmm."

"I did some more research on our geneticist. He was known for breakthrough research in the development of hybrid grains that were more heat tolerant. His research in botanical engineering changed the way farmers approached planting in drought-ridden areas of the world. I read up quite a bit on this guy. That man single-handedly turned a third world country in Africa into an exporter of grain. He was the reason that American troops didn't have to intervene in Southern Africa like they've had to elsewhere in the region. Our mystery clue: a Medal of Honor. Why? Why that item? Our biologist was killed exactly the same way. Brains scrambled, sucked out and spilled all over the floor. Mystery clue number two, or three, I should say, a pink cancer bracelet conveniently placed in the victim's right hand at a crime scene that I, of course, would be surveying. Luck of the draw, I guess."

"Thirty-seven years old, Cain. Why thirty-seven?"

"That doesn't necessarily mean anything. It's only two victims. That could be coincidence."

"What about an attack on intelligence?"

"But why these two? Why not some snob know it all who looks down on other people? Why a scientist who has helped to feed millions of people because of his research and a biologist working on a cure for cancer? And God only knows who number two is."

"And what the second clue is," said Ray.

"I don't know. I hate to see what person this world loses next if we don't find this guy and get him stopped!"

"Maybe he just happened to choose these particular victims, no thought about it, just random."

"Random? Ray, he made direct contact with their mothers. Do you really think that's random? I mean, how does a serial killer just happen to randomly pick people whose lives have had a significant impact on the entire world community? I think maybe it's something much bigger, more sinister."

"You mean like a conspiracy?"

"Yeah, maybe."

"Okay, now you're stretching things."

"Maybe there's more than one killer."

"Ah, that's a wonderful thought!"

Cain's cell phone rang. "Hello. Yeah? Okay, thanks." Cain hung up. "Initial lab results back on our biologist; pretty much the usual and nothing sexual."

"That's always good. At least now we know that our killer most likely just wants to savagely kill his victims for no apparent reason except that they're trying to save the world."

"I know. It would almost be better if he had another motive, something less cynical."

"Yeah, pretty pathetic, uh," said Ray. "Alright, change of subject. Talk to me about something less depressing."

"How's Holly doing, is she driving you crazy yet?"

"This time she seems to be handling the pregnancy better. I think with Kenny it was just all so new for her. I'll be happy when she finally drops this one. She's tired all the time."

"You'll make it, Ray. At least you're not hauling the thing around."

"The thing? You make it sound like the plague."

"You know what I mean."

"Well, we've got three long months left!"

"Are you gonna see if it's a boy or girl?"

"Hey now, that's like peeking at a Christmas gift. We don't want to know. It takes the fun out of it. Kenny's pushing for a baby brother."

"Yeah, I could see him wanting that. He's definitely all boy!"

"Is she worried about you going up for training this week?"

"Not really, everything's gone good so far."

Ray brought the car to a stop at a red light. Cain looked down the sidewalk past the light at the row of storefronts. People filled the sidewalks, scurrying about in different directions. The light changed and Ray crept forward in the slow moving traffic as Cain glanced upon Pelili's Bookstore. The smell of the bakery next door permeated the air inside the vehicle. They made little distance before the next traffic light on the short block changed to red, trapping them in the afternoon gridlock again. Across the street from the bookstore two men labored to hang a sign for a law firm near the front entrance walkway of a remodeled Victorian Era mansion. Beyond that, just a short distance, the parking garage for Crossroad's Hospital rose up in the air. Cars lined the street, parking meters guarding their stay. Trees grew up out of openings in the sidewalks and flowers poured down the sides of concrete planters. A young man rode past on a skateboard, swooping in and out of the planters, a guitar strapped to his back.

So busy . . . Cain thought. *So many people now.*

"Man, remember when we'd spend all day down here riding our bikes around," Cain said.

"We'd scrape up every ounce of change so we could afford a movie."

"And stop at the drugstore on the corner and raid the candy aisle, then slip out the front door when old man Crutz was busy in the back with customers."

"Oh, yeah, days aren't made like that anymore!"

4

Cain was dreaming. It wasn't violent, but disturbing. The clean-cut man stood looking up at a clock on the wall, his back toward Cain. In his right hand he held a shimmering object. The clock's second hand was rounding toward the number twelve and the minute hand toward the number eight. The hour and minute hand fell onto their eight-o-clock marks. The man spoke. "It's time."

The scene faded, then changed.

In his dream Cain now stood in a small lobby area, turned to his left slightly, and looked down at a young woman holding a little baby boy in a blue and white outfit. She looked up at him.

"Are you ready?" he asked.

"I guess so," she said back, hesitantly, turning her head downward, looking into the tiny blue eyes of the small child she held in her arms.

Cain reached forward and pushed open the red colored door in front of him. It opened to a long hallway. He walked through the door and down the hallway. The young woman followed.

The phone rang, awakening Cain from his sleep.

"Cain, this is Kenny," his little voice cracked as he spoke. "My mommy needs you. She says she needs you to come to the hospital."

"What's the matter, Kenny? What's going on?"

"My mommy's having the baby," Kenny sounded scared. Cain heard a siren in the background.

"Are you at the hospital?"

"No. We're at the store, my mommy fell down. Here's my mommy."

"Cain, I think the baby's coming early! I'm having heavy contractions. Can you go to Crossroads? I'll meet you on the OB floor. I called my mom and dad, but they might not make it there in time. I can't do this alone. I need you. They think I'm hemorrhaging."

"I'm on the way. I'll call the training center and get a message to Ray."

"Okay. Can you talk to Kenny? He's scared."

"Hey buddy, your mommy's gonna be just fine. I'm on my way there to meet you, okay. Is mommy with the fire guys?"

"Yeah, and she has a mask on. I don't think she can breathe cause I saw a TV show when they put those on people . . ."

Cain interrupted his anxious voice. "No, she can breathe. They just put that on her to help her and the baby feel better."

"Her eyes are closed, Cain. Is she dead now?"

"No, Kenny. She's alright."

Cain heard a voice near Kenny.

"Someone wants to talk to you."

"Okay."

"Hey, this is Si. I've got Kenny. I'll get him to the hospital."

"I'll meet you there. I'm giving Ray a call."

Kenny got back on the phone.

"Hey buddy, you remember Si, right?"

"Yeah."

"He's gonna give you a ride in the cruiser to meet me at the hospital, okay?"

"Okay."

Cain heard one of the paramedics in the background as they closed the door on the ambulance, "Roy, kick it up a notch. BP's dropping!"

"I've got to call your daddy, okay?"

"Alright."

Cain heard the wail from the siren as the ambulance left the parking lot. He knew it was serious.

"You keep mommy's phone and I'll try to call you right back."

Cain hurried and dialed Ray's cell phone. It was off. He called the division and told them to contact the training center and let Ray know what was happening. The training center was over half an hour away. It would be a drive for Ray. If Cain hurried, he would be able to beat Holly and Kenny to the hospital.

"Oh my God! Give me a freaking break!" Cain yelled as he brought his car to a stop behind a large line of cars at a traffic signal. "Come on, change, change!" Cain yelled again, as though the higher decimal pitch of his voice and pounding on the steering wheel would cause the mechanisms of the signal light to somehow respond to his frustration.

The light finally changed and Cain edged his way toward the intersection, the cars in front of him displaying a turtle's race performance. He brought the car up behind two other vehicles. As each car turned in opposite directions Cain broke free of the congested traffic like a race horse bounding from its gate. He swerved past a car at the other side of the intersection and nearly ran over a pedestrian who had used up his allotted time in the crosswalk.

Cain rambled on incessantly as he made his way to the hospital in the midday traffic. "Should've walked! Could've got there faster. Okay, that's it, move to the right. Great job, you idiot, good job signaling! Yeah, any other day you'd all be speeding, wouldn't you? The sidewalk looks pretty clear except for a couple people. Not a good idea. I can't believe this!"

Cain was now stuck at another light. The light had turned green, but the cars weren't moving. Nobody was moving. It was like the whole world had come to a grinding halt. Cain looked at the buildings on his left and right, feeling trapped. He growled.

Just a few seconds later an ambulance entered into the scene from the left with its lights flashing and blasted its siren. A police cruiser followed.

Cain thought of Holly and tried desperately to see inside the ambulance but was too far back from the intersection. He could barely see the top of Kenny's little head in the passenger side of the cruiser as it passed.

Great! That's them. I won't beat them to the hospital.

Several cars moved through the intersection before it turned red again and locked Cain in the fourth position for the next race. He could see down the streets in each direction and watched as the ambulance passed through another traffic signal and then disappeared behind some other vehicles. A moment later he could no longer see it or hear its siren. He was angry that he couldn't get to them.

Cain skid to a stop in front of the hospital, leaving his car parked just past the loading area.

Elevators, lines, lots of people; not what he wanted to deal with. He shot to the left and ran into the stairwell. Bounding the first three steps in one leap and then breaking into a run, he made his way to the fourth floor. He flung the door open and stepped into the hallway and jogged to the nurse's station.

"I'm looking for Holly D. . ." Cain started to ask.

"They just took her in for an emergency c-section. Are you Cain?"

"Yes."

"She asked for you. Follow me and we'll get you into some scrubs."

Cain turned to go with the nurse and then thought of Kenny.

"Her little boy?"

"He's fine. An officer has him in the waiting area."

Cain was about to say he should probably stay with Kenny when he saw Holly's mom and dad step out of the elevator.

"Kenny's in the waiting area!" Cain yelled and pointed to the room.

Herb waved back at Cain, acknowledging that he would get his grandson.

Cain watched Patricia walk up to the nurses' station with a concerned look on her face as the nurse ushered him down the hallway and into the floor's operating area.

Cain stood to the left of Holly, at the head of the operating table, watching as the doctors used a scalpel to cut a large incision across her lower abdomen. A plastic cover protected the area of the cut. Blood immediately began rolling off her belly and was dabbed up with gauze by one of the many operating room techs. The doctors talked as they worked, urgency in their voices, their hands steady. Something inside of Cain was aching, like he had no control over the situation. He desperately wanted to help, to do something.

"Alright, let's see what's going on in here," a doctor said.

"Do we have our blood?" one asked.

"It's been ordered up," a nurse in surgical garb spoke.

"Blood, why blood?" Cain asked.

"We'll try to avoid it, but it's here if we need it."

Cain listened, watching them work, his hand on her shoulder, hoping she knew he was there.

"Is she going to be alright?" Cain asked. "I thought people were usually awake for these things."

"Had to put her under fast so we could look for the source of the bleeding."

"Does dad need to leave?" one of the doctors asked.

"Oh, no! I'm not dad. Dad's at the police academy's training facility. I'm his partner on the force, homicide." Cain felt silly after saying what department they worked in.

"Well then, you should be able to handle whatever happens here. The baby's heart rate is elevated showing that it's in distress, but at least we have a heartbeat. Oh, here we go!"

Cain watched as the doctor reached into Holly's abdomen with his hands. A tiny little head emerged first, followed by the chest, belly, then two wrinkly legs and little feet. Cain didn't even notice the sex of the baby.

"We've got a little baby girl!" One of the doctors said.

Wow, that's insane. What a beautiful little baby, Cain thought to himself. *So small.*

One of the technicians took the baby from the doctor and walked over to a table with a warming light on it. Two nurses immediately began working on the baby, clearing her nose and mouth out and cleaning off her body.

"Okay, we've got bleeding from the uterine wall. Looks like the placenta tore free."

The doctor lifted the placenta from Holly's abdomen and placed it on a tray. He then reached inside of her and pulled out the uterus and placed it on her belly near the incision. The uterus had a long cut across it from the baby being removed. The doctor was trying to examine the inside of the uterus to determine how to stop the bleeding. Cain could see the fallopian tubes running from the uterus and then back down into Holly's abdomen.

"Bleedings not too bad. I think everything's going to be alright with momma. We'll get it stopped now that we've isolated it," the doctor said, looking toward Cain.

"Four pounds, one ounce," a nurse said from near the baby. "Let's move this little girl down the hall."

Another attending doctor looked at Cain. "She's going to be okay, if you'd like to go see if dad's here yet and let him know."

"Alright," Cain said. "What about the baby?"

"Baby looks good. It's a bit of a struggle for them at that size, but we have everything here for the little ones. We have our share of preemies. She'll spend some time in the NICU but she should be just fine."

"Do they have a name for her?" a nurse asked.

Cain felt like she asked the question to deflect his concerns.

"Why don't you come with me and I'll show you to the recovery room."

Cain walked out of the operating room. He pulled the mask down off his face and it hung on his chin, then grabbed the light blue cap from his head and peeled the gloves from his sweat covered hands, throwing them away. He pushed open the double doors to the main hallway and Ray and Kenny stood in front of him, along with Holly's parents. Cain lit up and then spoke quickly.

"She's okay!" He knew Ray needed to hear those words.

"Where's the baby, Cain?" Kenny asked.

"The baby's good too, but real little."

Cain looked at Ray as he spoke to Kenny.

"Do you think you can handle a little sister in the house?"

Ray's eyes teared up.

"Congratulations, Ray," Cain said.

Kenny piped in. "A little sister! Not as good as a little brother, but she'll do."

"Well, I guess I've got my granddaughter," Patricia said.

"Thanks for being here, Cain," Ray smiled. "It really means a lot."

A nurse walked up the hallway from the nurse's station.

"Okay, who's dad?"

"Right here." Ray raised his hand.

"And I'm the big brother!" Kenny said.

"Just wanted to let you know that the baby's doing fine for what she's been through. We'll come and get you when you can see her. It shouldn't be very long."

Another nurse stepped out from a door to their right. "Would the husband like to come into recovery?"

"Can my son come with me?"

"Well, we prefer dad alone to begin with. Your wife's been through a lot and she's very weak."

"Cain?"

"I'll watch him, you stay here," Cain said. "Come on, Kenny, let's see if we can find out where they took your new baby sister."

"Alright!" Kenny shouted.

Cain and Kenny walked down the hallway, Kenny half skipping, grabbing Cain's hand and holding it tight. Herb and

Patricia followed.

Cain stared down at the pictures lying across his desk. The killer's first victim stared back up at him, eyes wide open. It was as if the victim was staring straight through him and at the ceiling above, straight through his mind, his soul, resonating the call for Cain to vindicate him.

He shook the thoughts from his mind. "I can't solve these mysteries if I don't concentrate."

He opened the folder for the second victim. Her contorted and oddly twisted body lay across the floor of the lecture hall office.

"Hey, Greg, can you come here for a second?"

"Sure."

Greg stepped out of his office.

"Check this out," Cain said as he laid the pictures of the two victims side by side.

"I see it.".

"Shouldn't we find this a bit strange? I mean, our first victim's legs were pulled together into each other, nearly un-natural. The detached leg and torn foot were neatly pushed back into place. His arms were pushed inward, his right hand kind of coming together across his chest. His left hand at his side, the fingers set back in place. It's fairly obvious that he was forced into some kind of compressed composure. It seems that with the violence of his death, he would've just been left lying all over the room. That's odd when compared to our second victim. Shy of the bracelet placed in her hand, there didn't seem to be any sort of arrangement at all, and the killer left her intact."

"It's his second victim. He's just getting started. I wouldn't read too much into that kind of detail yet."

"I'm not. Just wanted someone else's thoughts on it," Cain said as Greg walked back toward his office.

Cain continued to examine the pictures: the close-up picture of the Medal of Honor, its blue ribbon stained with the blood of the victim's hand as it wrapped itself through the fingers that remained. The victim's button up shirt, recognizably torn open from the two buttons that had been snapped free, one laying on his abdomen, another on the floor. Another, ripped from its stitching, but not completely free of the shirt, hung by a loose thread, dangling at his side. And then finally, the parts, his body parts, all placed back in position, neatly, as if the victim was saying, "Don't worry, I'm all here," or the killer was saying, "Hey, I'm organized, I got this all handled, I kept him in order, no missing parts."

What is the killer trying to say? Cain thought.

His phone rang.

"Hello?"

"Hey, this is Karen. Do you have a minute to step into my office?"

"Uh, yeah, sure. I'll be right there."

Cain closed the folders on his desk and walked to the other side of the room along the far wall, peeking into the captain's office.

"It's exactly what you'd thought. You just about described this thing to a tee. I really don't know where you get this stuff from."

Karen had laid an evidence picture of the bracelet on the small table near the door for Cain to see. "Those are pink diamonds, like you said. The larger stone is a sapphire, a rather expensive one, actually. The chain and mounts are platinum. It's got an approximated value between eight to ten thousand dollars."

"So it not belonging to our victim is even more disturbing."

"Yes, very disturbing. It really bothers me that our killer was willing to leave something so valuable at a crime scene."

"I have a hard time believing the killer didn't know what he had."

"Well, I've got several officers checking around to see if a local jeweler handled it. I already checked online. There's really nothing like it that's produced in volume by any company. We'll have to see what our team comes up with."

"Alright. Thanks Karen."

"No problem. How's it going?"

"This isn't gonna move very fast. He'll strike again before we can do anything to stop him. I'd be shocked if we find anything significant enough to give us our killer any time soon. There's not enough here to figure him out. He's not stupid and he's already toying with us. It's obvious he's only leaving us what he wants us to have. It's almost as though he has one-up on us, like he's got an advantage. He knows something. He knows how to keep us from figuring him out. He's too clean.

"Cain!" Kenny shouted as Cain walked into the room. Kenny was wearing an adult-sized facemask that covered half his face and came up over his eyes.

"What's happening, buddy?"

"Baby's getting better!"

Cain looked at Ray and Holly. "How's little Ranae?"

"Doing pretty good. She's gained almost two pounds total, about seven ounces since you came by last week," Holly said.

Cain bent down to look at the tiny little girl in the incubator. She no longer had the oxygen and feeding tubes running into her nose that were there when he'd visited previously. There were still wires running out from under her little shirt. The wires wound across the cozy little blankets and out of the incubator to a monitor that showed her heart rate and oxygen levels, along with several other numbers and lines.

Every now and again the baby would stretch out her legs and arms and tug on one of the wires, causing the monitor to emit a continual beeping noise until a nurse walked into the room and silenced it.

"Wow, she seems so much bigger," Cain said. "Her skin is pink."

"They're saying just a few more ounces and she can come home. She's eating on her own now."

"That's great, guys."

"It's not like you didn't help," Ray said.

"I'm glad I could be there. I just felt like I was intruding on a sacred moment, almost like it wasn't my miracle to watch, you know?"

"No, Cain. I think it was your miracle to watch. I think it belonged to you. Out of all of us, you're the only one who saw her born," Holly said.

Cain felt privileged, blessed.

Ray spoke. "We want you to be her godfather."

"What? No! I mean. I don't think . . .wow! You don't know how much that means to me."

"Hey, Cain," Kenny said. "There's two babies born that are really little."

"Littler than your sissy?"

"Yeah," Kenny smiled, his eyes wide open.

Ray jumped in. "One pound, 11 ounces. They're tiny little guys, twins. They almost didn't make it. The nurse said they'll be here for several months."

"Can you imagine the bill on that one?" Holly said.

"Somebody's willing to pay it, huh?"

Ray looked at Cain. Do you remember that gal from over on Elm Street, the corner apartment, the one with the meth problem?"

"Yeah."

"They were hers," Ray spoke quieter.

"Hey, Kenny, go check on your sissy."

Kenny walked over to the incubator and Ray shook his head no.

"Didn't make it?" Cain asked quietly.

"No. No family has shown either. They can't seem to find any of her relations. And there wasn't anybody around claiming to be the father."

"Sad. They'll probably end up in foster care or get adopted out to somebody."

"Anything new?" Ray asked.

Cain understood what he meant. "No, I think he's gone quiet for a while. It'll be good to have you back. I'm getting tired of mulling over all this crap by myself."

"Should be Monday. They think the baby will be ready to go home this week and Holly's sister is going to fly in and stay at the house to help out for a few weeks."

Cain turned his attention to Holly. "How you feeling?"

"I'm sore. It took the last two weeks to start feeling better. One day Kenny flopped up on my belly on the couch. That got me good, and the incision's irritating, but it's healing. I can't lift anything, so that hasn't helped, but Ray's taking up the slack. Kinda nice having him do the laundry."

Cain finished with his visit and walked out and turned toward the elevator. As he approached the middle of the hallway he noticed a blind on a window open and he could see into the Neonatal ICU. Next to the window a door was cracked and he could hear muffled talking. He glanced into the window, then stopped to look. There were several life support stations and incubators, tiny babies in each one, warming lamps shining down on them and monitors at each unit.

Two of the stations stood side by side. Nurses were by the stations, one writing on a clipboard, the other pulling little pads off of the chest of one of the babies. She wrapped the blanket up and around the tiny little body. Another nurse reached up and turned off the monitoring system and the light above the baby.

Cain looked at the nurse tending to the other child. He could see her face and barely hear as she brought her face down close to the baby and gently said, "It's just you now *little guy*. It's just you."

⸙

Man, that sun is bright, Cain thought as he pulled the visor down. He could see a grove of trees near the end of the city block. The marker. Cain turned left into the drive. Beautiful rosebushes ran in a line across the front of the property near the street. Impatiens and other annuals slow-danced softly in the breeze, the ground around them freshly disturbed by a gardener's hand. A wrought iron fence stretched outward to his left and right, interrupted every fifteen feet by white stucco pillars. The fence appeared to sink into the stucco on each side. In a few spots on some of the pillars the old red brick showed through from its entombment underneath. There was a smell of earth, soil. Evergreens lined each side of the paths and small roadways on the grounds. Flowering trees sprinkled their petals into the air. It was an idyllic park-like setting, the filtered sunlight casting a soft shade upon the ground below the trees.

Death, Cain thought.

Tombstones rose around him in different shapes and sizes, each a seemingly separate symbol of individualized death. Bleach white buildings stood in the middle of the cemetery, a lying facade for the decay they held within. And, of course, there were the maintenance vehicles, hidden off to one side of the facility's buildings near several sheds.

Well, that's pleasant, no trucks with concrete crypts on them today.

Business must be slow, Cain thought.

The trucks bothered him. Dirty, scratched, no signs on the doors, just plain old work trucks. A large backhoe sat off to the far end of the sheds, waiting to do the gravedigger's bidding. The trucks, the machinery, they always reminded him of the reality of what the place was. A place where men worked, where men got their hands dirty. For them it had to be just a job, another day at the office, another body to put in the ground.

He stopped his vehicle just shy of the next corner near a fenceline of the cemetery. The fence was covered with vines, but Cain could hear the cars on the street just fifty feet away. He stepped out of his vehicle and walked toward the fence, passing a patch of freshly turned dirt and attempting to stay along some imaginary set of lines between the grave markers and stones.

He finally came upon a spot about four rows from the fence line. *Wish this wasn't such a hurried thing,* Cain thought. He and Delores hadn't planned for what happened. It just wasn't a thought. He'd had to settle for an area of the graveyard that he didn't consider ideal.

As he came upon Delores' resting place he noticed the freshly turned soil of a new grave, just feet from where he would lie some day.

There was a small metal marker plate over her grave. Cain ran his hand across it, feeling the grooves of the letters as though they gave the grave some sort of life, some existence.

"I've almost got enough money saved, hun. I'll be able to get your stone soon. The one you really wanted. The one we talked about, with the bench."

It bothered Cain that Delores was just right there, under his feet.

"I've been missing you a lot lately. Shoot, by now, you probably would've had me re-married or something. I just can't let go of you. It's taking a lot longer than I thought it would. You were my world, babe."

Cain knelt silently by the grave, memories of his wife scattering themselves across his heart and mind.

"I love you. I'll always love you."

"Hey, Nick, good to see you," Cain said to the young man in the military uniform standing at the entryway to the apartment next door.

"Oh, hi."

"Are you home on leave or home for good?"

"Just on leave this time, but it's a surprise. So if you see mom, don't tell her. I just want her to get come home from picking up sis and find me kicking it on the couch."

"I wouldn't spoil a surprise like that! So, you were in Africa?"

"Yeah. I go back for one more tour. There's some stuff we have to do in South Africa."

"The news hasn't had anything good to say about what's going on there."

"No. There's a lot of turmoil, a lot of people starving."

"How're your parents handling it?"

"I've been able to call home any time I want, but mom still worries about me. My little sister's always, you know, asking if I'll come back. Dad and I haven't been close since I was a teen, but he was even stressed about my last tour of duty. They see the news."

"Well, I don't get a chance to say this very often, but thank you! It's because of people like you that we have the freedoms we all seem to take for granted so much, and those who give their lives, nobody can ever repay them."

"Well, if you see my family, keep it hush, okay?"

"No problem. I hope to see you later. And listen, don't be a stranger to your dad. Dads can be stubborn. They just need a little time to understand what matters in life, you know?"

"Yeah, I know. He's been writing me a lot, so it's been a lot better. I'm gonna get inside and hide out before they get here. I'll catch you later."

"I hope so."

As Cain turned away he thought of the news stories about South Africa. *I really do hope I see him again.*

5

The crunching snap of the cat's neck silenced the subtle purr that had slid across the weathered beam and nestled itself against the killer's arm. He held it tightly, a cupped hand over nose and mouth as it squirmed, kicked, went silent. Its last warm breath pushed out against cold fingers, dampening them with condensate from the night's cold air, bringing an odd comfort. Quiet shadows, defined by a lone streetlight, sliced across the animal's body as it fell and lay lifeless on the garage floor amidst broken glass and dry rot timbers, themselves having succumbed over time, no witness to their disrepair.

In the stillness of the night the killer's face shifted slightly out of the shadows, eyes penetrating through the dirt covered broken window and onto the patrol car at the end of the cul-de-sac.

The killer's mind floated in a sea of emptiness, a dark void, an ocean of thoughtlessness . . .

Your fortified encasement will crack with just one blow. Familiarity breeds trust. In the shadow of the darkness I move. You won't see me. I turn down the gears of the gates of your moated place. Your sanctuary is breached. There is but one way to escape, no place to hide, no place to flee. Your safety, your ease, they deceive you. You're wrapped in the womb of your contentment. By the light of my darkness, my practice, I find you. The shadows hide the first blow of my hand. My skill is perfected. You are no match for my masteries. My art is refined. Pain awakens your sensory. My cause is righteous. You are obligated to partake. Your choice, my mind does not heed.

The killer slipped from the shadows.

Cain slept. He dreamt. It was a quick, violent thrust. The killer jabbed the weapon into the back of the little boy's head. He reached outward and savagely ripped the child's arm off at the elbow, pulling away the forearm, and then tore at the other arm until it pulled free of its socket. Then it was over.

He awoke to the phone ringing, his eyes trying to adjust to see the time on his alarm clock, his mind foggy and confused from the dream. He tried focusing on his cell phone. It was Ray calling. Cain fumbled with the numbers and answered it.

"Another one? What?"

"Yeah. A trooper."

"Where? At home?"

"No, he was on duty, just off the square, Nepel Street, a cul-de-sac. Some kids found him. Washington's saying it looks like he gave it the fight of his life. Apparently he didn't go easy."

"Well, won't their department be handling it?"

"Since it looks like our killer, we'll be working with them on it."

"So the same M.O.?"

"Yeah, by the sounds of it. I guess he's an awful mess, a little closer to what our geneticist looked like."

"I'll get ready."

Cain sat up and flipped the switch for the small lamp on the nightstand by his bed. He looked at the time; 4:05 a.m. *Man, why not an hour later. Kids should have been home sleeping. Somebody else could have found this guy at 5:05, or 6:05 or something.*

He stuck his legs into the legs of his pants, which were in a clump right where he had set his feet down, and pulled them up. He slid his chest holster into place. He looked around the room for his shoes, but didn't see them, so he walked out to the small living room area adjacent to his kitchen. He found one shoe by the couch and one shoe by the door of the bathroom. He slipped his jacket over the shirt he had worn to bed and went to grab his keys from the key hook by the kitchen. The keys weren't there. He looked at the counter. No keys. He walked back into his room and looked around. They weren't on the nightstand. He looked by the chair and around the rest of the room, nothing. He walked back into the living room area, looked again, then around the corner toward the front door and looked on the floor in the little hallway. As his eyes scanned the floor in the hallway he glanced upon the bottom of the door.

It was open! Cain quickly looked over the door. There was no sign of forced entry. He turned and looked at his apartment, almost as though somebody should be standing there watching him. It tripped him out. He remembered locking it. *Or did I.* He questioned himself. *But even if I forgot to lock it, I would have closed it.* He heard footsteps in the hallway just outside the door. He reached into his jacket and slid his hand over his weapon and backed away from the door. The door swung open as he went to pull his revolver from its holster.

"Come on, Cain." He heard Ray's voice. "Can't wait forever!"

Cain let out a deep breath and sighed. "Yeah! I'm coming.

Hold on, I'll be right out."

He slowly moved around the rest of his small apartment, checking every space for anything out of place or unusual. He shook off the flustered feeling and grabbed his spare apartment key from the drawer in the little table by the front door and stepped out, closing the door behind him and locking it. Cain didn't see the tiny little scratch marks around the keyhole for the deadbolt.

"Man, did it have to be so early?" Cain said as he slid into the passenger seat.

"Well, last I checked most people don't have a set schedule for discovering dead bodies."

"I'm exhausted. I didn't sleep good last night. I think somebody may have gotten into my apartment."

"Why do you say that?"

"Because the door was open when I got up."

"Like open, open?"

"No, just cracked, and I can't find my keys."

"Maybe you didn't get it closed all the way. Do you want to check your car real quick? Maybe you locked them in your car."

"No, let's just go. I'll look for them later. Besides, I would have noticed them missing last night. I don't get it. They're probably just somewhere in the apartment."

"Our victim's thirty-seven years old, Cain," Ray said in a calm, serious tone."

"Really? Thirty-seven?"

"The Captain said she'd do some research for me on that timeframe. Hopefully she'll come up with something."

"I've heard of this trooper. They called him Slammer at the local taverns. He liked to nail people down at the bars after they'd drive off. His little brother was killed by a drunk driver, so he was always working that angle.

Ray's phone rang.

"Yeah, we'll be at least another ten to twenty minutes. No, whatever you think is best."

He hung up. "Greg cleared the techs to start a preliminary work over of the scene."

☖

The long street ended in a cul-de-sac. It was an older neighborhood. A couple of houses at the end of the cul-de-sac had been condemned and another torn down completely, leaving an empty space with overgrown grass and an old dilapidated garage with its paint peeling off. Their headlights lit the inside of the old garage, its rafters hanging down and the fallen wood visible through the opening where the door once was. It had seen its usefulness. Now it stood as an empty shell, a near prophetic judgment of where the rest of the neighborhood was headed. A cold, lifeless body of a cat lay un-noticed on the floor just beneath a window against the garage's sidewall.

As they left the vehicle they noticed a newer officer discharging his last meal onto the grass by the sidewalk. Cain and Ray knew it wouldn't be pleasant.

They were right. The scene at the end of the street was horrid. The trooper had been dismembered, his torso leaning up sideways against the curb and blood draining into the gutter. Ray felt as though they were slowly losing evidence into the city's storm system.

"Beat you here! Chelsea teased as she approached them, almost too cheerfully. "I brought extra coffee. It's in the truck. We're still missing a forearm. Ana found his right arm in a trashcan on the other side of the cul-de-sac. The head's intact. Same wound to its base, though."

"The inside of his cranium is scrambled like the other victims," said Ana.

"Scrambled! I forgot to grab breakfast," said Chelsea, letting out a sigh.

"Really?" said Ray.

Cain shook his head. "Did somebody bag his weapon?"

"No," Chris said from nearby. "Missing. The kids who found him said a man was crouched over him. There wasn't any cash in his wallet. No bank cards, credit cards."

"Where are the kids?"

"They were searched as soon as we saw the weapon missing. They've all been questioned. They said the guy ran off before they got close. They're pretty freaked out, probably going to need some counseling. I don't think they were involved. One of them was curled up in a fetal position rocking at the end of the street when our first patrol got here. He hasn't said a word to anybody yet."

"Did they give a description?"

"Yeah. The guy was about medium build, kind of slender, didn't look overweight, torn jeans with lots of holes, a white sweatshirt with some sort of design on the back. He was wearing something on his hands, possibly gloves. He had on dark shoes that looked like boots. They said there was a heavy sound from his footstep. And get this: they said he ran fast, and by the way he ran must have been a teen or in his twenties."

"Great description," Cain said.

"Yeah, I think they did a little profiling on the running fast thing."

"Guess us old folks can't run, huh?" said Ray.

"Kayla, did we get any prints?"

Kayla looked at Cain with a why-did-you-wake-me-up-this-early-in-the-morning look on her face.

"Oh, yeah, the wallets covered with them. They don't appear to be from our trooper, but we'll see. You know, this doesn't seem to be our guy. The killing probably was. But the guy who ran off? If he actually left his prints on the wallet, I'd have to question it."

"Yeah, but the guy who ran off was wearing gloves?"

"That's what the kids said."

As they talked a commotion erupted to the left of them.

"Oh, come on!" Officer Kollasch yelled loudly as she rapped on the door of a nearby house, trying to awaken the occupants. They turned to see Si chasing a dog around the front yard.

"Come here, boy!" Chris said, making his way toward the fence.

The door opened and a man stuck his head out. He looked half awake.

"Sir, we need you to contain your animal for us."

The angry dog snarled behind her in the yard as the officers got too close.

"I've got to put my shoes on," the owner said.

"Yeah, that's fine, it's early enough," Kollasch growled. "Shoot! We've got the rest of the day, right?"

The owner of the dog winced from his porch light and Kollasch's flashlight in his eyes as he stepped from his doorway. "Get your stinking flashlight out of my eyes and maybe I can see to do something," the owner barked back.

"Come here, boy. Come here." The dog was reluctant to come to his master. "Oh, God! What's that?"

"Just get him to set it down," Chris responded.

The dog was angry, not wanting to give up his prize. He was prancing back and forth in the front yard with his head up high. Cain first noticed the bloody brown shirt sleeve, and then watched as the dog ran across the yard dragging the arm behind him, the fingers bouncing off the dirt and a shiny wedding ring reflecting the light of the officer's flashlights.

Washington walked up. "I just put a call into animal control. They'll be here in about ten minutes."

"This scene's the worst so far," Ray said.

"Well, anything unusual?" Cain turned and asked Ana, who was holding a large evidence bag in her hand with the trooper's other forearm in it.

"Unusual?" Ana answered as she gave him a stupored look.

"I'm not sure. I mean, usually this isn't how I have my breakfast and first cup of latte in the morning." She held up the bag as she spoke.

Cain rolled his eyes and shook his head.

"You mean other than a state trooper that looks like he's battled it out with a demon from hell? Yeah, actually, we did." Ana seemed to perk up a little. "Our killer is messing with us. In the hand on the arm we found in the trash he had a lock of hair, a shiny little lock of hair. It looks like it came from a kid, you know, delicate, fine hair."

"That's even stranger than the last ones," Cain said. "A trooper and a lock of hair? The killer's going somewhere with all this. I'm beginning to wonder if these aren't payback murders, you know, someone died and now he's going after the people he feels are responsible?"

"Do we have any idea how long he's been deceased?" Ray asked.

"He started his shift at eleven last night. From the looks of the trash in the patrol car, he'd stopped and grabbed some food, but that was probably closer to the start of his shift," Kayla said. "I checked with a couple patrol guys. They said this was a popular spot for them to take a break if they needed to get any paperwork done, so I'm guessing he was probably confronted by the killer in the later hours of his shift. He went out of service around two-thirty, which was close to his normal second break time. It looks like there wasn't a lot of time between the attack and the kids finding him."

Cain noticed as the dawn was breaking that a lot more people from the neighborhood were gathering toward the end of the street and that many in the houses nearby had come into their front yards to see what was happening.

"This is going to be another long day, isn't it," Ray said.

Cain turned and Ray caught a glimpse of his face, shadowed partially by the light from one of the vehicles, casting dark rings under his eyes, accentuating his exhaustion. He put his hand on

Cain's shoulder as they turned back toward the trooper's vehicle.

"Alright," Ray said. "Let's get this done."

Afternoon came quickly. The sun shot a warm glow of light through tree branches onto the cul-de-sac, creating tiny angled shadows in the asphalt. Ana and Kayla finished loading equipment into the tech van as Cain and Ray drove past.

"I have one more kid run out in the street in front of me . . . I swear, parents don't teach them anything anymore."

Ray was frustrated. "There's just too much correlation between the victims. Worlds apart, yet all of them were important to society or had some sort of research they were doing to make this world a better place to live or doing something significant that made a real difference."

"This trooper was well-liked in the community."

"Well, now we have his service weapon to deal with when we find the killer."

"He systematically rips his victims to pieces. I'm pretty sure that weapon isn't our main concern."

"How in God's name did this guy get the jump on a trooper? Fourteen years on the state patrol? He wasn't some idiot. You don't just sneak up on someone like that."

"Yeah, it doesn't look like he had a chance."

"Maybe it's somebody important. Someone in the spotlight, city official, well known, could get close to him without suspicion. Man, he really tore him up. It looked like a wild animal got ahold of him. I mean, Cain, his arms weren't cut, they were torn, the flesh was ripped."

"The number four."

"Yeah, I know. This just means that much more our number two is out there rotting somewhere."

"Maybe we'll get lucky and the guy has an aversion to the number two and didn't want to use it."

"Well, we don't stop this guy . . ."

"Number five, or nine, or whatever the heck number he wants to use next."

"Hopefully the victim's wife can give us something to run with."

"I really don't want to do this," Cain said as they pulled in front of the trooper's house.

"I know, feeling's mutual, but we need answers."

Their visit with his wife was painful and heart wrenching. They had to watch as she ushered her four teenaged children from a family meeting in the living room when they arrived. The anguish of the visit was compounded by having to see the five-year-old son, having broken free of his siblings in the other room, cling to his mom's side the whole time. They weren't terribly surprised by what she had to tell them.

"Sorry to bother you so soon. We're working with Public Safety on this because we think your husband may have been killed by someone who committed similar crimes over the past few months. There seems to be at least a few threads that run through each case to the next. One of them is that the mother of the victim . . ."

"Received a phone call from a man?" the woman asked.

"Yes!"

"His mom talked to somebody last night. He had already left for his shift. She called me to ask me if anybody had been by the house looking for him. I'll get you her information. I can call her and let her know it's important that you talk to her. She has a hard time remembering things, so don't be surprised if she can't give you a lot of details."

"Did she tell you anything about the call?"

"No, she didn't. Just that something didn't feel right after talking to him, that's why she called me."

"Do you have any idea what she may have meant?"

"No. I called my husband and let him know about it, but he didn't seem concerned."

"One more thing," Cain said. "Your husband held a lock of hair in his hand. It looked like it came from a small child. Is that something he may have gotten from one of your children?"

"I don't think so. He would have probably mentioned that to me. I could ask them."

"Could you let us know?"

"I can ask them now. Hey, guys, Come here."

Cain and Ray watched as the children slowly ushered back into the room.

"If you'd like to just call us later that would be fine," Ray said.

"Mom needs to ask you a question. Did any of you give daddy a lock of hair to keep with him at work?"

Cain and Ray watched as all the children silently shook their heads "no". There was tiredness in their downcast eyes.

"Thanks, guys," Ray said.

Cain turned back toward the mom. "I know your husband's department is there for you, but if you need anything at all you have our card. You can call us."

"Just promise me you'll get this guy."

"We will."

Cain and Ray stood up from the couch and turned toward the front door. Ray walked out first and Cain followed. As Cain crossed the threshold of the door, his eyes happened upon a family portrait just inside the door to the left. The portrait seemed to split, and shatter into a thousand pieces. Cain blinked his eyes, his vision returning as he stepped onto the front porch of the house.

The trooper's mother lived in a middle class neighborhood on the east side of town in a baby blue sided house with white shutters and a huge maple tree in the front yard. As they sat in the front room it was obvious that she was proud of her son and what he had accomplished in life. Several pictures of him decorated the living room area: one by the lamp, two on the mantle, some hanging on the wall. Almost all of them were of him in his trooper's uniform at some point in his career. There was what looked like high school and college graduation pictures on another shelf near the walk-through to the kitchen. Trinkets and knick-knacks sat here and there about the room collecting dust.

"Your son was very well known. A lot of people in the community respected him. We wouldn't be bothering you at this time if we didn't think it was important," Ray said.

"He was a strong young man. He told me he knew the risks of his job but wanted to protect people. When he was a child he always dreamt about catching the bad guys. You know, he had the highest number of drunk driving arrests for his division. I suppose I was just meant to lose both of my boys to tragedy."

Cain spoke. "We need to know about the phone call you received from somebody trying to contact him. It's extremely important that you try to remember as much as you possibly can. Can you tell us what the caller said?"

"Oh, no. There was no phone call."

Ray and Cain looked at each other, wondering if the poor memory thing had kicked in until she spoke again.

"My daughter-in-law must've misunderstood what I said. The man was here. He came to my door."

They were taken aback by what she said. This was new. This could help their case.

"Do you remember him, Ma'am, anything about him? What

he looked like? What he sounded like, his clothing?

"Well, my eyesight hasn't been all that good, and it was dark out. The light from the porch didn't really help because I had to squint to see him. I didn't have my glasses on. He was, oh, maybe about your age and height. I remember that he wore a button up shirt, like a dress shirt. He said he needed to meet me before he met my son. I thought that a bit strange, but the gentleman seemed so clean cut, so professional. He was dressed nicely. He appeared to be a fine young man. And he seemed to already know details about my son's schedule, and kept saying he wanted to make sure he got with him soon, before time ran out. The only information I gave him was that he would be on duty last night. But then he started talking kind of funny. He said that he couldn't just go straight to my son. That the puzzle doesn't fit together like that. That he had to meet with me first. That's when I told him I was tired and needed to go to bed for the evening. He kind of scared me. I called my daughter-in-law right away, once I knew the man had walked off. You don't think he had something to do with his death, do you? I guess we just can't trust anyone anymore. It's just not like thirty, forty years ago."

"There's nothing to show this man was directly involved in what happened to your son. We're just trying to gather as much information as possible." Cain thought of the young, clean-cut man from his dreams.

"There's something else we need to ask you," Ray said.

"What's that?"

"Did the man mention anything to you specifically along the lines of needing your permission to see your son or thank you in any way after he talked to you?" Cain asked.

"Yes, yes he did. I really hadn't told him much of anything, but before I closed the door the man said, 'Thank you, this just isn't possible without you.' Oh, God, what have I done?"

"Oh God, What have I done?" Cain repeated the woman's words to Ray after they got in the car and shut the doors.

"Poor woman," Ray said.

"Yeah, but too trusting. Let's face it. She really did just hand her son to our killer."

"I'm sure it wasn't her intention. No mother would purposely put her child in the hands of a killer, someone who was going to tear them apart."

"I know, but I think it should have been a bit more obvious to this woman that this guy was up to no good, that something was wrong with his approach."

"Well, now the only people that matters to are the next ones in line, right?"

As Cain and Ray pulled out of the drive a call came over the radio. "Is there anybody who can check on a situation taking place in the field near 2100 L Street NW. A lady says there's a fight or something going on with a group of kids. Area patrols are all busy."

Ray answered the radio. "We're not too far from there. We'll get it."

"Turn left, that's only a couple blocks down."

Cain and Ray pulled up to the vacant lot. A group of kids were gathered in a sort of huddle. They turned to look just in time to watch as a young teen boy lifted something over his head and threw it to the ground.

"What the heck are they doing?" Cain asked Ray.

Another boy reached down and picked up a large rock. He

lifted the rock up and over his head and smashed it into the ground beneath him.

A couple of boys were also crouched down in a smaller group nearby, surrounding something.

One boy kicked something hard, stirring up a dust cloud. A small object rolled across the ground out of the cloud. The little object came to a stop and Cain could see it moving.

"Hey!" Cain yelled.

The boys turned and looked, then ran toward the other end of the field as Cain and Ray got out of the vehicle.

They came upon the spot where the boys had been.

"This one's dead," Ray said as he looked down at a little puppy that couldn't have been more than a few days old. It had been crushed with a rock.

Cain looked at the one that had been moving. It was squealing.

"Is it hurt?" Ray asked.

"I don't know. Can't imagine it wouldn't be. Did you see that kid kick it?"

"No, I missed that."

Cain reached down, using one hand to gently roll the dusty and squirming little puppy into his other hand. He cuddled it close to his chest, cupping one hand over it and squeezing slightly in an attempt to warm the puppy and calm it down. He looked to where the smaller group of boys had been crouched down and saw another puppy cut in half at its mid-section just below the ribs and a small pocket knife lying on the ground next to it.

There was another whimper, this time from the inside of a five-gallon bucket that was laying on its side.

"Sounds like there's another one."

Ray lifted the bucket slightly, then reached in and removed a piece of towel to reveal another little puppy. "They chopped off this one's tail," Ray said.

Ray lifted the little puppy out of the bucket, careful not to touch its injured tail. The puppy was whining. "He looks alright, oh, pardon me little miss, *she* looks alright, other than her tail."

"God, I just don't understand these kids."

"Senseless! Absolutely senseless!"

Ray and Cain looked over the area for more victims. Cain used the piece of towel to pick up the bloody knife.

"We'll throw this away."

"I think that's it. I don't see any more of them."

"Yeah, I wonder where the momma is."

"Well, let's get you two fixed up," Ray said as they walked back toward the car.

"Who's driving?" Cain asked.

"Who's holding the puppies?"

"Well, I didn't really want to drive."

"You want to hold the puppies!" Ray said, laughing.

"Kind of…"

"You hold your puppy, I'll hold mine. I'll drive with my other hand."

"So, you're not giving up your puppy either! I'm not the only one that wanted to hold the puppies, am I?"

Cain twisted his body left and right, stretching out his back as he leaned against the car waiting for a spare set of keys to be dropped off by an officer from the division. As he stood there, a little girl from his apartment building skipped up to him.

"Hi, grandpa," said the little girl. Her curly hair bounced on her forehead as she giggled.

Cain looked down into her angelic face.

"You are so goofy, Elsie."

"You're goofy," Elsie said back.

Every time Cain saw Elsie she would call him Grandpa and

he would tell her she was goofy. He wasn't even old enough to be a grandpa yet, he would say to her. She was the kind of little kid that just got into his mind and made him think that the world wasn't so terrible. Her bouncy, curly hair and huge smile always cheered Cain's thoughts and made him feel good. Because of her mother's addiction problems Cain had taken a keen interest in making sure she was safe.

"I had fun at Kenny's last week," Elsie said.

"You always have fun at Kenny's."

"When are we going there next?"

"I'm not sure, honey. We'll have to see, okay. I've been really busy lately and your mommy has to say yes and sometimes she doesn't."

"Ask my mommy next time you go, okay?"

"I will, sweetheart, I promise."

Elsie ran off toward the apartment as a police cruiser pulled up to the curb, the officer dangling a set of keys in his hand.

"One too many last night, Cain?" asked the officer.

"Stayed here. Must've locked them in my car when I got home from work yesterday. Thanks, Chris."

Cain unlocked the car and grabbed his keys from the ignition.

6

Fire crawled up the floorboard of the car. The heat was intense. Cain felt a dull and continuous pain centered on the left side of his head. Each labored breath drew soot blackened smoke into his nostrils. His mind, his body, was unable to reject it.

He couldn't move. It was getting darker with bright flashes of orange fiery light illuminating the inside of the vehicle.

Then, suddenly, the face came through the black smoke, a flash of fire lighting it. Arms reached toward him. *No, no . . . get away.* He feared the arms. In his mind he pulled away, but couldn't move. He was locked in place, frozen. A scream was in his head, in his heart, breaking free from his inner soul, but it couldn't gap the distance between thought and actuality.

Cain awoke on his couch. He was still in his street clothes from the day before. The areas of the couch where his body had been touching were wet from perspiration. The lights in his apartment were on.

Ray stood over him. Cain tried to open his eyes and focus.

"Don't know where you just came from, but it couldn't have been anyplace good. You were shaking pretty bad. Man, you look awful!" Ray said. "You just don't wake up well in the morning, do you? Maybe you shouldn't leave modeling paints uncapped when you go to bed. The whole place smells like freaking enamel."

Cain gave him an early morning dirty look. "Son of a…that set of paints cost me thirty bucks!"

Cain sat up on the couch and grabbed one of the small bottles of paint from the coffee table next to a model he'd been working on. He examined the top layer of paint that had glazed over and dried, then poked at it with a paintbrush. The Corvette model sat nearby.

"You left your front door unlocked; don't know if that's the wisest move."

"I must have fallen asleep."

"Well, let's go get some coffee at Jacks."

"Can I at least change clothes and brush my teeth?"

"Go ahead. I'll just make us coffee here."

The sound of a symphonic orchestra filled the inside of the car, a violin solo followed by a blast of brass instruments and a soft percussion roll. The music turned the inside of the car into a miniature amphitheatre. The concerto spilled into the air and people gave Cain strange looks as they passed by.

He watched as a young girl in her teens approached a known drug dealer for the neighborhood. The girl looked like a high school kid and didn't look like she was from the area. She was wearing clothes that belonged in neighborhoods more toward the west end of town or maybe the Lake Estates. She handed the young man cash for which he gave her back two pills from crumpled up tin foil. She turned to where Cain could see her face.

"*Ah, you again!*" Cain thought.

As the girl started to walk away, Cain jumped from the car and flashed his badge, stopping her in her tracks. He held out his empty hand and gave her a stern look. The dealer looked Cain in the eyes, turned, and ran.

"What? You want to take them?" she said. "Write yourself a prescription!"

"You can give them to me or we can get a uniformed officer and a car down here and you can take a ride home to your mommy and daddy's house. I'm sure they'll be real happy to know that you're hanging out buying drugs on this side of town."

"I don't think my mom and dad would believe it. They didn't believe it last time. I just told them I was feeling sick."

"If you were my daughter . . ."

"You'd also be too busy with your life to care, just like them."

"So you want to take that ride?"

"No. But I just paid good money for those."

"What was your name again?"

"Beth, Beth Amphetamine," she said sarcastically.

"What's your name?" Cain asked again, more sternly.

"Kelly! Do you need a last name? It's Daniels. But you should remember that, right?"

She put the two pills into Cain's hand. Cain dropped them on the ground and crushed them with his foot and then scattered the powder across the sidewalk.

"I know you'll probably just spin the block and do this again, but you know, there are much better things you can do with your life."

"Like what, try to grow up and live in some adult world?"

"What about school, your grades?"

"What about school? Half the kids I know party. It's not that big a deal. You all act like you never did anything crazy when you were younger. You wanna tell us how to live! Are you done with me? Can I go now, dad?"

"If I catch you doing this again, I'll see to it you get some kind of court-ordered treatment."

"Yeah, okay, whatever. Can I go?"

"Uh huh, you can go. I don't really have time to deal with you right now."

Ray had walked up. "Here's your soda. I could hear that music in the back of the store at the cooler. Do you have to torture the whole neighborhood with it?"

"Somebody spent endless nights spinning together those wonderful masterpieces for us, Ray, creations of musical excellence!" Cain swayed his arms across the air as they walked to the car.

"Well, let's change the station to some oldies masterpieces," Ray said, emphasizing the oldies part. "I need something a little closer to my listening range." Ray dialed in a station.

"I was listening to that!"

"That stuff's just ancient. I can't handle it."

"That's not right."

"You aren't making a single difference in that girl's life. She'll just find another dealer. I'm not knocking what you did, but it's just sad. She's gonna need some heavy-handed intervention. But if I remember right, I said that to you last time you dealt with her."

"Well, this is my neighborhood and when it's right here, it's home and it starts to affect the people around me, so it's different," Cain said. "Her parents need to know where she's at. They're probably in some other world, thinking everything's peachy keen with their kid."

"Or they've tried and she won't listen. Sometimes there's only so much you can do. Kids have to make right choices on their own."

Cain and Ray edged along slowly, eyeing people on the sidewalks up and down the street.

"Do they really think our killer is going to be out walking?" Cain said.

"No, our killer has more sense than that."

"Well, not like he has to work at eluding us. He's had every scene meticulously worked out just as he wanted us to see it. He's not gonna to just throw himself at us. This killer's sitting somewhere quietly right now, thinking about and planning his next kill."

"He knows he hasn't given us anything."

Ray and Cain's speculating was interrupted by their radio squawking out information from a nearby patrol.

"We've got a runner, possible suspect on the trooper murder. Need patrols in the block area of 29th and Aurora."

"29th and Aurora, that's right . . . oh, crap," Cain said as they crossed the intersection of 29th and Aurora Streets and the suspect bounded around the corner in front of them, a patrol car almost broadsiding their vehicle.

The young man broke into a faster sprint, knocking two pedestrians to the sidewalk with the power of a linebacker.

"Come on, come on!" Cain yelled.

Ray sped forward up the street. The man left the sidewalk and ran across a front yard.

"Let me out, let me out!"

Ray slammed on the brakes and Cain jumped from the vehicle, leaving the door open. It swung shut as Ray pounded the accelerator to the floor. The car lunged forward, the tires smoking and the car fish-tailing around the next corner as Ray attempted to cut the man off at the next block.

The runner bounded over a wooden gate. Cain ran across the yard and approached the spot with caution, looking around the corner of the house and glancing over the gate. The man was still running, now in the back yard toward the far corner.

I'm too old for this! Cain thought as he swung open the gate and ran down the side of the house.

Ray circled the block, coming to the alley entrance at the other end.

Cain ran into the backyard and watched as the man made his way through a thicket of bushes and trees at the corner of the lot and then into an alleyway. He could see Ray crossing the alley in front of him and saw the young man reach into his jacket as he ran. *No, no, no. Don't Ray!* Ray slammed on the brakes and the car came to a screeching halt. He backed up slightly and turned into the alleyway, facing the suspect head on.

Cain pushed his way through the thicket of bushes and into the alley just in time to watch Ray come to a stop in front of the man. Ray stared straight ahead and then began to duck as the man raised a handgun and pointed it at him, firing a round into the driver's side of the vehicle. The man moved closer to the vehicle, firing another shot.

Cain's vision blurred as he reached inside his coat and pulled his weapon from its holster. "Stop!" Cain yelled.

Bam! Another shot rang out, the front windshield splintering into multiple spider webs of shattered glass. The suspect wildly released two more shots into the driver's area of the car.

Cain was at least fifty feet away. His vision went black, then blurred. Images of several of the murder victims flashed across his mind. Caboom! Cain's first shot snapped him back into reality. He had drawn down on the suspect and was now firing multiple rounds into his back. The suspect's body lunged forward, bouncing off the fender of the car and hitting the pavement.

Cain ran towards the vehicle, his handgun still pointed at the suspect. "Ray? Ray!" He looked into the car. Ray wasn't moving. He was lying on the front floor of the car, completely up underneath the dash as far as he could fit.

The patrol car that had nearly hit them pulled up and Si and Chris jumped out. They moved toward the suspect, Chris grabbing the weapon off the pavement and taking it away from him.

Cain swung open the driver side door. "Ray!" Ray didn't respond. "Ray?" Cain grabbed his leg.

Ray recoiled from his touch and pushed his body away from the firewall and from under the dash, rolling his body back toward the front of the seat and fumbling to grab the steering wheel. He had shattered glass all over him. He was panicked, grabbing at parts of the car trying to get out. He pulled the passenger door handle and opened the door, using the corner of the seat to pull himself backward and onto the asphalt.

He was breathing heavy, in shock. Cain moved to the passenger side of the car.

"Are you hit? I don't see anything. Do you feel anything?"

"No, I'm just having trouble breathing." Ray leaned against the car and crouched, bending his knees and then slowly sliding down to the pavement and putting his head in his hands. "Oh, God, that was close. That was real close."

"Tripped rescue already," Si said.

"I just need to breath."

"Just sit still and try to relax," Cain said.

People had begun to make their way into the alleyway. A police car blasted its siren to break the crowd up so they could drive through. Another patrol vehicle pulled up at the street and the officer started to do crowd control, moving the people out of the alley and onto the sidewalk area. Neighbors with fences adjacent to the alley started to pop their heads up to look at the scene. Cain walked around the vehicle as he holstered his weapon. Chris checked the suspect's pulse.

"Nothing?" Cain asked.

"No, he's gone. By the looks of it he was probably gone before he hit the pavement. I don't remember ever seeing you that accurate on the range."

"I don't remember pulling off the rounds," Cain said.

Si dropped to his knees next to them, cracking open the

medical kit he had retrieved from the car and pulling out large gauze rolls.

"Don't think you're gonna be able to help this one, Si," Said Chris.

"Cain looked at the shattered windshield of the vehicle and then at the handgun the officer had set on the hood. It was a police issue .40 caliber semi-automatic. It was most likely the trooper's weapon.

The suspect was wearing jeans with large holes in the legs. He had a white hoody on that was now beginning to show from the spread of blood how many times he'd been shot. He was wearing black, military style boots.

"I think we got him, Ray. I think this is our guy."

"Yeah? Well, he almost got me!" Ray said, still trying to catch his breath.

Greg pulled into the alleyway and brought his car to a stop about forty feet from Ray's car. He hurried from his vehicle to the side of the vehicle where Ray was sitting.

"You alright?" Greg asked.

"I came in on him too fast. I should've been more careful."

"We can talk about mistakes later. I'm just glad you're okay. This could've been bad." Greg helped Ray to his feet.

"I know." Ray ran his arm across his forehead and collected the sweat from his brow. "That was just way too close."

"Do you need medical?"

"No."

"Just sit tight, alright? We'll take care of the rest of this."

Greg turned and walked over to Cain.

"What do we have?"

"Looks like our suspect. The weapon's on the hood of the car. "

Greg examined the handgun. "Polymer .40 Caliber. Let's see if it belongs to our trooper."

Greg opened a folder he had set down on the hood of the

car and compared the serial number on the weapon to the paperwork in front of him.

"That's it. I'll call Jones and let him know we have his man's weapon. He'll be glad to know it's been recovered."

"And that we got his killer," Cain added.

"I'm not so sure about that. The guy looks like a punk kid to me."

"Well, I hope so," Ray said from across the hood.

"Wouldn't hold my breath or count on it if I was you," Greg said.

"Right now I couldn't hold my breath if I wanted to."

"Alright, Cain, you know the drill." Greg slid the folder on the hood to the side.

Cain reached into his holster and pulled out his weapon. He pressed the release button for the clip and let it fall into his hand and set it on the car. He held the gun over the hood of the car and pulled back on the slide, opening the firing chamber and carefully examining it. He set the gun on the car's hood next to the clip.

"Because of the way this case is going, make sure you go down to the armory today when you get back. I want another weapon assigned to you right away," Greg said. "This is probably going to shut you down for a few months."

"I know."

Greg called for one of the patrol supervisors nearby.

"Washington!"

Washington walked over to the vehicle.

"Ralph, could you have someone watch these items until our techs get here? They'll need to go into evidence. I've got the OIS team from the DA's office on their way. They should be here fairly soon. Cain, are you ready for this? Do you remember everything?"

"Some of it's blurry, but I'll have it all straight by the time they get here."

"Ralph, I'll need the two officers who were on scene also.

Have Karen pull them over here."

"Alright."

"They need to stay close by."

Washington started to speak into his radio as Greg walked toward the front of the car, taking in the whole scene again and looking closely at the shattered windshield. He blew out a deep breath.

"I want a debrief back at the division in the training room as soon as we all leave here. Nobody goes home until that's done."

As Greg was talking the investigative on-call from the DA's office walked up.

"Greg, how are you? What do we got?" he asked.

"Good. My men just survived a serious incident; that's always good. We've got an officer involved shooting with one officer. Two officers un-holstered but didn't fire. One was taking cover in the vehicle."

"Well, my team will start gathering what they need. They'll collaborate with your collection of evidence. We'll need the usual from you."

Cain was worn out after giving his statement to the DA's team member. Moments later, Ray turned away from another interviewer. They walked toward each other.

"Well, that was fun," Ray said.

"Yeah, a true pleasure." Cain ran his hand across his brow.

Greg motioned for them. "Come on, guys. I'll give you a ride.

After the debriefing at the station Ray and Cain sat at their desks eating halves of a pastrami sandwich that had been delivered from the little deli across the street. Cain watched as an extension light on the phone flashed for several minutes. Nobody was answering it. He got tired of looking at the flashing light. He picked up the phone.

"Hello, can I help you?"

"I hope so. This is the chief editor from the Crossroad's

Chronicle. I want to talk to somebody about the murders that have been taking place in the city."

"Well, ma'am, as a matter of policy I'll have to give your call to my supervisor, okay?"

The lady on the other end of the line didn't like his answer. He looked in and saw that Greg was on the phone so he entertained himself listening to her while he ate his sandwich.

"I don't understand why you guys aren't cooperating with our reporters," she said. "They've put several calls in to your information officer. Nobody would talk to them at today's shooting incident."

Greg hung up the phone. "Let me put you through to my supervisor," Cain said.

Cain watched and listened to one side of the conversation as Greg picked up the phone and began speaking.

"Mrs. Greve, been a while. How's married life treating you? Today's? Yes, I did. I thought it was great. I like the way you have the ability to be so tactful in your words while you're slowly driving in a knife."

It was obvious from the tone of the conversation on Greg's end that the two had dealt with each other before.

"Yes, can you give me just a couple of days? I'll have something put together for our IO and have her get in touch with you. Alright, talk to you later."

Cain could see Kenny looking out the front of the large bay window as he made his way up the walkway to the front door. Kenny was kneeling on the couch that had its back against the window. He had his arm pulled back toward his face, squinting his eye near his little hand, which he had formed into a gun and was firing off pretend gunfire at Cain.

Cain knocked and swung the door open at the same time, looking at Kenny as he entered the house.

"Bam, bam, bam," Kenny yelled.

Cain wanted to reciprocate as usual but some of his playfulness was lost in the incident from a few weeks earlier.

"You got him, Cain! You got the bad guy!" Kenny said.

"Yeah, I got the bad guy, Ken."

"You shot em, Cain."

Cain felt a little awkward.

"You shot em dead!"

"Kenny!" Holly yelled from the kitchen. "Stop!"

"He's alright, Holly." Cain ruffled Kenny's hair.

"Kenny, come here. Come get a snack."

"Mom, Cain got the bad guy!"

"I think he knows that, honey."

Cain crossed the threshold into the kitchen. Holly walked up and gave him a gentle kiss on the cheek, a deep sincerity in her eyes. "Thank you," Holly said.

"I did what I needed to do."

"Well, I'm just glad you were there to do it."

"Cain, where's Elsie?" Kenny asked.

"I can't bring Elsie unless her mommy says yes, okay. Her mommy doesn't always say yes. She wanted to come play with you but she couldn't."

"Ah, man!"

"Come here, buddy. I've got something for you."

Cain reached into his pocket and pulled out a pound sized candy bar.

"Chocolate!" Kenny said.

"You've got to share it with mom and dad. That's if you can keep your Grandpa away from it."

"Grandpa loves chocolate," Kenny said.

"Yeah, you better hide that from him," Holly said.

"How's your mom doing?" Cain asked. "Ray said she had another strong episode."

"She's alright. She wasn't feeling well enough to come. They're both so independent. They just won't let us help them. I think they feel like some kind of burden. But they're not. I'd give them the world if I could."

"Well, give her my love."

"I thought you were going to bring Elsie. You know how much my little boy likes her."

"It's hit and miss. Her mom said she could come yesterday and changed her mind today. I just wish she'd straighten out her life."

Kenny broke into their conversation. "Man, you're awesome, Cain. You brought me candy and saved my dad!"

"Kenny?"

"What Cain?

"Listen to me, okay? I'd do the same thing tomorrow if it happened again, but we don't like to have to do that. We do it because it's our job. That man made a bad choice. Then I had to do my job and stop him from hurting your dad. Do you know what?"

"What?"

"We even want the bad guys to get better. Sometimes they just need time to realize what they're doing is wrong. Everybody can get better, no matter who they are or what they've done."

"Sounds good. Now let's eat some chocolate!"

Cain looked at Holly and she smiled. "I don't think he heard anything I just said."

"How're you doing?" Holly asked.

"I'm okay. It took me a couple days for the numbness to wear off. That's when I actually started to process the situation and what had happened. We came real close to losing Ray. I can't imagine not having him around."

"Well, why don't you go out there and relax with Ray and dad. I'll bring you guys some tea."

"I can get the tea," Cain said. He grabbed the tea from the

shelf and slid a canister from next to the wall across the counter.

"Where's that gallon pitcher?" Cain asked.

"Bottom shelf, right," Holly said.

"So where's my little baby girl?"

"She's napping."

"You know I need my Ranae time."

"Well, you can hold her later. I don't need a screaming baby on my hands right now."

"I can wait. Hey, Kenny, carry one of these glasses for me, buddy. Hand this one to your dad."

Cain pushed open the screen slider for the back patio. Ray was tirelessly slaving over an older, built in brick grill, trying to find some sort of balance between the concept of cooked through and severely charred as he shuffled brats and hamburgers between hot and cold spots over the fire.

"Herb, how are you?" Cain asked.

Holly's dad answered Cain by rolling his eyes and smiling a little as he took a shot at Ray. "I told him he should have made that grate adjustable. Now, Ray, Cain here's going to have to eat those burnt ones."

"Tea?" Cain asked.

"Kenny, set your dad's close to the grill there in case he needs to put out those brats," Herb said.

"Those smell good," said Cain.

"Yeah, they do. And they're about done."

"I think a few of them were done a while ago," said Cain.

"It's that grate," Herb said.

"You and that grate!"

"Every time we barbeque you burn half the food."

"I promise. The next grill…you can supervise the building, deal?"

"That might be a good idea," Herb said.

Ray had turned around to talk with Cain and Herb.

"Dad, look! That one's on fire!"

"That one's yours, Kenny," Cain said.

"Nuh uh. It's yours!"

Ray quickly moved the burning brats to one side of the grill and then switched the conversation to a more serious subject.

"Have you heard anything?" he asked Cain.

"Well, you were there on Thursday when Greg told me it would be about a week. He said yesterday that the DA's office was moving this one along quickly. You know, I almost didn't shoot him?"

"Huh?"

"I almost didn't shoot him. It's a miracle you're alive. I couldn't focus. Went totally tunnel vision. It's amazing I even got a shot off. I definitely don't remember firing that many rounds."

"Yeah, well, our vehicle had every last round from the trooper's revolver in it. You won't have any problem getting cleared by the DA's office. I don't understand why it's taking this long on such an obvious situation," said Ray.

"It seems like they're just about on schedule. I've never seen them issue a final report under a month's time. They had enough witnesses who watched the entire thing unfold. They've got a dashboard full of rounds. He wasn't messing around. I told him to stop. He didn't stop. I stopped him. It's pretty cut and dry, but you and I both know these things can take time."

"Well, as much as I like the free time there's something inside me that's biting at the bit wanting to get back to work."

"We'll be back before you know it. Alright, give me one of those brats. I'll take the one on the far right. No, no, the other one."

There was a faint sound of the beginning whimpers of a crying baby coming from inside the house.

"Oh, Cain," Holly said. "Somebody wants you!"

"It's my girl! Come on, give her to me."

Cain set down his plate of food and reached out for little

Ranae, who was now in a full cry from having just awakened.

"You just need your Cain, huh baby? That's right, yes, you're so beautiful. You're a doll, that's what you are. Yeah, I love you. God, she's so precious!" Cain pulled her in close to his chest, her tears soaking into his shirt shoulder.

He sat down on one of the patio chairs, holding Ranae in one arm and juggling his plate in his other hand.

"Hey, Kenny, can you squirt some mustard and ketchup on this brat for me?"

Kenny held each bottle over Cain's plate one at a time and squirted out far more of their contents then Cain preferred.

"Now put some of that sauerkraut on there."

"You guys are gross," Kenny said.

"What do you mean?"

"Sowgrats gross," Kenny said, mispronouncing the word. "It tastes yucky! And Grandpa said it's made out of pig's tails."

Ray and Cain looked at Herb, who gave a contorted smile that seemed to say "Who? Me?"

"Well, I like it," Cain said.

"That's because you're a grown up."

"Now, that's a matter of opinion," Ray piped in.

"Someday when you're grown up you'll like it too, Kenny."

A gentle breeze lifted the scent from the pine trees. Cain inhaled, enjoying it. This was one of his favorite places to come and sit, especially on a warm summer's afternoon when the trees cast a cool shade over the bench that was placed in the midst of the little grove. The grove of Ponderosa pines had been planted many years earlier, in memoriam to someone whose name had been reduced to a smoothly worn, illegible plate on the back of the bench. Cain remembered when the trees were just mere saplings, tiny. Now they towered over his head upwards of fifty feet, their branches dense with needles.

Just in front of the little grove were two small clusters of rose bushes. From where Cain sat he could see rows of fruit trees in full blossom to his left. The shoreline of a pond at the end of a short slope spread out in front of him. Ducks swam at the pond's far edge.

Cain leaned his back to one edge of the bench against the side arm and turned to look at the old worn metal. Once again, as he had done in the past, he attempted to interpret the worn-down inscription on the plate. He ran his fingers over the letters, but still could not distinguish them.

He looked out over the land and thought of his father's acreage, it's pond alive with waterfowl and small orchard covered with fruit . . .

"Hey, do you want a peach or an apple?" his father asked.

"I'll take a peach," said Cain.

Cain's father reached into the nearby fruit tree and pulled a perfectly ripened piece of fruit from one of it's branches and tossed it to Cain, who was resting against the trunk of another tree and looking out over the acreage.

"This is a beautiful piece of property, son. You two should consider holding onto it when I'm gone. The house isn't much, but you both could build something newer. There's enough room for that. The pond there would be great for your kids. These trees will last several years if they're taken care of. It would be a wonderful place to raise your families."

A piercing shriek pulled Cain from his thoughts about his father. He looked across the field, just in time to watch the shadow of the large bird rippling across the grass in the field below. The shadow grew smaller in size as it's speed increased and it came closer to the ground.

Cain's eyes moved forward, instinctively, almost in a pre-conditioned response, his eyes searching the field until they rested on the seemingly unaware creature foraging for food. The rabbit's ears raised upward. It placed its feet and legs in a strong stance, then immediately bounded forward to the right and then left toward a stand of field grasses. It overshot the grasses, running past them into the open field, slid and stopped briefly, then turned sharply and leaped toward a hole in the ground.

The little mammal had just crested the top edge of the hole, and then it was over. The pursuer and its shadow came together above the hole. There was a flutter of wings and dust, and then, after a brief struggle, the great bird lifted itself once again into the air, the weight of its prey clutched tightly in its talons. The legs of the small mammal kicked as it struggled in the predator's grip and then stopped moving.

As the great bird flew away, Cain closed his eyes and breathed, listening to each breath as he inhaled and exhaled. He struggled to open his eyes. Fear gripped him. He looked toward the trees to his right behind the bench and then back out into the field. The bird was gone.

Oh, there he goes! Cain thought as Kenny threw off his towel and made a mad dash for the five foot section of the swimming pool, springing off the concrete edge and leaping into the air. He nearly landed on top of a little girl as he plunged feet first into the shallow area of the pool. Water splashed up and over the edge, rolling across the "No Diving" sign painted on the concrete at Kenny's point of entry. He disappeared briefly under the water, then came up between two other children a few feet from where he had gone under. He flailed his little arms as he dog-paddled back to the edge of the pool and flopped his arms over it, holding on.

"Grandpa!" Elsie's voice was muffled through all the activity. Cain could hear her, but not tell where she was.

"Grandpa, up here!"

Cain hurriedly ran his eyes across the area of the pool where her voice was coming from, looking along the edge of the pool and at the diving board. He had just seen her before Kenny dove into the pool.

"Grandpa!"

His eyes finally met with Elsie's voice. She had made her way up the steps of the concrete high dive that extended over the deep end of the swimming pool and was now standing right up against the edge, the first in a line of kids preparing to jump into the pool twelve feet below.

"Oh, hey, that's too . . ." Cain tried to stop her.

The last thing he saw was a blur of pink and orange swimsuit mixed with a giant grin on her face, her eyes wide open as she plunged into the water below. *She's gonna go deep on that one!*

By the time she re-surfaced, Cain had made the distance from the lounge chair he'd been sitting in to the edge of the pool near the deep end.

Elsie inhaled as she surfaced, then started hacking and coughing, frantically trying to push out the water she was gagging on.

Cain dove off the edge of the pool, flying through the air, then gliding forward through the water and arriving quickly at Elsie's side. He wrapped his arm around her and lifted her upward. She continued to cough, now holding one hand over her mouth and nose and locking the other around Cain's neck in a tight grip, spitting out chlorinated water. She looked down into Cain's eyes and then stuffed her face into his cheek, tired but no longer scared.

Cain reached the poolside with her.

"Are you okay?" he asked her.

Elsie quietly shook her head yes, a concerned look on her face.

"I'm not mad at you," Cain said.

Elsie wiped more water from her face, her eyes tearing up, then laughed slightly and became more relaxed.

"That's why we have the deep end rule when we come to the pool. Silly girl! What were you thinking?"

Cain looked up toward the lounge chairs and noticed Kenny had gotten back out of the pool. "Are you ready to go?" Cain asked Elsie.

She shook her head yes.

"Alright, come on."

He moved her along the edge of the pool toward the ladder.

"Kenny, we're gonna take off, buddy. Gather up your stuff," Cain said as he and Elsie walked up.

"We're leaving already?"

"We've been here for hours!"

Cain wrapped Elsie's towel over her shoulders and started gathering their belongings.

"Okay! Do we have everything?" Cain asked.

"Yep," said Elsie.

"Don't forget your goggles," Cain said as he picked them up

from under a chair and handed them to Kenny.

They walked toward the shower areas.

"Alright, Elsie, don't come out the other side until I yell for you, okay sweetie?"

"Okay."

"We'll try to hurry."

Elsie walked to the right into the women's changing area and Cain and Kenny to the left into the men's.

"Wasn't expecting that last dive into the pool," Cain said as he and Kenny walked out to the entrance area and he started to towel off again.

Cain shouted past the concrete walled entrance to the women's changing area.

"Did you have fun?" Cain asked Kenny, crouching down to his eye level.

"Oh, yeah!"

"Elsie, you ready?"

Elsie walked out. Cain cupped his hand over the side of her head. "You okay?"

"Uh huh," Elsie answered, shaking her head.

"Alright. What do you two say we stop at the candy wagon on the way to the car? Some cotton candy sounds pretty good right now."

"And fruity rollies!" said Kenny.

"And tangy twisters," said Elsie.

Just past the corner of the pool fence along the sidewalk stood the candy wagon, nestled under a group of shade trees. It was a child's dream. There was row upon row of different selections of candy across several bottom shelves, cotton candy hanging from the carts frame above, and not a single ounce of real food.

"Can I get some tangy twisters?" asked Elsie, pointing to the five cent candies.

"I'll tell you what. You two pick out ten small candies and

we'll all share some cotton candy. Sound good?"

"Sounds great!" said Kenny.

Cain dropped the children off at Ray and Holly's, then headed home. The route he chose took him into the heart of the city, quiet for a Sunday afternoon, few cars moving about. Crossroads Cathedral rose into the sky ahead of him, breaking through the monotony of the buildings surrounding it, majestically declaring its stand. Cain stopped just short of the stop sign and edged his way around the corner slowly, scanning the scene of parishioners striding up the steps of the cathedral. Little girls wore flowery dresses. Men in suits, women, pantsuits or dresses, some long, some shorter. A torn pair of jeans on a young man wearing a faded rock band t-shirt caught his eye, his long hair curling at his shoulders. A man with an old shopping cart pushed it up against a street sign near a grass area, grabbed a small bag from the cart, and walked toward the door. A greeter put his hand on the man's shoulder and smiled.

Cain looked up at the cathedral's towering gothic steeple and its ornate carvings. Faded angelic images stood carved into the stone, weathered by years of harsh elements. An equally worn cross, centered in the old building's facade, seemed to draw his eyes inward toward itself, pulling his attention away from the rest of the scene before him. He thought of Delores, hesitated for a moment, then lifted his foot from the brake pedal and turned onto the empty street.

7

Cain lay in bed searching the ceiling for some blank patch of space he could stare at to flush the images from his mind. He was drenched with sweat again. He halfway felt like he was losing his mind. Another nightmare had intruded upon his sleep. The soft sound of a symphony rang through a small room. It was an aesthetic looking space. It wasn't veiled in this dream. He had stood, staring down into the face of the lifeless body of a naked, newborn boy, the number five dangling from his arm on some sort of tag with a date on one end. Bloody fluid oozed from sunken eye sockets across pale, torn facial flesh, rolling down the sides of the child's face. The infant boy's eyelids twitched. Cain could tell the eyes were moving underneath. The child was attempting to pull apart, to open, a tender eyelid. Coagulated blood and crusted fluid around his eyelid moved, split, and broke free. Suddenly, the child's eyes opened wide and he looked straight up at Cain. The little boy convulsed. Then, as quickly as his eyes had opened, they slammed shut. The music went silent. The smell was terrible. Cain awoke, trembling and clutching his pillow like a frightened child. Something inside of Cain was telling him that if he stopped the killer, he stopped the dreams. The dreams were some sort of clue. He had a deep gut feeling that these two worlds were intricately woven together, some mystery he had to figure out.

"He wasn't our guy!" Greg said. "I could have told you that from the beginning. Shouldn't have jumped to that conclusion anyhow. It was obvious the guy was just some punk."

"We didn't think so either, but kinda hoped he was," Ray said.

"He wasn't. A con, yes, serial killer, no. A thief, that's about it. He had our trooper's credit cards and about fifty bucks in cash, which we couldn't confirm with the trooper's wife, but most people tend to carry a little cash. This guy was known for pawning stolen stuff at the local shops on a regular basis. He'd tried to sell the gun at two shops that morning. One of the shops called the department right away because they recognized it as a service revolver. That's why we blanketed the area with patrols."

"What about the kids seeing him? He was hunched over the victim," Ray said.

"You and I both know that doesn't mean he killed him. A lot of young people run these streets at night. The lab checked out his clothing. When you shot him, he was wearing the same outfit as the night before, the one the kids described, yet he had hardly any of that troopers DNA on his clothing. There was way too much blood at that crime scene. It was too violent for him not to have blood on him from that trooper. We contacted his family. He'd been at his dad's house for almost a year. He just got back in town three weeks ago. That places him out of state for all the other murders. We also searched the room he was staying in at his grandparent's house and didn't come up with anything except a laptop just reported stolen from the campus."

"That doesn't mean he didn't travel back to commit the crimes," Ray said. "Nothing's happened. It's been over three weeks."

"From the coast? The guy thieved and pawned stuff off for money. That was his history. He'd been busted for it before. You really want to put credence in the idea that a petty thief made special trips hundreds of miles back here to commit serial killings? Doesn't fit. Not to mention the description we got from the trooper's mother. He wasn't our killer. I'd love to think he was. But you believe that, you're rolling dice for the next victim. Don't think this is over. Set this guy aside as the suspect. If he was, the killings will stop. If he wasn't, you'll be wasting precious time feeling like you got him. You need to move forward with the case as though the killer is still out there. The DA's pushing their paperwork through this afternoon. They said their office should have you cleared by next week. Just keep looking hard at everything until then."

As they spoke, radio traffic started bouncing through the room behind them.

Si yelled. "County's got a hot one in the Canyons! Victim's still alive, guys!"

"Greg?"

"Go, just go!"

It was after rush hour, so they were able to jaunt north a short distance and miss traffic and get on the bypass. They were doing over a hundred miles an hour on the highway that encircled the city. Cain's head was reeling. He had an insane, jittery adrenaline rush going on inside his body. They couldn't believe what deputies and rescue were saying on the radio. It was clearly another victim of their killer. But this one was still alive! Ray almost put the car into the back of a trash truck, barely slipping between its tail end and another vehicle. Their siren blasting and little rotational light seemed like a waste of electricity. By the time anybody saw or heard them, they had come and gone.

As sad as it seemed, they were desperately trying to beat the paramedics to the scene, hoping to extract some sort of information from the victim before EMS wouldn't let them near him.

"I guess this settles the idea that our shooter wasn't the killer, huh?"

"Yeah!" Ray yelled against the sound of the air rushing in through the open windows.

"Oh crap, man, you're making me nervous!"

"It's always been my job to make you nervous!"

"Well, that was alright, whoa, when we were teenagers."

Cain was relieved when Ray left the bypass and slowed down to around seventy miles an hour, although now it seemed just as fast because they were on surface streets. Ray made a hard left onto Canyons Road as they left a business district. They were immediately consumed by wooded areas on each side of the road. Cain was barely able to see the address numbers as Ray sped by. He caught a glimpse of the number they needed on a short marker partially obscured by some low tree branches and a bush. They went whizzing right by as Cain yelled, "There it is!" Ray slammed on the brakes a hundred feet past the drive, as if in some delayed reaction to Cain's yelling. The tires smoked as Ray spun the car around and headed back the other direction.

He nearly missed the entrance to the property again, losing control on the gravel drive and almost side swiping a tree. Overgrown branches smacked the sides of the windshield as they sped down the long driveway that finally opened up into a larger parking area in front of the house. There were several patrol cars and a patrol division supervisor's vehicle along with a sheriff's vehicle parked in front of the house. Cain and Ray could hear EMS coming up the road in the distance and knew their time was limited.

The house was tucked back into the trees. It was very secluded. "Seems like the perfect place for a murder," Cain said as they hurried from their vehicle. For a split second, Cain's mind was consumed by the sight of a mint condition 1953 Corvette in the driveway. They heard someone yell, "Back here!" They jogged around the side of the house. A deputy was hunched down over the victim trying to comfort him. Sergeant Washington started spouting off information as they walked up.

"Neighbor found him. Says he was out for a walk on the trail and heard some groaning from the patio and decided to investigate."

The neighbor, looking visibly shaken, stood in the back yard talking to another deputy, who was urgently writing in a notepad.

The victim was lying on an expansive stone patio at the back of the house. He was barely conscious. Cain knelt over him and the man seemed startled. "Sir, did you see who did this to you?" Ray asked.

He was shaking. Deep, intense fear filled his eyes. Cain could barely tell a faint 'yes' and a slight nod of his head. His eyes shifted to Ray and then back to Cain. He didn't look good. He was turning an ashen pale color. Blood gurgled with each breath and rolled out of the edge of his mouth.

"Was it someone you know?" Cain leaned in, closer to his face. His shaking worsened, and he seemed to be almost whimpering. He looked at Ray and then back at Cain again.

"M . . . M . . . Mom . . . D . . . D . . . Da . . . Daddy, why?"

He convulsed sharply. His eyes went straightforward into a blank stare. His body stopped moving. Cain heard the tires from the ambulance rolling over the gravel in front of the house. They were too late.

The killer was sloppy this time. He didn't do a good job. It was as if this was his first victim and he hadn't learned how to keep it clean yet. A partial shoe pattern was stamped across the deck wood in the victim's blood. It also appeared that he had actually stepped on some of the brain tissue that was scattered around the deck. If they caught the killer and he hadn't cleaned it off, DNA could now place him at the crime scene. There was blood coming from the back of the victim's head and the number five was carved into his chest. Cain and Ray looked at each other in shock.

"What the heck? What did he do, decide to give us the murder weapon?" Cain said.

"Was he spooked or something?"

"That's not a clue we expected to find."

Near the man's right hand was some sort of tool. It was a stainless steel rod with a handle on one end and a circular looking loop at the other.

"What is it?"

"I don't know. Deputy, could you come here?"

"What do you need?"

"Have you ever seen a tool like this? Do you have any idea what it might be?" Ray asked.

"Doesn't look like anything my dentist comes after me with."

"Is the house cleared?" Cain asked

"Oh yeah, first thing after we got here," another said. "I've got a team doing a final sweep-through right now."

"Ralph, get a call out on mutual aid. We'll need an assist on searching the area. The killer could still be close: neighbors, woods, surrounding areas. Try to determine if there was another vehicle here in the driveway. Let's look for people on foot also. No description, just anything strange."

"Got it."

"Blood's coagulated to at least three to four hours. This guy laid here suffering for a while. Probably happened early this morning before dawn."

"Our killer's long gone."

The house was beautiful inside, including a large living room with a grand piano off to one side. Its glossy black color shined in contrast with lighter colored floors. Cain was envious. What appeared to be a large study area was filled with musical instruments, resting quietly in their stands. Pictures lined shelves, awards lined the walls. In one picture, a younger man in his teens played a cello, the same young man with a violin, again at a piano. There was a larger picture of the victim conducting the city's philharmonic orchestra. Not far from that was a photograph of the victim standing with the Mayor and the Governor and several other familiar faces of prominence. On the credenza was a picture of the victim as a teenager standing next to an older couple outside what looked like a medical practice. The sign read: Crossroads Planned Parenting Clinic 924 North 25th St. A smaller picture of the victim and a young woman sat nearby on a shelf. Scribbled across the top of the picture were the words, "Luv Ya, bro, thanks for listening, Ke . . ." The name trailed across the photo, illegible. The older man's face was familiar to Cain but he couldn't place him. The young woman in the second photograph seemed familiar. *Maybe I've seen them somewhere,* Cain thought. He continued to look around the room.

"Okay, It's not like I'm a doctor or anything, but I'm

guessing this doesn't belong here," Cain said.

"What is it?" said Ray

Cain was looking down. Sitting in front of the photograph was a cylindrical plastic tube, about eight inches long, covered in blood.

"Is it a part of one of the instruments?"

"No, I don't recognize it."

"Are you sure?"

"Unless it's something new, I don't think so. Four years of band in high school, I would know."

"Looks like our killer is giving us a little more than we planned."

Cain's eyes scanned the room. It was obvious the victim had made a career with his music. Cain's enjoyment of classical music made it even more difficult to take in the scene. It made him angry at the killer. He began to question what the victim's true passion in life was as he looked over the bookshelves. There was book after book about depression. Lying across a large table were several pages of sheet music, hand-written, rough drafts with symbols crossed out, notes added. On the same table sat a large book.

"The Power of Music to Heal." It was a rough draft, incomplete. Cain thumbed through the pages. Chapter 2 – The Effects of Music Upon Clinical Depression and Addiction. The dedication – For my sister. The book was filled with hand written notations and drawings of notes and line music. "There are exact mathematically figured notes of music that when struck may affect the physical, the emotional, the psyche of the individual. Music has the ability to draw someone out of the realm of depression, physical illness and even addiction," read an excerpt at the front of the book.

Cain's thoughts were interrupted by Ray's voice, "Director of the cities philharmonic. This guy was really well known. Saw him on public TV one time explaining how he had formulated music in a way to battle clinical depression. His father was a doctor and he . . . "

Cain interrupted, "I know. I feel like I should know him. I just didn't recognize him on the porch. He looks just like the man in this picture."

"Here I thought he kind of looked like you with all these instruments. And that could be an older you."

"I got some gray, but I'll dye before I go completely white!"

Ray moved toward the kitchen area.

"Cain, come here!" Ray said.

"What is that?" Cain asked.

"That's not some druggy's syringe. That's different. Look at that needle. I wouldn't want my doctor sticking that thing in me," Ray said.

"The needle itself is really thin."

"It has something in it."

"Do we need to close this scene and get a hazmat team in here?"

"Have the techs look at it first."

"Three items, three clues, one victim. Our killer's talking a little louder here. We just have to figure out what he's saying!"

"Hey, you guys might want to come upstairs," a deputy yelled.

Cain and Ray left the kitchen and walked up the stairs.

"In here," the deputy called from a bedroom.

"Check this out," the deputy said, pointing to something on the middle of the bed.

"Those are forceps. Now that one I do know," Ray said.

"Guilty?" Cain nodded toward the head of the bed.

Ray looked at the pillow. Scrawled in blood across it was the word "guilty". Drops of blood were sprinkled across the pillow, accenting the word in an artistic fashion. "Guilty. Someone is guilty of something. The killer wants everybody to know. How does all this fit together?"

"Okay, five clues: that's three downstairs and two up, plus the pillow writing. Let's keep looking."

Ray's cell phone rang. It was Chelsea. "Oh, you're here? That was quick!"

"You guys missed a hot one down here. It was mixed in with the papers on the desk. Apparently our killer's rather poetic. And there's blood on these papers, so I think it was meant to be found like this."

"Chelsea's got something else downstairs," Ray said to Cain.

"Okay, yeah, we'll look at it in just a second. The place is full of stuff. This time the killer is definitely making a statement of some sort."

"Don't touch anything here. We'll have a tech come up and work the room," Cain said. "Let's all get downstairs. Can you make sure all the people from your agency are out of the house?"

"Yep."

"Our sergeant will need a list of your responding deputies."

"Already done."

"Doesn't look like anything else in this area," Ray said from the bathroom off the bedroom.

Cain and Ray walked downstairs. Chelsea was just about to point out the papers to them when Ana poked her head in the back door from the patio area.

"You guys are really starting to slack off some. Did the paramedics talk to you yet?" Ana asked.

"No."

"I left it in place. We've got the weapon. The crew just found it as they checked him over for vitals. It's in the back of his head. You wouldn't have found it unless you had put your hand around his neck. It's pretty far in. The handles sticking out."

"Hold on, Chelsea," said Ray.

Cain and Ray walked onto the patio as Ana lifted the victim's head and rolled it to one side, exposing what appeared to be the shiny rounded handles of yet another instrument or tool of some sort. It was covered in blood, with just small areas of the stainless steel showing through.

"Wow, this is like the treasure chest of crime scenes!" Cain said.

"Is it?" Ana retorted. "Or is it not? Looks more to me like he's done all of this on purpose."

"Can't hurt to be in his head just a little more," Chelsea said from the doorway.

They all looked at her puzzled. "What?" Cain asked.

"The killer." Chelsea said. "At least he's letting us get to know him a little better. Wait until you see his writing skills. This guy's got a vendetta or something."

"Where is it?" Cain asked.

"Right where you missed it!" Chelsea led them back to the table that had the sheet music setting across it. "It was just partially hidden, you know, kind of mixed in with the rest of the papers here but showing just enough to where it should have been caught by someone who was paying attention." She opened her eyes wide and looked at Cain.

"Don't know how I missed that, but I would've found it the second time through."

Chelsea spread three sheets across the table in front of Cain and Ray. There were drops of blood on the edges of the papers. She read what set before them.

He draws down the hammer that strikes death's blow,
implements of destruction, a one man show.

Crushed and tangled bodies weave. Innocent? Guilty? His mind
deceived.

He drowned their voices in gurgling blood, but he can't deny
their resounding flood.

From the safety of the sanctum womb, he dragged them to a
shallow tomb

His own flesh he chose to destroy, tormented now, his little
boy.

The helpless die, the children cry, vindicate, vindicate, their
justice denied

Each child fought to get away, but he, he had the final say
Murderous killer, with seed to sow, the hunted had no place to
go

Seed sown by this reapers slave, destinies lost, his family not
saved

"I don't even want to begin to try to decipher this," Cain
said.

"He draws down the hammer that strikes death's blow," Ray
read the first line.

"Is he talking about himself or someone else?"

"I think this is all payback, revenge," Chelsea added.

"He drowned their voices?"

"The victim's voices?"

"Each child fought to get away? There haven't been any
child victims," Chelsea said.

"This guy's talking about child victims like they really
existed," said Ray.

"From the safety of the sanctum womb," Chelsea said. "Is
the killer talking about unborn children or maybe children taken
from the womb?"

Cain's mind was reeling in confusion. He couldn't help but
think about the children struggling to get away from the man in
his dreams.

"Sanctum or place of holies, a holy place," Ana said. "The
womb is thought to be a sanctuary by a lot of people. This
could put a whole new meaning to these murders."

"God, I hope this killer doesn't think there's something holy about what he's doing," said Ray.

"He may be trying to say exactly that," said Chelsea.

"What do you mean?" asked Cain.

"Children cry, vindicate. These might be some sort of revenge killings," said Chelsea.

"Or this idiot feels he has a holy calling."

"Alright, we'll look harder at this at the lab. We need to get through the rest of the house."

The sun had dropped to the horizon, streaming itself through the trees surrounding the property as Ray and Cain made their way toward the car. It was a peaceful setting, quiet. One would never have known the violence that had taken place in the midst of it. Ray motioned to Cain and looked at the Corvette. Cain took one last look at it as he flopped down into their vehicle. He shaped his fingers into an 'O' shape and viewed the car through them.

"Someday."

"Keep saving your pennies Cain, you'll get there."

They got into the car and slowly rolled up the drive to the road.

"Hey, turn left here. Let's take the old road back toward downtown, you know, catch a little scenery."

"You and your countryside dreams," Ray said.

"You know, these weren't really canyons at all."

"I know, I know. You told me the whole story the last time we were out this way.

Cain thought about the area. The Canyons weren't actually canyons at all. They were a large area of countryside estates scattered through a wooded area about ten miles from downtown. A young developer had purchased the land from the city and Cain had kept an eye on it as each estate was built among the trees. The only reason they were called "The Canyons" was because the woods had grown up around several acres of large slab rock that had been deposited there twenty years earlier from a nearby quarry. The quarry had long been shut down. Erosion had taken its toll and created little streams and creeks around the rocks. The setting was beautiful, idyllic, with a quiet peaceful feel of a deep deciduous forest, a retreat of solitude tossed into what had become the outer developing urban sprawl of the city. *If only I could escape to this place.*

Cain looked down each long driveway as they passed by, trying to get a glimpse of the houses that were now barely seen through the thick vegetation.

"A geneticist, a cellular biologist, a trooper. Now a conductor. What the heck is this guy thinking? What's his game?" said Cain.

"Who knows? They're different types of people, I mean, they all impacted the world in a different way."

"Well, we have to get inside this guy's head and figure him out!" Cain said, frustrated.

"Try to get some good sleep tonight? You seemed a little out of it today. Have you talked to anybody about the dreams?"

"You know I can't do that. I get put on sleeping pills for something psychological and they'll pull me off this job for six months. You're the only one that knows about the dreams and you're the only one that's going to know."

"You've got to do something. You're losing too much sleep. You really need to get all those people out of your head!" Ray pointed his finger at Cain's forehead like he was poking it from a distance.

Cain wondered if he should tell him that he thought his dreams were some subtle message from beyond the grave, pointing to their killer. He decided to keep the thought to himself. *It's better I went this one alone.*

8

"Move a little faster. You'll get one!" Cain said.

"It's not about being fast. It's about skill. I've been doing this a long time, you know."

Elsie swung a long arch with the butterfly net at a tiger swallowtail that had glided past her head, seemingly swooping in close to toy with her already frustrated ranting. "Missed!"

She slapped a foot down and sighed.

Cain watched from the steps nearby.

"Those butterflies are not too fast for my little Elsie. Come on, now, you can get one. No giving up!"

Elsie bounced back and forth, brushing aside a tall stand of zinnias as she danced through the apartment's courtyard flower garden. A small fountain trickled nearby, a centerpiece to tumbled brick walkways, it's pump struggling against the moss and algae that had taken over its tiny ecosystem.

"There's one!" Cain said.

Elsie swung at a small butterfly, its reactive movement

bouncing it straight up in the air and over her head, out of reach.

Cain stood up from the bottom of the concrete steps and walked over to Elsie just as she dropped the net down hard and fast on a beautifully blue accented, black butterfly that had not moved quickly enough to escape her grasp.

"Got it!" said Elsie, exhaling excitedly as she cupped her hand over the net, butterfly and the flower it was pinned against.

"Now what, Elsie?"

"I need my jar."

"Where's your jar?"

"Uh, it's over there," Elsie said as she motioned toward the jar, which sat nearly fifteen feet away next to the front door of her apartment.

"Well, that creates a problem, I suppose, doesn't it?" asked Cain. "How do you plan on holding onto that butterfly and going and getting your jar?"

"I'm not. You are!"

"I am? What am I, the jar guy?"

"Yep!"

Cain looked at her jokingly, as though he wouldn't get it.

"Grandpa, come on, it's going to get away!"

"I don't know…"

"Now!" Elsie said in her sweet yet demanding little voice. "Please?" she added, slumping her shoulders down.

Cain retrieved the jar from near the apartment and brought it over to Elsie, cupping it under the butterfly.

"Be careful not to smash him," said Cain.

"I've done this before! We have to get him sugar and water right away."

"I guess the flower nectar wasn't good enough?" Cain laughed at her.

"Quick! Put the lid on," Elsie said. "Close it, close it!"

"Ah, trapped forever in Elsie's jar of paradise, like a little genie in a bottle."

"Is not, I'll set him free tomorrow."

"That's what you said about the one last week, remember."

"I gave that one too much water."

"Well, Elsie, he sure is a pretty one!"

"It's a she, silly."

"Oh, I guess I didn't realize."

"The pretty ones are girls."

"I must've missed that chapter in the butterfly book."

"The boys are ugly moths!"

"I apparently missed that chapter too."

"You're not very smart."

"And you, my little girl, are very smart, aren't you?"

"Yes, I am."

"We gonna catch another one?"

"Yeah, I want one with some green on it, like a pretty green dress."

"Alright, a green one it is, with a pretty green dress! Ready?"

"Uh huh."

Elsie began to move about the courtyard again, making her way through the rows of the twenty foot garden.

"I like the garden," said Elsie.

"Why's that, honey?"

"If the wind blows, it's like the flowers are dancing princesses."

"Maybe they dance like princesses because you're here."

"Sometimes."

"No, hand me the bacon one," said Cain.

"I thought you liked sausage," Ray said.

"I've never liked sausage, you know that."

"Well, I bought you the sausage one."

"But I don't really like sausage."

"Just give me the sausage. I'll eat that one," said Ray.

Cain and Ray shuffled their two sandwiches back and forth as they walked downstairs to the lab area. It was dark.

"Okay, no Kayla," Cain said as he turned on the light.

"Maybe she's running a little late."

"She's got a copy of the poem next to the computer here."

"I'm ready to get going on this."

"Now we're waitin' on a woman."

"You know, Holly doesn't take very long getting ready in the morning, but it still seems like forever."

"Yeah, Del was always a good forty-five minutes."

"Kayla's probably still sitting there curling her hair or something."

"I'm ready for you!" Kayla sort of yelled down the hallway as she made her way from the stairs. "And I heard you. Women don't waste half as much time as you men on your little boys, toys and buddies stuff. And styling your hair every now and then doesn't hurt, Cain. You might get a date."

Kayla gave him an eyes-wide-open look as she set an armful of items on the counter and held out a tray of coffee cups from a café.

"Here I go taking care of you two and you're standing down here bagging on me."

She pointed to three different cups. "Regular, double, triple. Triple's mine. You two can fight over the others."

"I better take the single," Ray said.

"I guess that leaves me with the double."

"Sugar and creamers are in the bag. Just give me a minute and I'll pull up the projector."

"Thanks for the coffee, Kayla," Cain said, now feeling a bit guilty about the sandwich he was eating and had slid down toward his side so she couldn't see it.

"That's okay, Cain. I'm not hungry. Besides, I don't like bacon *or* sausage."

"Kayla sat logging onto the lab's computer until a background screen appeared and she clicked on the mouse a few times. She shuffled around several items on the table near the desk, grabbing the remote for the projector and pointing it in its direction. The projector came alive, illuminating the screen on the wall, showing her computer desktop. The mouse curser bounced around the screen until she selected a folder and then opened another file inside of it. The poem from the conductor's house appeared on the screen.

"Well, some of this seems to be a no-brainer, but let's try to pick it apart. Maybe we'll come up with something," said Cain.

"It's written in third person." Kayla rolled the cursor across the screen.

"Right, so read the way it appears, it's one of just two or three things," said Ray.

"The writer of the poem is probably the killer. I checked a database of literary works and didn't come up with any apparent matches. The writer is either talking about himself as the killer or somebody else who has obviously killed."

Cain leaned forward. "We have adult victims. He speaks of child victims. Maybe they've killed both children and adults."

"We haven't had a bunch of dead children turn up around here and nobody's reporting missing children," Ray said.

"What if the children weren't from around here?"

"What if the children were killed at another place or time, maybe even years ago?" said Kayla. "You can't turn back time."

"Alright, let's try to look at it from some different angles. Let's start with the idea that the killer is talking about himself."

Ray pointed at the first line.

"Switch the words," Kayla said. "See if it works in first person."

Cain read the words of the poem in first person.

"I draw down the hammer that strikes death's blow, implements of destruction, a one man show."

"Okay, that could fit," Kayla said.

"Crushed and tangled bodies weave, innocent, guilty, my mind deceived, hmm, yeah, those go together," Cain said, then continued reading."I drowned their voices in gurgling blood, but I can't deny their resounding flood. From the safety of the sanctum womb, I dragged them to a shallow tomb. My own flesh I chose to destroy, tormented now, my little boy." It bothered Cain to read the words. "God, this is just wrong. The helpless die, the children cry, vindicate, vindicate, their justice denied. Each child fought to get away, but I, I had the final say. Murderous killer, with seed to sow, the hunted had no place to go. Seed sown by this reapers slave, destinies lost, my family not saved. Fits well, but I really hope it's not first person," said Cain after reading the poem aloud.

"Well, we're either dealing with somebody who, one, just wants to tell their story, which wouldn't be good, two, is dealing with a lot of guilt about something." Ray sipped from his coffee cup. "Oh, that's too hot."

"Or, three, is angry about something and transferring his anger to our victims," Kayla said.

"I don't know which is better," said Ray.

"Alright, now let's look at it just as it sits." Cain pointed at the screen.

Ray picked up a hard copy of the poem from Kayla's desk and started scanning over it.

"Well, if he's talking about somebody else then that person is just as bad as our killer," Kayla said.

"Maybe it's completely symbolic?" said Ray.

"He says, 'He draws down the hammer,' then uses the word

implements. He's talking about killing with more than one weapon, or a gavel. He holds the power to judge, to condemn to death."

"Our victims had crushed and tangled bodies. That fits our crime scenes," said Cain.

"He drowned their voices, yet in the second half, he can't deny their resounding flood. He's being tormented with guilt, I think," said Kayla.

"The next one seems obvious, but I hope to God it's only symbolic." Ray nodded at the screen. "Sanctum womb, or holy womb, dragged them to a shallow tomb. Now I know we haven't had any killings like that around here. If somebody takes a baby from a womb they usually kill the mother in the process. It's normally some woman who's desperate for her own child, but can't have one. Doesn't seem to fit."

"He dragged them to a shallow tomb. That sounds more like the babies were buried," said Cain. "A shallow, quick grave."

"His own flesh? The killer has killed his own child?" said Kayla.

"Which could be causing a psychotic snap into the killings we're dealing with," said Ray.

"You kill your own child, it would sure make it easier to kill other people," said Kayla. "It also says that he's tormented by it. He's tormented by his little boy. I think he's over-run by guilt."

"And some sort of vindication is being called upon for the victims," said Cain.

"Each child fought to get away," Kayla pointed out. "Does he see these victims as children?"

"He had the final say. He controlled the situation. He was in control of whether they died," said Cain.

"He had seed to sow in his killing," Ray shook his head, shrugged his shoulders. "Seed sown by this reaper's slave, this man of death, brings about an end result."

"Destiny's lost, his family not saved. Whose family not

saved?" asked Kayla.

"It definitely gets confusing at that point," said Cain.

"I'm thinking it's just plain confusing from the beginning." Ray tossed the copy he was holding onto Kayla's desk.

"The killings bring about an end result. When you sow a seed a plant grows. When you sow an action, you cause a reaction. Everything affects something else," Kayla said.

"The question here, I guess would be, is that his message or is that what he's actually trying to do?" said Ray.

"Well, so far, all of our victims have had some sort of impact on society. They weren't just ordinary people," said Cain.

Ray was bothered. "It wouldn't matter if they were just ordinary people. I'm just an ordinary person, but I make a difference in the lives of those I care about. Every person matters to somebody. Every person is meant to make a difference in this life, whether it's great or small!"

"So our killer is probably trying to make a statement," said Kayla.

"And leaving us with all his talking points!" said Ray.

"Well, hopefully we'll turn up something out at the lake today when we talk to our conductor's family."

The morning sunshine seemed to be making headway against the blanket of fog that had entrapped the city in a mystical shroud in the overnight hours. Beams of light broke through in scattered patches, exposing the blueness of the sky above. Ray turned left off the winding road into the long drive. Tall sculpted cypress trees lined both sides of the driveway, rising upward, yet constricted to their columnar growth by some master's hand.

"Nice piece of property," said Cain. "I wouldn't mind

building my house here."

"Uh, huh. Well, save your pennies. If you can afford the house, I might be willing to give you my half of the land."

"Someday, Ray, someday. You watch. I'll get it done."

At the end of the drive was a circular turnaround centered with a beautiful fountain and an expansive mansion, it's front facia covered with slate and gray colored stone. There was an older Jaguar to the far right sitting in front of the forth stall of an attached garage. A Volkswagen Jetta sat next to the Jaguar in front of the next stall. Next to that was a 1969 Mustang convertible covered in dust.

"Well, would you look at that," said Cain. "There's your car."

"You gonna buy it for me?"

"If I did, I'd have to keep it here at the house and just let you drive it every now and then."

"Maybe they'll trade you for all your little toys."

A puzzled look came to Ray and Cain's faces as they noticed the one car actually parked in the circle drive. It was a common man's car, an older 1980's Chevy with rusted fender wells and a faded paint job. A taillight was cracked and had been fixed with red vinyl tape. The vehicle didn't fit the scene.

Ray rang the doorbell. Cain stepped to the side and looked through the sparkling inlaid decorative glass at the side of the door. Shiny rainbow prisms shot light from the glass across Cain's face and eyes. Inside the front entryway a winding staircase led to the second story of the house and a majestic chandelier hung from the ceiling, splattering light at the walls and onto the marble floor.

"Well, if we're lucky, this woman heard from our killer also."

"Wow, these people aren't hurting, huh," Cain said.

"Maybe not financially but you can bet they feel the loss of a son just like anybody else would."

"I'd trade them my apartment."

"I'll bet you would."

"Think anybody is home?"

"Don't know. I don't really understand the car in the drive. These people don't look like they drive old rust buckets."

"Maybe it's a relative or something."

As Ray and Cain were speculating over the car Cain noticed some movement upstairs just to the right of the staircase. A teen girl emerged and came down the stairs. She was dressed in a casual jean outfit with a t-shirt and a vest that seemed too small for her. She walked up to the door and looked through the crystal glass. She didn't open the door but gave them a 'hello, what do you want' look and put her hands up in question.

Ray pulled out his badge clip and showed it to her. She opened the door.

"Can I help you?"

"We're from Crossroad's Police Department."

"Yeah, I kinda got that from the badge."

"Is the lady of the house available? We need to speak with her."

"What about? She doesn't really feel like talking to anybody."

"Well, it's really important that we speak to her. We need to know if anybody contacted her about her son . . ." Ray was interrupted.

"Son, what do you mean? She doesn't have a son."

Ray and Cain looked at each other puzzled.

"Are you here to talk to Kelly or to her mom?"

"Probably her mom."

"Her mom died of cancer two years ago."

"Really?"

"Yeah."

"Is her father here?" Ray asked, looking at Cain.

"No, he's definitely not here right now. You guys..."

Cain interrupted the girl, slightly irritated. "We need to know if anybody attempted to contact them or if they received any kind of phone calls asking for information about her brother."

"Messages are forwarded to her cell phone. I'll ask her, but she hasn't said anything about a call like that. I mean, that's kind of weird. Why would anybody do that?"

"Well, under the circumstances, why would that be so strange?" Ray asked.

"Listen, here's the situation. Kelly's it. She's the only one left in the family you can even talk to. But she doesn't want to talk to anybody. Right now she's a wreck. She's lost her mom. She lost her brother. Now, her dad's . . ."

Cain's cell phone rang and he answered it.

"Can we contact him there? What? Really? Alright, have the hospital call us the second he comes to."

The young girl finished her sentence with a frustrated look on her face. "Her dad's in the hospital in some kind of coma. I can't remember the name of it. He was in an accident. He's been all messed up ever since. So why would they send police officers to talk to Kelly about her brother? I don't get it. I thought you guys were here for something to do with her dad, you know, with the accident."

"That's normal procedure."

"What would the police have to do with a military death?"

"What do you mean, military death?"

"Her brother was killed in the military."

"Are we talking about the same brother, here?"

"She only has *one* brother! He was killed in a firefight in Africa about three years ago trying to deliver food on some relief mission. He got a medal of honor for it. Do you guys watch the news? How could you miss a story like that in Crossroads?"

Cain turned toward Ray with a questioned look on his face.

"I'm sorry. There must've have been some sort of mistake here with the information our department gave us," Ray said.

"Does that Medal of Honor happen to be somewhere in the

house?" asked Cain.

"I don't know. I'd have to ask Kelly."

"Could you please do that for us? Then we'll leave you alone."

Ray looked at Cain strangely.

"Something's not right here," Cain said as the young girl turned away and jogged up the large staircase. She returned a few moments later.

"She says the last time she saw it her dad was sitting in the chair in his study holding it and looking at it, but hasn't seen it since. Her dad was pretty tore up by her brother's death. He was his only son."

"Okay, thank you," Ray said.

"Can you tell me what her dad's occupation is?" asked Cain.

"Sure, he's a doctor. An OB GYN. Listen, she's been through this when her mom died. My mom and I helped Kelly then, we'll help her get through this. We've been best friends since we were little. She spends a lot of time at my house. Her uncle has somebody come in a couple times a week to check on things and clean this place so she doesn't really have to worry about it much."

"Can you check the messages on the phone, that kind of stuff, just in case something is mixed up here?" Cain re-iterated.

"Yeah. We will."

"Please call us if she says she's received any calls like we talked about." Ray handed her a business card.

"Or if she remembers anybody trying to contact her father," said Cain.

Cain and Ray drove down the long drive.

"Why would any of what we just asked that girl matter? It's not like that's our victim's family. Who did the next of kin information on this? They botched it up somehow!" Ray said.

"Maybe it was a glitch in the system, some information got

crossed up. Data, you know, faulty, broken computers; I've always hated those things, never enough memory, whatever. We need to take a hard look at this guy in the hospital. Maybe there's something in his head that will help us."

"The Medal of Honor thing could be a coincidence."

"Medal of Honor? OB GYN? Africa? Wife who died of cancer? That seems like a few too many coincidences. Maybe somebody's trying to hide something, to clean up a mess. We need to get a warrant for this house and figure out who the conductor's family really is. Hey, go right so we can pass the statue."

Cain looked to the left toward Lake Berryessa and the long line of trees against the edge of the river. Most of the properties in the Lake Estates were small acreages that backed up against the river or lake and included private shorelines. Some residences had long drives and weren't visible from the road. Larger homes sat at a distance, their domineering glory rising into the blue skyscape or facades showing through the woods surrounding them. Smaller acreages seemed scattered between them as a nuisance.

On the city side of the large lake, which was hardly visible from the private waterfronts, were public access areas for boating and picnicking. The bike trails were always buzzing with riders in shorts that revealed too much for most people's comfort zones or rollerblade clad speed jockeys swooshing in and out of people walking their dogs or kids.

"What time is your appointment?" Ray asked.

"I've got two hours before I have to be there. Just drop me off at the apartment and I'll meet you back at work when I'm done."

"I could just take you and wait for you."

"No, that's okay. I kind of want to check on Elsie. Her mom was pretty trashed last night. I want to make sure she got in from school alright. I could use a quick nap also."

9

"I'm telling you, the listing was here! And there was a phone number one of the techs pulled from a bulletin board at the victim's house. All records in the system as of yesterday showed them as next of kin for the victim. Now the listing is completely gone. It's all out of the system!"

"You're positive?"

"Come on, guys. I'm not some idiot. I get this kind of information for your section all the time."

"This isn't good," Ray said. "Can you access who changed the record?"

"I can try, but the whole records gone, even our victim. It's almost like somebody wanted him to never exist."

The tech pounded at the keyboard. "It's not showing any kind of change of record. It just looks like the record never existed to begin with."

"Who has access to these things?" Ray asked.

"Lots of people. People like me, people at city, county, state levels. If we can't pinpoint a source computer for the change, we're looking at hundreds of people. Let me go into county records. Let's see, titles, birth certificates. No birth certificate in the county records. He could've been born elsewhere, but I'm nearly positive when I looked at his records yesterday it had this county as his place of birth. I think your killer knows exactly what he's doing and now he's found some way into our data system. He's trying to erase memory data."

"Alright," Ray said. "Pull up the other victim's records!"

The tech shuffled through some papers that he had slid out of a green hanging folder that was sitting on his desk by his computer, then started typing in a case number.

"It's not here. The record's not here!"

"What?" Ray said.

"It's not here for this one either." He ran his hand across his face, flustered.

He typed another number in.

"Or this one."

The tech re-typed a case number into the system. "No, nothing. They've all been removed!"

"Cain?"

Cain shook his head, "I'll call Greg."

"We've got hard copies of everything, right? The crime scene? The evidence information? The photos? Right?" Ray asked.

"Well, that's our protocol. Everything gets backed up twice also, outside of our local intranet and firewall. Gone! All the local stuff is gone for these cases."

"Do you think we've been hacked into or is this from the inside? Can you get me the back-ups?"

"Slow down, Ray. Yeah, I mean, I don't know about your first question. As far as the back-ups, those are kept off-site downtown on a different server. I don't have access, but supervisors do. I'll make some phone calls. It's not likely that somebody could have removed them completely from the server. Once they're backed up, it's pretty hard to erase them. There's hidden restore points."

"Alright."

Cain was getting ready to speed dial Greg when his cell phone rang. It was Greg.

"Greg, you're not gonna believe this!"

"Oh, you've heard already?"

"Yeah, we just noticed. The files, the cases, every last one of them gone from the system. This isn't good at all."

"What? No, no I hadn't heard that. Crazy!" Greg sounded completely frustrated.

"Anyhow..."Cain started to speak.

"No wait, listen, Cain." Greg interrupted. "The victim's house, the conductor's, it burned to the ground this afternoon!"

"What? Were they able to save anything?" Cain asked as Ray and the tech looked at him, puzzled by his question.

"No, it was almost completely gone by the time the fire department got there. I need you guys up here right now!"

"Okay, we'll be up in a minute."

Cain looked at Ray and let out a deep sigh. "Our last victim's house just burned to the ground."

"Serious?"

"Yeah! Greg wants us upstairs."

Greg had gathered several supervisory people from the department in the main office area.

"Alright, I don't know what's happening here. We need to get a team back out to that house to work with the fire marshal and see what we can come up with for evidence."

"I told you something wasn't right with this," Ana spoke up.

"Yeah," Ray said. "First he gives us more clues than we could ever hope for, then he burns the house to the ground."

"He's mocking us," Greg said. "Ralph, Karen, pull together a team. Work the surrounding area all night if you have to. I want every neighbor re-questioned and the woods gone over again.

Don't leave anything for granted. We're gonna have to look a lot harder at that property now that he's come back."

"Done!" Ralph turned and motioned to several officers along the side of the room and they followed him downstairs.

Cain sat at his desk, then looked over at Ray and down at the blinking light on his phone signaling he had a voicemail.

Greg spoke, "Do we have anything from IT? Jason, what did you guys figure out?"

"Nothing yet. I've got three people working on it and we're talking to the department that handles the server downtown. We know that the original files appear to be missing from the entire system, with some trace data still there. They were nearly wiped out, but not completely. The back-up records should be there somewhere. There's too many safeguards in place for this to happen. Whoever did it had an interest in these people never existing, or a strange sense of humor."

"Are all the records affected for every victim, you know, birth records, etcetera, or was it just the crime files?" Greg asked.

"Just the crime files on three of them. But the victim from the Canyons, whose house just burned, his are completely gone. We can't find any record of him anywhere. The killer did a good job at making his records go away. It's almost like our victim never existed."

Ana spoke. "There was a case a few years back like this in the southeast. The killer murdered his victims, then went about destroying everything that ever existed to do with the people he killed. They finally caught him. It was a year or so later I was watching a show where they profiled his case and they interviewed the guy. He told the interviewer that there were no victims. He didn't understand why anybody would be upset with him or why he was in trouble. This guy had somehow worked it out in his mind that if he got rid of everything to do with his victims then they never really existed."

"I watched that case unfold," Ray said. "The scariest part

was that the killer said he had a clean conscience. He believed that since he made them go away in his mind, that he hadn't really killed anybody."

"I hope to God that we're not dealing with somebody that whacked," Cain said.

"It's starting to look like it," said Ana.

Another IT supervisor stepped into the room.

"What do we got, Sean?" Greg asked.

"They're back in the system."

"The records?"

"Yeah, all but the last victim."

"Somebody put them back?"

"We're not sure. We're looking at it all and trying to figure it out. Maybe it was just a glitch somewhere."

Jason's cell phone rang. "Hello, uh huh, yeah. Really? Okay." He hung up. "Alright, a little more information. The records were definitely tampered with on several levels across the system. They don't have an ID on the specific location or computer, but they're working on it. They'll let you know as soon as they come up with anything else. What they're seeing is that the person just didn't get far enough into the mainframe to completely wipe out all the restore points. But it's obvious they were trying to erase the records, to get rid of them completely. We safeguard against that type of thing. Nobody can just come in and swipe the mainframe clean. The Administrators are the only ones able to wipe records completely from the system, the only ones that can clear the main servers and there's certain protocols for that type of action. And there's only three Administrators who have that kind of access and control, and all three are involved when core memory is dealt with."

"Is it all secure now?" Ray asked.

"There's a problem with that. Downtown is saying that it doesn't look like it happened from outside the system. The firewall wasn't compromised. Whoever it was, well, it looks like the records were changed from within the city's intranet."

Jason's phone rang again. "What's up? Okay, thanks."

"Second to the last victim's records are all in. I'm gonna head back downstairs. I'll let you know when I have specifics."

"Thanks," Greg said as Jason walked out. "Alright, everybody, I want reports back immediately on anything the teams turn up at the house. Just keep in mind that we could have different evidence now and it may be even more significant to our investigation. It might not look like evidence, either. Our killer had to have spent some time there to do what he did. Maybe there was something at the scene he wanted to hide, even though it didn't seem that way."

"Maybe he got scared about all the evidence he gave us?" Cain asked.

"Maybe he planned on burning the house from the beginning," said Ana.

As the meeting dispersed Greg motioned for Cain and Ray to come to his office.

"Shut the door," Greg said. "I'm sure you know what I'm about to say. Everything new comes to me immediately. I want you guys to start looking local, but don't make it obvious. Try and think of anything that might apply here."

"Alright," Ray said.

Cain shook his head in agreement.

"That's all."

Cain sat down at his desk and reluctantly picked up the phone, dialed his voicemail, and put the phone on speaker.

"Cain, this is Kenny. When are we going to work on the Corvette again? My dad says you like to procas . . . procastrat...pro...cras...stinate. Call me back . . . but don't let my dad know I called you at work cause he might get mad."

Ray looked at Cain as he shook his head and smiled. The next message played. "Cain, that bottle of wine you ordered on Wednesday is in. You can pick it up any time."

Next message: "Cain, the killing . . . it's only gone until you remember it. You just can't get it out of your head."

Cain and Ray sat up in their chairs.

"Play it back, play it back!" Ray said.

"Greg, come in here!" Cain frantically punched at the phone for a replay.

Greg came into the room.

Ray motioned toward Cain's phone for Greg to listen.

The muffled, distorted voice played again. "The killing, it's only gone until you remember it. You just can't get it out of your head."

Greg looked nervously around the room and motioned with his hand. "Turn it down."

They listened to it again.

"Let the lab know. Have Chelsea get with the system guys and figure out where that call came from. I want to know immediately!"

"Alright, this is starting to creep me out. It's too close. This killer just got way too personal," Ray said.

"He's probably been at one of the crime scenes and just knows we're working the case," said Cain.

"I understand that, but you guys need to be careful here," said Greg. "Was that the only message?"

"Yeah," said Cain.

Ray spoke the obvious. "Now we know it's a man."

"You need to watch your backs. I don't like that he left a message on your voicemail, that he chose yours. That means whoever this killer is, he is well aware of who you are in the play of things," Greg said.

"Just stay at my place a couple of days. It's not like he left any messages for me."

"Yeah? I'm gonna put Holly and the kids in danger? I'll be fine. The guy doesn't know everything about me. Besides, maybe somehow I can draw him in with this. I'd love for him to show up on my doorstep. He'd have a bit more of a fight out of me then his innocent victims. I'll shut him down for good."

10

Cain pushed the rickety old shopping cart down the Italian foods aisle at the little corner market two blocks from his apartment. The cart kept repeating a slap, slap clicking sound. Slap, cluck, clap, wheel wobble wobble, slap clack wobble.

After setting two cans of tomato paste next to the box of pasta in the shopping cart, he started around the end of the aisle. "Whoa," he said as Elsie nearly ran right into his cart. She gave him a funny giggle and laughed at him. There was ice cream on her face. It looked messy. He wanted to wipe it off, to clean her face.

"Grandpa!" Elsie said in her playful little voice.

"There you go again, silly girl. What's all over your face?"

"Ice cream!"

"You're messy."

"You're messy, silly!"

"Is your mommy here?"

"No, I walked."

"You walked? What's mommy doing?"

"Sleeping. She says she doesn't feel good. She was mad at me for bothering her and waking her up, but she gave me a dollar for icecream."

"Oh," Cain said, sighing inside.

"Do you know what my mommy told me today?"

"No, what's that, honey?"

"She said that my grandpa once told her that I should have been taken care of before I was born. How can you take care of somebody before they're born? Even I know you can't take care of a baby before it's born. You have to wait till after."

"Honey, you just forget about that. I'm sure your grandpa wouldn't have said that if he could see you now."

"See you later, grandpa!"

"Be careful walking home." Cain practically had to shout at her as she ran off down the next aisle. "If you wait till I…"

He was going to offer to walk her home, but she was gone. Cain stood there in the aisle looking at the food in his cart, thinking about Elsie's mom. *God, how could she say something like that? You don't repeat something like that to a child.* More than once he had walked into the little corner market and seen Elsie's mom, a counter full of alcohol in front of her at the check stand, some food mixed in. She often looked high or stoned. It seemed that she was always either sick or sleeping. Elsie hung around a lot of the kids and families at the apartments. Most everybody knew the situation. People were always inviting her for lunch with their children. Elsie's Grandpa made regular stops by the apartment and checked on her and her mother. Her father wasn't involved. Neither were the other grandparents.

Cain finished his shopping and walked up to the cash register. The elderly woman behind the register smiled.

"Esther, how're you doing?"

"Pretty good for an old lady."

"Where's Harry?"

"I think he's sleeping in the back. He said he was going to get some refrigerator items stocked, but I think he's back there enjoying the cold air and getting into the ice cream."

"You know, I think this cart here's on its last leg."

"Sounds like me," Esther laughed. "If I don't get something done with this hip of mine I'll need someone to push me around in one of those!"

Elsie bounced by both of them toward the front door.

"Elsie!" Esther stopped her.

"Yes, ma'am?"

"You be careful walking home and watch out for cars. Here, take this bag of apples and bananas with you." Esther handed her a bag of discounted fruit that was near the end of the counter. "You eat those up right away, okay?"

"I will."

Elsie disappeared into the flutter of people walking past on the sidewalk.

"I worry about that little girl," Esther said as she grabbed the final can of tomato paste and put it in the bag Cain had already started. "You've got to stop bagging your own groceries when you come in here. You're stealing my exercise! How do you expect me to stay looking sexy for my husband?" She lifted her eyebrows and winked at Cain. "I never see that girl's momma unless she's in here buying booze. A couple of times I refused to sell it to her because she was obviously half drunk already. Isn't there something more you could do for that little girl, Cain?"

"Her mom's just now letting people be a part of her life. I hate to say it, but a lot of times kids like that just end up being raised by someone in the system, a foster parent, a relative, an aunt, maybe a grandparent," Cain said. "I just wish her mom would snap out of it and change her thinking. For now we all have to just take what we can get."

Cain scooped up his bags of groceries into his arms.

"Tell Harry I said hi."

"I will. I better go check on him and see where he's hiding. He's into something. I just know it."

"Have a good day, Esther."

"You too, honey, take care."

Cain stepped out the front door and turned right off the corner and headed down the street. It was a warm, sunny day. The smell of the fresh vegetables in his grocery bag captured his senses. He was pulled back several years, instantly taken to a more innocent time in his life. His mind wandered as he walked.

He remembered himself as a child standing in the middle of a large garden. He held seeds in his hands, and dropped one of the seeds into a thumb-sized hole that his father had just pushed into the dirt . . .

"Here, do another one," his father said, crouching down near his son. Cain squeezed the bean seed between his little six-year-old fingers and dropped it into the next hole in the row.

"Okay, let's put these ones over here," his father said.

Cain bounced across the soft dirt to another place in the garden.

"Carrots."

"Carrots!" Cain repeated his father's words.

"Three rows of them. Here, push these down into the dirt in the corner over there."

"Daddy, what are these?"

"Big, giant flowers that get really tall."

"Really tall," Cain said as he reached his hands upward and jumped up and down. His hair bounced against his forehead, his eyes gazed upward into the clear spring sky.

"Come on, let's go plant something for the rabbits."

"Okay!" Cain said as he jumped again.

Cain's father reached down and took his little hand. They walked between the three long rows they had just planted, his father stepping over one of the rows and then lifting Cain up and swinging him over the same row. The little handcrafted wooden gate was latched as Cain pushed on it. His father unlatched it.

"Push on it," he gently said to his son.

Cain pushed open the gate, his little hands wrapped around the twisted circles of willow that his father had worked so tediously to create two years earlier. The rest of the fence, hand cut from fallen trees along the north edge of the property, stretched outward from Cain and his father to the left and right. Behind them, the gate sprung shut with a clang as the catch snapped into place.

"No rabbits in there," Cain said.

"No. No rabbits in there," his father repeated.

No rabbits in there, Cain thought. *Huh*. Once again Cain's mind bounced from that moment forward several years to a time when he had stood in the same garden as a seventeen year old working the ground with his father. It had been an especially warm summer and the garden was flourishing. He was covered in sweat that was mixing with dust from the garden, causing little lines and splotches to form on his bare chest and stomach. He swiped his arm across his forehead, not realizing the dust on his forearm and leaving a large patch of dirt across the top of his face and eyebrows. . .

"I can't believe you still plant all those greens for the rabbits, Dad," Cain said.

"Never hurt us, son. They stopped trying so hard to dig their way through the fence to the main garden once I started throwing some seed onto that patch of dirt for them."

Cain watched his father rake the salad green seeds into the ten foot square patch of ground which his father had set aside for the wild rabbits that wandered their property, then looked up at the beautifully framed greenhouse. The greenhouse seemed to be his father's one great novelty in life. One could see an abundance of plant life through its beveled cut rectangular glass surrounded by a tightly constructed white painted wood frame and siding. A red brick base wall made the distance from the ground up to the first framing of glass. Venting windows were open in various places across the top edge of the greenhouse, and two pinnacle towers crowned the rooftop, one at each end, arrows crisscrossing at the top of each little structure. Cain stared at one of the pinnacles. Across the white wood, beneath them, were darkened patches, stained in.

"Do you think we'll see him again this year?" Cain asked.

"We'll see him," Cain's father said. "This seems to be one of his favorite spots."

"Why here?"

"Oh, there's that perfect time of the season, you know, when the gardens aren't all grown in yet. The younger rabbits are foraging across the acreage. There's just not that much coverage for them. It makes them easy prey. Now with the garden all grown, it's a little harder for him. But he'll be back. If we don't see him again soon, we'll see him in the fall."

"I hate it when he takes them up to the pinnacle."

"I know, but it's just part of life, son. That seems to be the place he's chosen to take his prey."

"I wish he'd take them somewhere else, so we don't have to see him pick at them and tear them apart."

"Why's that?"

"I watched him one time. He swooped in and chased one around the fence line of the big garden. It couldn't find a way in. We closed it up so tightly. He got it eventually. It couldn't get away. It didn't stand a chance."

"Well, there's only so far those little fellas can run and hide. A little more weeding in the big garden and we should be finished. Then we can take a sit down under the maple tree and enjoy some of that lemonade."

The apartment manager spoke as Cain walked across the small patch of lawn in front of the building, pulling him from his thoughts. "It's a beautiful evening, Cain, isn't it?" the man said.

"Oh, hey. Yes, it is."

11

Cain lay on his couch, restlessly slipping in and out of sleep. His eyes fluttered, closed, then it was dark, quiet. He was aware, yet asleep. A dim light tried to break through into his mind, to flow into his eyes. It was distant, a pinpoint in the darkness. He heard shuffling, movement, and muffled voices. The light became brighter, stronger. A small, faint voice called his name. "Cain . . . Cain." He felt something pushing lightly, tapping on his chest, but saw nothing, just the darkness around him.

"Cain . . . come back." Cain looked at the light. The light dimmed, then went black. He awoke on his couch, wondering.

"Si took an interview from the house adjacent to our last victim's. Apparently, there was a vehicle with county plates there just before the fire. They're checking to see who had someone out there. It's probably nothing. I've also got the report back from the fire marshal," Greg said. He tossed the report onto Ray's desk. "This is getting stranger by the moment."

"Why's that?" Cain asked.

"Just read it. You'll see."

Ray glanced over the report quickly, trying to see what Greg was talking about.

"What is it?" Cain asked, now feeling a little kiddish and not wanting to wait any longer.

"This is wild. They're saying that a concentrated heat source was used in one spot to start the fire. The heat source may have been identified and has been retained as evidence. This heat source is possibly a lighter that was found. Chemical composition at the start point shows residue that is similar in make up to typical fuel source for the lighter taken in evidence, determined to a seventy-eight percent match rate. See lighter with Asclepius symbol. The house appears to have burned from corner to corner. The entire house burned to the ground except…"

"Except what?"

"Near one corner of the house they found the lighter containing a small corner piece of paper."

"I'm already confused."

"Let's see . . . It says that near one corner of the house was what appeared to be the remains of a desk drawer. The lighter was setting on a small rock, the drawer burned in place around it. In the lighter was a tiny piece of paper, apparently protected within its lid from the fire, which is in evidence," Ray rambled on. He turned the page and viewed the picture of the lighter, then handed it to Cain. It was a typical chrome flip-top lighter and it had a medical symbol on it.

"Go on."

"The paper inside the top of the lighter had a layered carbon copy on it. There was a clear fingerprint impressed on the top and bottom of the papers, a thumb print and forefinger, as though somebody had been holding the corner of the paper when it burned. The paper edge was burned all the way up to that place. The paper is approximately one inch across. Fingerprints were also found on the lighter itself."

Greg, who had gone back to his office, yelled out to them, "What'd I tell you, huh?"

"Strange," Cain said. "Our killer had to have chosen it for a reason. Why this symbol? Why even a lighter? And gave us a print?"

"Well, given all the other medical stuff we found at the house I'd say there's some obvious tie in here," Greg said.

Ray continued. "At the farthest corner of the house, directly across from where the lighter and paper was found, was where they say the fire was started."

"That's it? There's nothing else?" Cain asked.

Greg stepped into the doorway of his office, "Nothing more from our teams at the scene either. Chelsea said they pushed out the perimeter by about eight hundred feet, overlapping several properties. They didn't come up with anything. Ralph's team canvassed every house in the neighborhood and several businesses nearby and came up empty handed. Nobody saw anything. Everybody near our victim's house was either not home or inside their houses and didn't notice anything until the house was well into burning down."

"Maybe we're dealing with a ghost?" Cain said.

"Ghost, apparition, phantom. Maybe it's all just a big nightmare," Greg said.

"No, the cannula is attached to a hose, which is essentially attached to a vacuum pump. We use electric here. The pump, that is." The doctor patiently explained and described the items in the evidence pictures laying across his desk in front of him. "It's called aspiration. Generally, the procedure will be attempted with just a vacuum process. Now, sometimes, a suction curettage needs to be done. That would be one use of the tool in your second picture here. That tool is called a curette, which is used to scrape away remaining fetal matter from the wall of the patient's uterus."

Cain kept picturing Holly's c-section, the precious baby girl being so carefully and meticulously pulled from her womb and the caution taken during the surgery to protect the baby from harm.

"Now, there's the D and C, which is dilation and curretege; this basically involves the same procedure without suction. The cervix of the woman is dilated and the curette is used to scrape out the fetus. The mother is sedated for this type of procedure. Sometimes certain chemicals may be used instead of the other methods. Now, I probably don't have to explain to you what this one is. It's simply a pair of forceps."

"Please explain. I'm interested," Ray said.

"Okay," the doctor continued. "A larger dilation is done."

"And why's that?" asked Cain.

"Well, when the pregnancy is further along, suction aspiration is no longer an option, due to the size of the fetus. The amniotic sac has to be ruptured. Then, well, piece by piece the fetus is removed from the uterus using the forceps."

"Our victims had their brains kind of scrambled and brain tissue had been purposefully spilled out around their heads. Is there any significance to that?" Ray asked.

"The calvaria sign! When the brain has been sufficiently

dealt with, brain matter will flow out into the uterus. This tells the attending doctor that the skull will be easy to remove. The curette is then used to clear out any remaining matter, and the suction can once again be used to remove the remaining pieces. Either that or it would be a significant example of what we call D and X, or dilation and extraction."

"Why's that?" Cain asked.

"Well, D and X is used in later term abortions. This method is the one in which you would see the scissors used."

"The scissors were stuck into the back of our victim's head, pretty much as deep as they could be placed," Ray said.

"That would be similar to a D and X procedure. It definitely sounds like your killer had something to say about abortion. Maybe you need to be looking at, well, someone who had a botched procedure done. Maybe your killer lost a spouse or a daughter. When these procedures aren't done properly, somebody can be hurt. Not just anybody can perform an abortion. It takes training, a mastery of skills."

"So why the wound to the head on our victims?" Cain asked.

"During the D and X procedure the attending doctor positions the fetus into a breech position. The baby's, uh, fetuses, body, is pulled from the uterus and the head left just inside the birth canal. The doctor then pushes the scissors into the base of the fetus's skull and creates a hole. He inserts a suction tube into the hole and removes the brain tissue. The fetus is then removed from the patient's body."

Cain shuffled the pages around on the desk. "So what's this big syringe?"

"Those are generally used for what we call a ditch. The needle is used to inject a chemical into the heart of the fetus, usually digoxin. The fetus dies, and then a feticital agent is injected, which causes the tissue to soften, making the removal process easier."

The phone on the doctor's desk rang. "Yes, okay, I should be finished up here shortly," the doctor said. "Well, gentleman, if you don't have any more questions, I have a patient waiting."

"No, that should be it, Doctor Moran. Thank you for your help."

"My pleasure. It's nice to be able to educate people some. There's a lot of folks out there who just look at us as monsters or something. They don't seem to understand the work we do."

§

"I don't understand why we can't get a search warrant at some point. The family was in the system as his next of kin. Our tech saw it. You'd think they'd let us look into it," Cain said.

"I'm just as frustrated as you, but since there's no solid connection between the victim and estate you went to, judge won't give us a warrant," Greg said.

"What more do they need?" Ray asked.

"Once the father or whoever this guy actually is to our victim comes out of his coma, maybe we can get one. Whatever's in that man's head is significant. We just have to wait until he comes to."

"There's a definite connection here, Greg. Records showed them as his next of kin. Doesn't that count for something?" asked Cain. "What does it matter if the records have been tampered with since then?"

"You mean his birth certificate? Because there's something new that seems to have come into play here."

"What's that?" asked Ray.

"No birth certificates in county files for a single victim of our killer. They just called me with that one today."

"What?"

"That's right. We don't know if they were wiped out when somebody messed with the records or not. That's one record

146

for each victim that's eluding the IT guys. Explain that one," said Greg. "They're just not there."

"Okay, but come on, there's more to this case than that. There's a lot of evidence that seems to pull that family in and link them to these clues," said Cain.

"I mean, shoot," Ray said. "The Medal of Honor, the mom dying of cancer, the dad's an OB GYN and the items found at the last victim's house relate to the man's work and he could very well be his son. Our last victim and possibly every other victim was killed with tools used from that line of work."

"There's a few things you're not putting into consideration, Ray. First of all, let's not take coincidence out of this. It could simply be just coincidence. Secondly, the man's been in some kind of a coma for several weeks, so how could that place him as the killer or being involved at any of these crimes? He obviously didn't have anything to do with the death of our conductor and probably at least the last two of our other victims."

"But Greg, what about the daughter? There was some planning here," Cain said. "There's a connection and something to this, mark my words."

"Here's the facts. The last thing we need to be doing is going after a family whose face was plastered all over the local papers a couple years ago because their son was a war hero. Most people in the community aren't going to be happy with something like that. Tyler knows better than to attach her name to a warrant like that. So until we have more to give her, she said there's no way she's touching this one."

"What about the picture of our victim in front of the clinic? We need to at least check and see if the man at the hospital is the same person," said Cain.

"The house burned. The picture's gone. There's no telling now. Nobody thought of that. The house burned right after you guys realized the problem with the records; it's all moot now, isn't it."

"Nobody's come forward to claim this man as their relative. Doesn't anybody find that a little disturbing?" Ray said.

"Did we get any information from the civic center?"

"Karen's doing some checking. Some of it's going to bother you. His co-workers said his father was a well known doctor. They didn't know where the father lived, so she's trying to find a correlation. Other than that, he was apparently a rather elusive individual. He performed for his work, went to a few public functions, that's it," said Greg.

"God, this is irritating!" Cain slammed his fist onto his desk.

"I know guys. If you can figure out the mysteries on this victim you may solve the case entirely."

"Just cuff us," said Ray.

"Listen, it's your Friday. Give it all a break. Enjoy your weekend. It's crazy. But what can we do. Gotta separate the job here from our lives. Let it go for a few days. I know there's a future victim counting on us to stop this guy, but we've got families too. Maybe the one in the hospital will come out of it soon or we'll find something to connect the dots."

Cain stood in the doorway of Elsie's apartment.

"I'm alright with you all being in Elsie's life now. It's taken me a while, but I know I have some serious issues to deal with. My problems aren't going away overnight. I know there's a lot of people looking out for her. I trust you. I trust a lot of the families here, too."

"I've never seen you looking this worn out. You look like you haven't slept in days."

"I haven't slept in days. That's one reason I'm sending Elsie with you to Holly's. She'll watch after her."

"You really need to do something here, don't you think?"

"Got a meeting tonight, that's a start. I go to my counselor a couple times a week. I'm not winning this battle. It's not as easy as you all think. When this poison gets its claws in you, it doesn't just let go."

"What do you think about some inpatient treatment, maybe something more structured? Holly and Ray would watch Elsie for a few months while you get some help, nothing permanent, just long enough for you to get the help you need."

"When that little girl was born, nobody came to our rescue. Nobody was busting down the door to help us. It was almost as if we didn't exist. It wasn't until she had grown some that people noticed I had a problem. I'd pass out and she'd end up at a neighbor's door or call you, her grandpa, somebody else. I feel terrible about that. Now I'm trying. But it was then I needed everybody the most. Dad and mom weren't around then, were they? Nobody wanted to be a part of it. I was a young, eighteen-year-old, single parent. Why is it that now all of a sudden people are more interested? Everybody's coming at me, concerned about Elsie. I raised her to this point, didn't I? She's made it this far."

"I know, but there are things we can do to help you. You just admitted you're a mess."

"It doesn't mean I can't take care of my child!"

"But…"

"Listen, like I said. You can all spend time with her. Be a part of her life. But don't expect me to just hand her over to somebody. It's not gonna happen like that."

"Holly's already said she'd watch her so you can get better. She gets along great with Kenny. Why don't you take her up on that?"

"Why? So I can satisfy everybody else's requirements about how I should be living my life?"

"Just give it some thought, okay?"

"Elsie, come on. It's time for you to go to Kenny's."

Cain realized he had just lost the argument.

"Come on, baby, let's go! Mommy wants to lay down." She looked at him, exhaustion in her face, her eyes darkened, tired, a clear depression upon her.

"I'm coming," Elsie said.

"Will you think about it a little?" Cain asked again.

"When are you bringing her home?"

"Well, I think the latest movie we'll see is seven-thirty or so. I'll probably have her back by nine-thirty."

"Fine, that'll work."

"Bye, mommy."

"You have fun, okay," she said as she crouched down to Elsie's eye level.

"I will! Kisses?"

"Kisses and hugs!" She held Elsie and rested her lips against Elsie's temple. "I love you, baby."

"I love you too, Mommy."

"I'll bet your mommy would like that one," said Holly.

"It's really pretty!" said Elsie

"Alright, let's try these three on, okay? We'll see which ones fit you best."

"Okay."

"Hey, boys, we're gonna hit the dressing room."

"Alright, we'll be hiding in electronics."

Holly and Elsie made their way through the circled dress racks in the girl's section of the department store. Ranae turned a little in her car seat in the shopping cart, looked up at Elsie and then started to suck on her pacifier again, gripping it toward her mouth with her tiny little hand, then falling back asleep again.

"Alright, which one first?" asked Holly.

"The blue one!"

"You really like that one, don't you?"

"I like the lacy stuff."

Holly lifted Ranae's seat out of the cart and set it on the little bench in the changing room, then hung the dresses on the hooks.

"Pull that door shut, hun."

Elsie went to work pulling off her shirt as Ranae started to fuss again. Holly laid her hand on Ranae's belly and it calmed her.

"I don't think we have much time," said Holly.

"Nope, and boy, can she cry!"

"Here, up and over," said Holly as she helped Elsie pull her dress on. "Let's get the zipper."

Holly zipped the dress up in back, looking forward at Elsie's sparkling eyes in the mirror. She was clearly ecstatic.

"Well, I do believe I am looking at the prettiest little girl in the whole world."

"I like it!"

"And it fits perfectly. Okay, that's definitely a yes. Let's try on the pink one."

"Green!" Elsie pulled the dress from where it hung.

"Okay, we'll try that next."

Holly and Elsie repeated the steps, pulling off the blue dress and putting on the green one. Ranae started to turn and fuss in her car seat and looked up at both of them.

"Uh oh," said Elsie.

"Yeah, we better hurry. Our little fire alarm is awake. Oh yeah, that one looks cute, although I think any dress would look cute on you."

"Holly."

"What honey?"

"I love you."

"I love you too, baby."

Elsie laughed hysterically. Cain rolled his eyes around in his head, making a funny looking smirk with his mouth and causing her to giggle even more. A third twist of his head, puffed out cheeks and crossed eyes and Elsie was nearly unable to control her laughter. Her face turned dark from being bent forward giggling so hard.

"Elsie, come on!" said Kenny, tapping her on the back. Elsie turned and gave Kenny a gentle, playful push, then ran down the hallway after him.

"Hey, you two need to eat more of your sandwiches!" said Holly.

Kenny and Elsie trotted back down the hallway to the little square dining room table. Elsie immediately grabbed a handful of cheesy puffs and shoved several in her mouth. Kenny picked one up and threw it across the table at her, the puff falling to the floor.

"Kenny, stop!" Holly said.

He grabbed the cheesy puff from off the floor, looked at Holly and Elsie, and then tossed it into his mouth.

"Eewww, gross!" said Elsie.

"Kenny!" Holly shouted his name again, looking at them both and shaking her head.

Kenny and Elsie started to giggle, then looked at one another grinning. Each chomped down several bites from their sandwiches and then slipped away from the table as soon as Holly wasn't watching.

Cain and Ray sat with Ranae in the living room.

"It wasn't too bad," said Cain. "I might actually have to read the next one. That puts me, like, what, three ahead of you in the series in your set of books? Makes me wonder why I bought them for you."

"We've been a bit busy the last few months, if you know what I mean!" Ray nodded toward Ranae as she used his lap and legs as a springboard to bounce. Ray held a lightning grip around her little body.

"It looks like she's going to be as rambunctious as Kenny."

"Oh, she's completely her mommy's baby. You should see when she gets mad!"

Holly walked into the room from the kitchen. "And what's that mean?" she asked.

"She's always been like that," said Patricia.

"Who, the baby or Holly?" asked Cain, laughing.

"Holly is my baby, so I suppose I could answer 'yes' to both. When she was little, boy could she throw a fit! Now, Holly, where's that bathroom of yours?"

"I'll show you, Mom." Holly said. She gave Ray a tired, concerned look. She helped Patricia down the hallway and then in through the doorway of the bathroom her mom had used only thirty minutes earlier.

"Make sure you lock it, mom," said Holly as she walked back toward the living room.

"Is it about the same, or getting better?" Cain asked quietly.

"It's leveled out. It's amazing what the right treatment can do. I just wish we'd caught it sooner."

A burst of laughter echoed through the air as Kenny and Elsie ran into the house from the back yard. Elsie stretched to reach cups in the kitchen cabinets as Kenny opened the refrigerator and struggled to pull out a gallon jug of chocolate milk. The two of them went to work, filling the cups to nearly overflowing so they had to sip milk off the top before they could move. They spilled anyways. Kenny grabbed a rag from near the sink and wiped the milk from the countertop. Elsie walked slowly, balancing the two cups in her hands and pushing the door open with her back as she went outside. Kenny started after her.

"Kenny," said Holly.

"What, Mom?" Kenny answered, frustrated.

"Put the chocolate milk away!"

He sighed. "Okay."

Cain could hear the refrigerator door open and close and then the back door slam as Kenny went to join Elsie on the patio.

He spoke up, "Holly, how'd you know it was chocolate milk and the milk was still out?"

"I don't need to see the kitchen to know my little boy will leave something out. He has a love for chocolate milk lately and I just watched him and Elsie run around the front yard with those two puppies for the last fifteen minutes. So they were thirsty, and that's his choice of drink now-a-days."

Ray pulled Ranae into his shoulder and began rocking her as she began to fuss.

"I'll get her a bottle," said Holly,

"Oh, hey, I'll feed her," said Cain.

"Okay," said Holly. "Let me grab the bottle."

"No, you sit down. I can get it," Cain said, standing up.

Cain reached out for little Ranae.

"Don't you want to make the bottle first?" asked Ray.

"No, I can do this."

"Great, he's gonna try to juggle the baby and the bottle making," said Holly.

"Only takes one hand to make a bottle!" said Cain, snuggling his cheek up against Ranae and hugging her, holding her tightly with one arm and walking into the kitchen.

"Hey, Cain?" said Holly.

"Yeah?"

"If you have to drop something, make sure it's the formula."

"Yeah, yeah, I got it!"

Kenny and Elsie walked in from outside.

"Hey, big guy," said Cain. "Whatcha doing?"

"Playing with the puppies! They got real big."

"I saw that. What did you guys decide to name them?"

"My mom said we should call them The Keystone Cops, after you and dad, but Dad said no."

"So, what did they name them?"

"They let me and Elsie name them."

"Yep," Elsie said. "I named the girl and Kenny named the boy. I named the girl Stubby."

"Stubby? I don't think I want to know why you named her Stubby."

"The boys name is Roller!" said Kenny.

"What? Stubby and Roller?"

"Well," Kenny said. "Stubby has a stubby little tail and my dad said the first time you saw Roller he was rolling across the dirt!"

"Oh! Does mom and dad know what you named them?

"No, not yet."

"Grandpa?" Elsie said to Cain.

"Elsie," Cain said back, giggling inside at being called Grandpa by Elsie and trying to position the formula scoop over the bottle.

"Are we still going to the movies?"

"That's the plan. As a matter of fact, I need to check with Kenny's daddy to see what time the second one starts."

Formula powder dribbled down the outside edge of the bottle as Cain attempted to put in the three scoops. Ranae's face was wet from tears and her eyes red and tired from crying. She started to pout again, sniffling.

Holly yelled from the living room. "It's okay, honey. Cain's not trying to starve you. He's just slow!"

Ranae barely lifted herself up straight in Cain's arms, rubbed her eyes and forehead with her arm, and tiredly looked at Cain.

"Almost, baby," Cain said as he held the bottle end with his finger and shook it up. Ranae leaned forward into Cain's chest and did her best to grip the bottle with her little hand as Cain fed her.

Cain and the children walked into the living room.

"Hey, when's that second movie start? It looks like we already missed the first one."

"Seven-twenty," said Ray. "We better take off soon if we want to make it on time."

"And get popcorn!" said Kenny.

"Cain, you want to head out with the two kids. Holly and I and the baby will catch up. We've gotta run Patricia home," said Ray.

"Sounds like a plan! Looks like she's just about out," Cain said as he handed Ranae to Holly. "Elsie, Kenny, come on, let's go!"

Cain and the two children headed toward the car.

"Cain, can I drive?" asked Kenny.

"Uh, no! You need about four more feet of growing before that happens."

"Maybe by then you'll have the Vette!"

"Yeah, keep dreaming with me, buddy."

Cain opened the passenger door and Kenny and Elsie slid

across the seat. He got in the driver's side, started the vehicle, then began to back the car into the street.

"Seatbelt check!" Cain yelled out.

Kenny grunted. "I wasn't ready yet! That's not fair! I had it in my hand!"

"Looks like Elsie won."

"Ah, come on, I was close!"

"Alright, since you had it in your hand and you were trying."

"What do we get?" asked Elsie.

"Oh, open the glove compartment. I think I have some candy in there."

Elsie opened the glove compartment and pulled out a long tube of hard disk shaped candies.

"You two have to share."

Elsie and Kenny went to work tearing open the waxed candy package as Cain made his way down the road.

12

Cain tossed, nearly convulsively, in his bed. His eyelids flickered, then partially opened and closed as salty sweat from his face rolled into his eyes. It stung.

The dreams had variations to them, but they were always the same children, the same boys, same girls, always the same number of children. The same numbered tags hung from their bodies. But then a new child would be added, a new number. The new numbers bothered Cain. With each new number came a new victim of the serial killer.

It was always the same person, young and businesslike, the blank stare, his eyes visible, his face clear. There was always blood on his hands, the same brutality, a smell, a stench, not rotten, an aesthetic stench, unexplainable, and helpless victims. Cain had learned to accept the dreams as a regular part of his sleep schedule, each character like some morbid visitor, ever wishing upon him their memory, never to be forgotten. They haunted him. They wanted his attention. They demanded his attention. They wanted him to hear them.

He was lucky if he had a week of freedom from them. There were never any new clues. He had started to discount their supposed message as a little piece of insanity, dismissing them as some result of his work. He didn't think he'd ever be free of their torment.

Tonight's dream was particularly confusing to begin with. Cain stood on his father's property, staring up at the pinnacle on the greenhouse roof. The bright early spring sun shone around him. A shadow covered the sun and shaded Cain's eyes. There was a flutter in the shadow and suddenly he was there. The large bird of prey fastened its talons around the edge of the pinnacle, then immediately launched again, swooping across the property in a hurried dive.

Now Cain was inside the vision of the great bird, a sharp tunnel vision focused on movement near the fenceline of the large garden. The bird's eyes caught up with the movement, and for a split second Cain saw the frightened eyes of a young mammal turn toward the bird. A talon widened and came down hard, driving the claws through the body of the small mammal, sticking it to the ground. The vision faded, and Cain stood silent, looking back at the pinnacle.

He felt himself blurring in and out and then found himself standing in view of the hallway room from his other dreams. His hands were free, but he couldn't move. Previous dreams overlapped each other, as though they belonged together. Except this time something different happened. Each child's face overlapped with the face of one of the adult murder victims from the case. Tags and numbers hanging from the children corresponded with the numbers carved into the victim's chests.

Suddenly, as if transported by some unseen force, Cain was now standing in the partially opened doorway, watching helplessly. The killer stood over his little victims, his hands resting on the shiny table before him. He was slumped forward.

Cain could see sweat collecting on his face. He looked tired and for just a slight moment Cain felt an odd pity for him, questioning his own understanding of this man. Again, he was transported forward.

Now Cain stood directly behind him, moved through the room in a flash of an instant in his mind. *Show me your whole face, you sick* . . . , Cain thought. *You senseless coward. Preying on victims that can't defend themselves.* Cain wanted to grab him. He wanted to plunge all of his anger through him like a sharpened sword. He wanted to stab him in the heart, to execute him, to stop this murderous rampage, but he couldn't move.

A tear rolled down his cheek. He felt trapped in this insanity with no power to stop it. His heart pounded in piercing shock as he noticed the unspeakable. On the table, directly in front of the man, lay a little boy, a baby, alive, his arms and legs moving about.

No. No! Cain screamed in his mind. *Close your eyes. Close your eyes. You don't need to see this!* He closed his eyes, only for them to appear open once again, still seeing everything, as though he had no eyelids. He wanted to escape, but couldn't. He was being moved along completely outside of his will. Cain would witness this terrible thing. It was unstoppable.

It was when the man reached for his killing implement that Cain saw his rubber gloved, blood covered hands. What Cain had thought was a blade was something different. It had a different shape to it. As he brought it forward it appeared to be like the pair of scissors from the last murder scene.

An intense blackness began to fill the room, a powerful darkness, swooning over the space and shadowing everything he could see. In the darkness Cain felt a presence, an evil, a deep void. Then there was emptiness in the room. With the darkness there was a vacuum, a loss of all feeling, all emotion. The darkness seemed to fill the place, yet emptied it at the same time. It was moving, swirling. There was something in the darkness, something indistinguishable, something evil.

All at once the darkness shot inward toward the killer, swirling around him, then vanished into his body. Cain felt a deep sadness come over his soul. Then the killer struck, hard and fast. Cain watched as he thrust the weapon forward into the little boy's head, twisting and turning it as the child's body writhed in convulsive pain, his tiny arms and legs violently thrashing about before this beastly killer. His little body shook. The killer held the child's head. There was a flash in Cain's mind, an explosion of bright light. Now, in place of the child was a full grown man, his body thrashing about just as the child had been, except in the child's place.

The killer reached outward, grabbing the victim's right arm, savagely pulling and tugging at it like a maddened ravenous animal trying to tear his prey apart. The arm ripped free of the victim's body. Blood shot outward into the room in an unreal slow motion swirling pattern, like dye shot into water or cigarette smoke streaming across the air. It puddled on the table, glistening. Through the blood Cain noticed the texture of the table. It was shiny and had a metal, polished look to it. As the victim flailed his arms and legs about, the tiny bodies of the other victims were knocked to the floor from the table, each one making a thumping sound as they hit. And then it ended. The victim's struggle went out of him. He had nothing left, drained of his life by this maniac! Cain watched and cringed as he saw the killer unbutton the man's shirt and, with what appeared to be a scalpel, began to carve something into his victim's chest.

"I'm gonna quit!" Cain said.

"What?" said Ray.

"I don't think I can do this anymore. Between you and me, last night was the worst it's ever been. I woke up this morning covered in my own excrement and urine. I crapped myself, and I had thrown up all over my bed and on the carpet. That's how scary it was. It's too much. I think not stopping this guy is more than I can handle. I could transfer to traffic or a desk job. Try something different."

"Oh, you mean like the guy who lost it last year after responding to that accident on the bypass where the little kid got decapitated. Yeah, that's your answer! Listen, maybe something will break soon. It's starting to wear on both of us."

"Both of us?"

"Yeah, trust me. It's affecting my life, too."

"Probably not quite like me."

"You wanna get some coffee?"

"I could handle that. After last night, I could use the caffeine."

Jack's Donuts — any time of day you had to wait in line. They made black coffee that looked like old oil and seemed to taste the same. If the caffeine didn't awaken you, then the taste rolling across your tongue would. It was clear from the flavor that they left the old soot from each day's coffee in the bottom of the pot to strengthen the next batch.

Cain stood staring at the metal counter while Ray ordered their coffees. The shiny countertop reminded him of the table in his nightmare. The smell of fresh baked donuts filled the air.

Jack's was a classic scene of Americana. One reason the coffee was so good was because you had to stand outside to place and wait for your order. In the winter, by the time you got your coffee you were just ready for anything hot to drink, which made it a lot easier to handle the taste.

There was an outdoor eating area. Someone's dropped soda was splattered across the ground near the tables, its long winding trail looking like a river on a map. A hot dog holder sat on the ground next to the base of a table where the legs met at the center. Little plastic seats too small for the average person's behind were attached to bars that came together in the center and then up to a tabletop that wasn't quite big enough to handle a spread of food orders.

Cain's eyes traced across the ground from the soda spill to a bent cigarette butt and then to a tray at the top of a trashcan. Sticky solidified ketchup ran down its side from a little packet that had spilled its contents.

"Sir, here's your coffee." The worker's voice shook Cain from his thoughts.

It was only a few seconds after the man handed them their coffee and they had managed a bite of their donuts when they heard the police radio squawking at them from their vehicle. "We need crowd coverage at Crossroads High School, report of a body found." Ray's beeper signaled the same message.

They fumbled with their coffees as they got into the car. Cain bounced his head off the door jam. "Ah! How many times? You need a different car!"

Cain held one hand on his coffee, trying to keep it from spilling as Ray swerved in and out of traffic. His donut fell off his leg, bounced on the seat and rolled across the dirty floor. For a brief moment he considered reaching to pick it up until he smashed it with his foot trying to brace himself as Ray made a hard right turn.

"Ray, they found a body. Slow down, man! The person's still gonna be dead when we get there."

It was probably best a janitor found the victim. The scene had been secured before any of the faculty or students showed up for classes.

It appeared he had been killed either late the night before or in the early morning hours. His body lay across a stainless steel table in the school's biology lab, a wound to the base of his head, his brains churned into liquid and spilled out. His right arm had been torn from his torso. His shirt unbuttoned. The number six was carved into his chest. Cain's mind was numb from the scene.

"Alright, give us the mystery clue," Ray said.

"Somehow I knew that would be your first question. A photograph," Kayla said.

"A photograph of what?" Cain asked.

"You mean of *who*? It appears to be a photograph of a girl. It looks like a high school picture, you know, wallet sized."

"What do you mean, 'it appears'?" Cain shrugged his shoulders.

"Well, it's covered in blood. It was in the victim's right hand. It looks like he had it clenched tightly. Obviously, he let up his grip at some point. The killer made sure it stayed there though. The hand was hanging off the table and the arm was turned upward so the picture wouldn't fall out."

"Can we tell who's in the picture?" Ray asked.

"No. Lab's gonna to have to spend some time with it. Parts of the photo were lifted by the blood. Did you notice the chalkboard?"

"Whoa, nope, didn't see that!" Ray said.

"What?" Cain asked.

"The board, check out the chalk board." Chelsea pointed at the chalkboard.

"3, 6, 7, 5, 2, 1, 4. I thought it was just math or lesson

stuff," said Cain.

"He speaks again, huh," said Ana.

"Yeah," Ray stepped in closer.

"3, 6, 7, 5, 2, 1, 4 . . . The numbers don't matter, it's just one more," Cain read the poem out loud. "5, 4, 7, 6, 3, 2, 1 . . . Can't turn back time, you killed your son." It bothered him.

"You killed your son," Chelsea pondered out loud, repeating the phrase again. "You killed your son."

"Somebody's child was killed?" Ray asked.

"I wonder if our killer's son was murdered," Cain said.

"Maybe our killer is speaking to the victim's parents," said Kayla.

"You killed your son," Ray repeated it again. "Mmm, this victim or another?"

"Who knows?" Cain said, confused.

"The numbers don't matter," said Ana. "These numbers are just symbolic, random."

"Random, yet in order. There's order to what he's saying. He made it rhyme. Rhyme is order," said Cain.

"Rhyme can be chaos, disorder, also," said Ana.

"He's obviously just messing with our heads," Chelsea poked at her temple. "And it's working."

"These numbers aren't in order now, but he's counting his victims in order," Ray said. "His numbers show an intent to have more victims."

Cain looked over the words again. "He's saying that the numbers don't really matter, just that there are numbers, that there's a body count. But the age of the victims, there's something more to that. Do we know his age yet?"

"Do you even have to ask?" said Chelsea.

"This guy was one of our best educators," the principle said as they sat in his office. "The kids really loved him. He was their inspiration. You know, that kind of person."

"He didn't have any problems with his students?" Ray asked.

"Problems with the kids? Not a chance! He grew up in Crossroads. He won MVP two times in college and had three national teams interested in him. He chose to come here, back to little old Crossroads and teach kids math and coach a small city team that nobody will ever hear of. He won a league award for being coach of the year and for the last three years the kids nominated him for teacher of the year for the state. He could have had anything he wanted in life, but he had a passion for showing children they could succeed. This young man had kids that we'd practically given up on getting nearly straight A's. He gave them hope. He insisted they could have a future, that they could go beyond and rise above the norm. He made them dream. He worked with two of our girls in starting a peer group to help kids deal with the pressures of being teens." The principal got angry. "My God, what is this world coming to? What am I going to tell those kids? We spend years of their lives teaching them character and the value of each and every student, every life, then they have to be witness to such an atrocity. How can we expect kids to care about anything?"

As they left they walked past the usual commotion of public interest created by a homicide scene. A scattered mass of people had gathered across the street. The sound of the coroner truck's back-up signal beeped in their ears as it made its way close to the nearest entrance to the biology lab.

Teachers were organizing students into age groups and moving them back toward busses that had returned to the school.

Some of the students pulled together in small huddles and held each other, their cheeks covered with tears.

One young teacher who had collapsed onto the grass sobbing uncontrollably was surrounded by other faculty as they attempted to comfort her.

Several weeks and nothing solid enough to put them in the right direction toward a suspect. *This guy's good*, Ray thought. *He's slick. He knows just what he's doing. He knows something he shouldn't. He knows too much!*

◊

"Oh, Cain, come here!" Ana yelled for him.

Ray looked at Cain with a silly grin on his face. "I already had my turn."

"What's up, Ana," asked Cain.

"You know my name's not really Ana?"

"Really? Must be something far more beautiful."

Ana ignored his flirtation. "It's actually Christiana. You can call me that when you've realized I'm frustrated with you. "Come here," she said, like she was talking to a small child. "Come here, Cain." She had her eyebrows raised.

As Cain walked up to her she reached for his left hand and grabbed it, pulling him ten feet across the room to a scanning machine and flopping his hand down palm first and pressing a button.

Here we go again, Cain thought to himself.

"I don't know how many times I have to tell you guys. Get the gloves on as soon as you start to process a crime scene and keep your hands off things you don't need to touch. You're going to compromise evidence. I got nearly a full print from the window sill at the High School. It's not the victim's or a child's, but since we've all had this talk before, I'm guessing it's yours,

Ray's or the killer's. If it's another teacher's or student, then, well, that creates a huge problem. Hopefully the killer was the one that wasn't thinking this time. I've already scanned Ray's hand. And the winner is. . ."

The light scanned across Cain's hand as he gave Ana a silly 'I'm the culprit' look and watched as the scanned images came across the computer screen. A window opened matching his handprint to the one on the screen. A pulsating border signified the match.

"Ooops?" Cain said.

"Gloves! And you shouldn't be touching things anyhow. You think after this many years it would have sunk in somehow. You guys need to be more careful. Drop the sloppy!" she said, shaking her head. "I should've saved you guys' prints in a file a long time ago. This is like the fourth time."

"So, does this mean you'll finally go out with me?" Cain asked the lady ten years younger than him. "You know, I left that there just so I'd have a chance to ask you out."

"Remember, you're at a crime scene. Ana smiled. "Apparently you guys are getting a little *too old* to be careful."

"Oh, ouch!" Ray mocked.

A slight smile and tilt of her head gave Cain his answer.

Kevin Patrick Smith

13

The back screen door slammed against its frame as Kenny bolted into the house.

"Hey, mom," Kenny said to Holly.

"Yes, honey."

"Can I ride my bike?"

"Sure, but remember, you have to stay on the sidewalk!"

"I will!"

"And don't go any farther than the stop sign!"

"Can I ride to Cain's?"

"No! That's too far! You're only to do that with daddy on the trails."

"Come on, mom!"

"No! Do you need to stay in?"

"Noooo."

"Besides, Cain's at work."

Cain heard it on the police scanner first. He had a sickening feeling as he pulled onto his street. He saw the flashing lights of two police cars and then watched as paramedics covered a little body in the roadway.

They were directly in front of his apartment building. He found himself running pictures of neighborhood kids through his mind, hardly believing that he was choosing one child over another to live or die, as though he would have some sort of power over the situation.

It wasn't until he came closer to the scene that the full impact hit him like a hard blow to the gut, sucking the wind and strength from his body. His heart immediately sank inside him. An ache set itself into the pit of his stomach as he watched a sedan from the coroner's office pull away from the scene.

Standing on the sidewalk with the police officers just past the ambulance, was Elsie's Grandpa. His head faced down and hand held over his forehead tightly grasping his hair. He had a look of anguish on his face.

"No." Cain's eyes filled with tears and they streamed down his cheeks. His heart teetered on a precipice of despair. He couldn't even think. *Oh my God, not my precious little girl. She's one of the only bright lights left in my life.* Cain froze up. He was dizzy. He couldn't breathe, couldn't seem to move.

Cain watched as the paramedics retrieved the stretcher from the ambulance. He took in the rest of the scene from down the street. A police officer questioned a man who was probably in his thirties near a vehicle stopped in the middle of the street by the ambulance. The man had a distraught look on his face as he shook his head and pointed to other vehicles along the side of the street. The police officer was writing information on a clipboard as the man spoke. There was just a small dent on the front of the car, hardly noticeable, and a bike in the street.

Cain pulled his car hard into the curb. He was reeling inside. The pain was almost too much to bear. He laid his head forward and rested it on the steering wheel, closing his eyes. He heard the people around him outside. He thought of Elsie. He was tired. *I have to see her.*

He was out of the car as soon as he thought it, making his way toward the little body covered in the street. His mind was cloudy. Everything around him seemed to stand still. He knelt down and grabbed the corner of the fabric covering and started to pull it away from the body.

"Grandpa!" Elsie yelled.

Cain's lungs filled with air as his mind awakened, trying to sort his thoughts, which were now confused by Elsie's little voice. He looked up. Elsie's Grandpa was turning to scoop her up from the lawn of the apartment.

"Oh, honey, I told you to stay inside," he said to her. "You should have listened to me! Officer, are you done with me? I don't want her to see any more of this. She's seen enough already."

"Yes, sir. I think this statement will do. If we have any more questions about what you saw, we'll be calling you. I'm sorry you had to experience this. If you need to talk to somebody about it you can call the number on the card I gave you."

Elsie and her Grandpa walked back toward the apartment building as Cain let go of the covering and stood to his feet, exhaling, his heart still pounding painfully in his chest, a flush feeling rolling over his body.

He gathered his composure, wiped the wetness from his face, and then walked toward the apartment. He nodded to one of the police officers. "Hey Tammie, tough one, huh?"

"Yeah."

Several of his neighbors were gathered near the street and on the sidewalk.

"Cain," one of the neighbors said. "Terrible, huh?"

"Yeah," Cain said, wanting to know whose child it was but feeling kind of strange asking after what his mind had just been through. "Who's kid?" Cain asked.

"Nobody knows, some little boy. He's not from this neighborhood. I think they're still trying to figure it out, trying to find the parents."

"Too bad." Cain said. Cain thought of Elsie and how he was glad it wasn't her, second guessing what he felt was an apparent coldness of heart toward the child laying in the street. *Wasn't anybody I know, right? I shouldn't feel anything, necessarily. People die every day. Kids die every day. It's not really my problem. It doesn't affect me.*

Cain watched from his apartment window as the ambulance pulled away and drove down the street slowly, now as a morgue transport rather than a life support unit, no urgency in its purpose. He felt sympathy, but not for the child or the parents who lost him. For the paramedics and the un-invited layer of callousness that had once again most likely tried to wrap itself around their hearts. *All just part of the job,* Cain thought.

His phone rang.

"Hello."

"Cain, this is Holly. Have you seen Kenny? she asked anxiously.

"Kenny? No. Why would I have seen Kenny?"

"He asked to ride his bike and then asked if he could ride over to your place. I told him no, to stay on the block, but I can't find him and I've looked everywhere."

Cain's body went flush.

Holly listened as Cain's keys slammed onto the counter on his end before she could say anything more.

Cain flung back the curtains and looked out the window.

The ambulance was nearing the end of the street. He ran from his apartment and nearly jumped the first flight of stairs in one leap, then ran down the rest of the steps.

He turned as he came out the front door of the building and started to run toward the ambulance, which was now at the corner of the block and preparing to turn into traffic. He broke into the best sprint he could accomplish, only to watch it turn left into heavy traffic and disappear.

He crouched down, winded, trying to breath. He felt dizzy. He thought of using his cell phone, but then remembered his car's radio. He jogged back toward the car. *My keys are upstairs!*

It was then that he noticed the officer loading the crumpled bicycle into the trunk of the patrol car.

"Hey, hold on," he said.

She closed the trunk, not hearing Cain's request.

"Tammie!" Cain repeated.

This time she heard him. "What's up?"

"I need to see that bike!"

"What? Why?"

"Just let me see the bike!"

"Alright, alright, no problem."

"Can I ask you why?" Tammie said as she keyed the trunk of the car.

"Ray's kid is missing and Holly said she thinks he might have ridden over here to see me."

"Ray's kid?"

"Just open the freaking trunk!"

"I'm opening it, I'm opening it."

Tammie opened the trunk.

"Relax man. It's not his, Cain."

Cain looked down into the trunk of the police cruiser. The bike was blue.

"Kenny's bike is green," Cain said, letting out a sigh of relief.

"I was trying to tell you that. I saw the kid. It's not Kenny. Kenny and my nieces are in class together. Holly and I see each other all the time at school events. Besides, we got an ID on the parents a few minutes ago."

"I'm sorry."

"That's okay, I understand. Holly's told me how close you are to the kids now."

Cain reached into his pocket and pulled out his phone. He was about to dial when it rang. It was Holly.

"Cain?"

"Yeah, hey, he's not here. I can come over and help you find him."

"Well, I found his bike. It was shoved over into the bushes on the side of the house. He actually put it right where we've told him so it wouldn't get stolen. He's probably next door playing with the neighbor's kid. He's just so darned stubborn. I thought for sure he'd tried to ride out to your place. He thinks he can conquer the world."

"Call me back as soon as you're sure he's next door."

"I will."

Cain walked across the apartment lawn and started up the stairs, thoughts of Kenny's boyish, fun loving face bouncing across his mind. *Man, I don't know what I'd do if I ever lost that kid.*

"What about the chest carvings? Did Chelsea give us an answer on those yet?" asked Cain.

"She said it looks like a scalpel or a razor of some sort, they're not sure yet. It was a clean, straight cut," said Ray. "The wounds were tight and even through their entire depth."

"Maybe a box cutter."

"They're doing some more imaging to see what they can come up with." Ray said.

"What makes a person do that to another person? I mean, how twisted, how far off do you have to get to cut, to mutilate like that?"

"And I don't think these numbers are significant. He's just counting his victims and letting us know which ones are his."

"Gotta hand it to him, he's clean," said Cain.

"Except for our conductor. It seems like he made it a point to be messy with that one. Why would he do the conductor the way he did? It just doesn't fit. I mean, he walked through the blood. That's not like him."

"It's like the conductor was his first. Not enough practice."

"This guys good. Maybe some medical background, knows how to clean up after himself," said Ray.

"Yeah, I just wish he'd clean it all up. Dump the bodies in the river so we don't have to deal with the mess. Let them float downstream and be somebody else's problem."

"That's pretty sad, bud," Ray said.

"We live in a sad world."

"The phone calls and contacting the victim's moms before he kills them? He didn't have to do that. He could have gone straight to the source. He could have found the victims the same way he found their mothers, the phone book, whatever."

"These people were well known. He didn't have to go to their mothers or a phonebook. It seems like it has to be a part of some weird ritual. He included their mothers as a part of his ritual. They're the beginning of the murder, the beginning of the ritual. He has to somehow feel like he got to the victim through them."

"Exactly!" Ray said.

"So why? Why would he being doing that? What's in this guy's mind that makes him think like this?"

"Maybe something happened to him. Maybe something to do with his mother. Is there a chance he wants to somehow mentally place the blame on the mother? Somehow if he goes through the victim's mother than he's not really responsible?"

"Do you really think this guy cares whether he's responsible or not? I doubt he even has a conscience left," said Cain.

"Can a person be that devoid of guilt?"

"Yes, a person can be that devoid of guilt. Have we looked at locations as an issue?"

Ray shrugged his shoulders. "I mapped it a few weeks back. There wasn't anything significant. And the last two wouldn't change that. He went totally off the grid on those. Obviously, he's not staying in the more prominent neighborhoods anymore. He's willing to pick his victims from elsewhere, so your whole conspiracy thing is out the door. He's pretty much hit entirely different areas, social groups and occupations."

"Doesn't seem to be discriminating anymore, does he?"

"Nope." Ray shook his head, then looked down at his plate.

"Nobody stands a chance if he shows up."

We need to put out a notification to border states and see if he's hit in other locations. Maybe they're finding victim's in other states that have been ripped apart in the same way. For all we know, there could be a whole slew of dismembered bodies out there."

"Karen's already running that for us. We'll see," said Cain.

Cain and Ray looked up from their breakfast plates and the conversation they were consumed in to notice that the people sitting at the next table had disgusted looks on their faces. The mother was shielding her child's ears from their conversation, her hands cupped at the sides of his head.

Cain set down his coffee and put his hand up and gestured, "Sorry."

"Maybe we should switch topics."

"Yeah."

Cain walked past the outside corner of the building and through the short hallway that entered the courtyard of the apartments. A strong scent arose from the small grouping of lilacs at the edge of the garden. He turned toward the stairway that led to his apartment and glanced at the lower level apartment directly under his. The curtains on the window blew in the afternoon breeze. As they flowed inward he caught a glimpse of Elsie playing in the front room of the apartment.

I'm not doing anything tonight. I should try to hang out with Elsie. Maybe I could get her mom to do something with us.

"Hey sweetie," Cain said as he walked up to the door. Elsie was now in the window, her face pressed against the screen, her nose slightly crunched into it and her eyes following him as he walked up. What are you doing?"

"Playing," Elsie answered through the window screen.

"What's your mommy doing?"

"I don't know."

"Can you get her?"

"Yep."

Cain heard Elsie fiddling with the door knob and the door opened. Elsie bounced off into the apartment.

"Mommy, Grandpa wants to talk to you," said Elsie.

"Mommy," Elsie repeated, now knocking on the door to her mother's room.

The door slowly opened and Elsie's mom leaned into the edge of the door, looking exhausted, a concerned tension showing in her face.

"How are you doing?" Cain asked.

"Okay," she replied, looking at him tiredly.

"I was thinking maybe we could all go for something to eat, my treat."

"I'm kinda wore out today. I had an early appointment."

Elsie immediately jumped into the conversation, as if she didn't want to let the moment pass.

"Come on, mommy. You can have fun. We'll all have fun."

"What do you say?" asked Cain.

She hesitated, thinking, and looked at Elsie.

"Hmmm, maybe."

"Yes!" Elsie was excited.

"But I need a few minutes to freshen up."

"Okay," said Cain.

Elsie turned toward Cain.

"Where?"

"Where? Well, that's no fun if I tell you. It'll spoil the surprise."

"Is it where I got the fudge cake with Kenny?"

"So much for a surprise."

Elsies' mom stepped out from the room and walked into the bathroom and shut the door. Instinctively, Cain tuned his ears on the bathroom, worried about what she may be doing, but a moment later the door opened. The sink was running. She turned off the water, dabbing her face with a towel, looking at Cain and reading his concern.

"Life's not perfect, but I'm trying."

"Good, good. Shall we go?"

"Uh huh," She said.

She looked at Cain. Her eyes landed with his. He knew what she was thinking. It was a questioning look, an asking why look. He'd tried to break through before, tried to insert himself in her life. He understood the struggle. He wanted to help her so much with it. She had been cold to his interest. Elsie, yes, Elsie, was allowed outside the wall, the wall of her heart. She knew Elsie needed other people. But herself? The latches were holding strong on the gate. Her fortress was several years in the building, and nobody was easily entering. She had protections in place. Hardened. Tough. Hurt. Not willing.

"Elsie, you're not between the lines," her mom said.

"Grandma always told me I didn't have to stay between the lines."

"You loved your grandma, huh?"

"I miss her."

"I miss her too, honey."

Cain teared up.

"Elsie, look at these here. You have to decide what you want."

Elsie set aside her crayon and began to fiddle with her menu.

The waiter walked up.

"Are you guys ready for some drinks?"

"Yeah. I'll take an iced tea, how about you?" Cain looked across the table.

"I'll take whatever cola you have. Elsie, honey, what do you want to drink?"

"Can I get a milkshake like last time?" Elsie turned and asked Cain.

"That's fine, sweetheart."

"Like last time? What are you doing, spoiling my little girl with these outings you go on with Ray and Holly?" she jested at Cain, smiling.

"She might just have me wrapped a little itsy bitsy tiny little bit around her little fingers," Cain said as he pinched two fingers together in the air.

"Uh huh," she said, shaking her head.

"Alright, well, I, um, I'll be right back with your drinks," the waiter said, turning to walk away, but not before hesitating as he looked back at the table one more time.

"I caught that," said Cain.

"Caught what?"

"He likes you!"

"I noticed," she said, uninterested. "Are you giving me fatherly advice now?"

"He's cute."

"Uh huh."

"You should get his number."

"I have not got time for that right now."

"Hmmm."

"So what's good?" she looked at Cain.

"On the menu?'

"Yeah, on the menu."

"A lot of them."

"And the other?"

"Well, you know, that's always a toss up, right?"

"Oh yeah, always!"

"The cavetelli's good. I love the stuffed pork chops. The rib-eye is absolutely amazing. It's doused in this bourbon glaze rub . . .'"

She started laughing. "Are you serious. Oh, my God, you sound like a waiter. What do you do, eat here every other day?"

"I eat here, enough." Cain smiled.

"Apparently."

"They've also got great salads. What do you like?"

"I'm kind of a sandwich girl lately. She ran her fingers through her hair. Elsie, did you see something you want?"

"I'll take that," Elsie pointed to a picture on the kids' menu.

"Looks like three-cheese ravioli for Elsie."

"I'm gonna get the stuffed pork chop," said Cain.

"You're a stuffed pork chop," said Elsie, giggling.

They all laughed. Inside, Cain felt an ease he'd never felt before. It was good that they were all having fun together. There didn't seem to be the usual tension.

"And who had the tea? the waiter asked as he walked up.

"Here," said Cain, looking at the waiter, then across the table. "And she wanted your cola there."

She tipped her head slightly and gave Cain an angry but fun

look, teasingly like a sister asking a big brother to stop doing something.

"And . . . a milkshake for me," the waiter said as he walked off with the milkshake.

"Hey!" Elsie let out a yell.

The waiter stopped.

"What?"

"That's mine!"

"Oh, well, let me see here," the waiter looked at his ticket book. "Nothing on here says the milkshake belongs to the adorable little girl at table four," he said as he set it in front of her and winked as he walked away.

"Wow," she said.

"Flirting through your daughter," Cain said.

"What's flirting?" Elsie asked.

They laughed.

"Don't worry about it, honey. You'll know soon enough."

"Did he forget to take our order?" asked Elsie.

"Yeah. Little too much of his head in the clouds," said Cain.

The waiter walked back down the aisle toward the back of the restaurant and the kitchen area. Cain lifted his hand, motioning him to stop.

"You guys real busy?"

"No, not at all. It's actually kinda slow right now."

"How long do you think it'll be till our foods ready? I've got somewhere I have to be."

The waiter looked at Cain, then Elsie, and across the table, his eyes meeting the eyes of the one closest his age, a look of embarrassment coming over his face.

"Oh. I am so sorry. I was a bit distracted."

"You're alright," she said, and looked at Cain.

He turned toward Elsie first.

"What does this little princess want?"

Impressive recovery attempt, Cain thought.

"Ravioli," said Elsie. "This one."

"And you sir?"

"The stuffed pork chops."

"And you," he hesitated with his words. "What do you want?"

"I think I'm gonna play it safe and stick with *just* the stuffed pork chops today."

The waiter looked disappointed. Cain smiled.

"I forgot how beautiful it was."

"It's been right here all these years. You should spend more time here. Elsie and Kenny love feeding the ducks."

"When I was little, mom would hold my hand and we'd walk down the shoreline together." She was visibly hurting.

Cain saw her pain and his eyes swelled with tears and he blinked to make them go away. He wasn't used to her showing this much emotion and feeling around him. The few times he had managed an outing with her and Elsie, she had been more cold, distant, closed up, especially after her mother had died.

Elsie flung another handful of crumbs in the air, half of them landing on the ground at her feet. Several ducklings left the water and surrounded her, pecking at the breadcrumbs. She screamed and then giggled hysterically, lifting away from them whatever foot they got too close to. One nipped near her toes and made contact. She screamed again in excitement.

"Life just jumps up and slaps you in the face. When I was that little girl, I would never have imagined being trapped like I am now. This is good for her. You, Ray and Holly are good for her. Kenny's like a brother. Right now it's a good place for her to be. This is safe, around all of you." She hesitated. "Will you promise me something?"

"What's that?"

"That if anything ever happens to me, if I don't beat this thing, that you'll watch out for her. Holly and Ray, you know, you'll all stay close to her."

"That's not ever something you need to worry about. We all love that little girl. But hey, brighter days are ahead, right? You'll be okay."

"I suppose I could lie to you. But I don't know. Sometimes I'm not sure. Sometimes the joys in life don't seem to outweigh the pain. I was finally getting close to mom and since losing her, I've just never been this low."

"We're all here for you. You just have to ask."

"I know. I know now."

Cain wasn't sure what she meant by her last words and it bothered him.

"Well, six-o-clock, we've just about lost the sun, and it's a feeding frenzy with the mosquitos once that happens. They attack in squadrons out here."

"Come on Elsie, baby, we've gotta go."

She turned toward Cain again.

"Thanks."

"I wouldn't have wanted to spend my evening in any other way. I'll count today as a treasure."

She smiled and looked him in the eyes. It was a comforted look, a look a daughter gives her father. A look of feeling safe, protected. Cain cherished it.

The three of them left the side of the pond and walked up the grassy area, past the small grove of trees surrounding the bench with the worn placard. Elsie latched onto her mom's hand, then Cain's.

14

The numbing deadness of the killer's psyche blocked out even the minutest feelings of human empathy. A darkness swooned over him, invading the inner cavities of his conscience, and like a cold sun setting over some distant arctic region, slowly dimmed any light that remained in his mind. The coldness, the darkness, the process, always won. And then there was blackness, no anger, no rage, just methodic motion, that of a machine, running through a preset program, a routine, just another part of his day.

"I'll be with you in just a second," the mechanic said. "This brake line doesn't seem to want to cooperate with me. These older fittings can really seize up good sometimes."

The little bells jingled against the door as the killer stepped into the mechanics bay.

If I hurry, I can be home early, the killer thought. *But the kill has to take place. I have the permission. I have a job to do.*

In his hand he held the papers, the kill orders he had so

carefully prepared. At the top of the papers was a small tag, the number seven written on it sloppily. There was type of various sizes and spaces that had been filled in. At the bottom were two signatures. The killer looked carefully at the signatures. The signatures authorized the kill. He slowly and methodically moved across the repair bay until he stood next to the man hunched over working on the car. In the grip of the killer's hand was a long pair of stainless steel scissors, sharp, pointed, and slightly tucked behind him.

The mechanic looked up from his task.

"Oh, hey. Can I do something for you?" The mechanic asked.

"Your father sent me," the killer replied.

It was one of the biggest crowds they had seen gathered at a crime scene. They were in an older part of town, the original Main Street of the city. Many of the buildings were in disrepair. City officials had been trying to get the area either cleaned up and looking nicer or condemned and torn down. Several of the storefront buildings facing the street had been vacated years before. Others were filled with miscellaneous small businesses that looked like they were trying to build something in a place where dreams had long been forgotten.

On the corner at the east end of the business district sat an old mom and pop service station with a little convenience shop and a two stall repair bay. There was a car in one of the stalls and several cars sat outside the shop in the faded asphalt parking lot. There were stacks of old tires with a sign on them that read 'free'. Two older gas pumps stood like dedicated workers. They seemed to be saying, *"How can we help you, no extra charge for full service, would you like your windows washed? Check your oil?"*

Crime scene tape was attached to an old barrel on one side of the gas station, connected to one of the old pumps, then strung all the way across the asphalt to the farthest corner, blocking access. Sergeant Washington stood with Officer Kollasch at the street making sure no one crossed the sidewalk onto the property. Another officer stood near the door to the mechanic's bay.

An air hose sat coiled in front of the repair bays like a snake ready to strike. As they entered odors of gas and oil took over their senses.

Ray gave a half smile to Ana and Chelsea as he and Cain walked into the bay.

The victim was lying on the concrete floor, a puddle of blood pooled around his head, parts of brain matter sitting in the blood. It looked like the struggle had started while the victim was hunched over inside the engine compartment working on it. There was blood on areas of the engine compartment, on the front left fender of the vehicle, and then smeared across the grill and bumper, like the victim had tried to hold on as he went down to the floor. His eyes were open, staring straight upward at the ceiling, but sunken back slightly in his head, having no brain matter for pressure. His arms and legs were intact and his blue mechanic's scrub shirt was unbuttoned. The number seven was carved into his chest.

"Do I have to ask his age?" Ray asked.

"No, same," said Chelsea.

"What's this in the blood?" Cain asked Chelsea. "Looks yellowish. Maybe brake fluid?"

Cain crouched down and examined the liquid that was not mixing with the blood.

"There's a bottle of it in the engine compartment that looks like it spilled during the struggle. I'd say with the box over here and the badly worn brake pads on the floor by the front wheels, the mechanic was obviously changing a set of brakes on this car." Chelsea looked at Cain dumbly and shook her head in a yes motion as she spoke.

"It's not uncommon to see a car this old around this end of town. This one's in decent shape. That's back when they actually put some steel in the fenders. What is that? Maybe a sixty-eight, sixty-nine?" Ana asked.

"I think it's a sixty-nine," Cain said. "Don't ever wanna get hit by one of those. That's a solid machine."

"Hey, guys," Chelsea said. "When you're done with him there, you won't want to miss the featured poem of the day back here."

"Our poet strikes again, huh?" Ray asked.

"Oh yeah! Except this time he mixed a little poetry with art."

Cain reached down and pulled back the man's clenched fingers as Ray stood over him watching. They weren't expecting what they saw. In the man's right hand was another lock of hair, the same color, size, and shape as the one found on the trooper.

"Well, there's a direct connection for us," Ray said, slowly shaking his head and looking around the room.

"Wasn't expecting that. Now we might have a clear link between two victims. Just need a DNA match," Cain said.

"What would a state trooper and a mechanic have to do with each other in a way that links them to a lock of hair?" asked Ray.

"My initial thought would be an accident? Mechanics work on cars and troopers are around cars. Maybe somebody, maybe whoever's hair this is, died," said Cain.

"And somebody's mad about it," said Chelsea.

"Do you guys realize the significance of this location?" the officer near the door asked.

"What do you mean?" Cain asked.

"This was your trooper's main patrol zone. He worked the bigger surface roads around this area and the road that runs out to the Canyons and The Lake Estates."

"No, we hadn't put that together yet. That's a good one.

Maybe you should come work homicide. God knows Cain and I are getting too old for this!"

Cain continued to investigate the scene as Ray turned to talk to the young rookie officer standing in the doorway that separated the repair bay from the office and the convenience shop. This was the officer's neighborhood. He worked here on his patrols and lived just a few blocks down the street. The officer spoke again.

"We grew up right here in the neighborhood together. I ran these streets with him when we were kids. I don't get it. All he ever did was help people. He kept his prices low so people could afford it. He took care of people's cars for free, especially the older folks in the neighborhood or if a family was hurting financially, you know. He did a lot of simple things that made a difference."

"It's important that we talk to his mother as soon as possible."

"Can't! She died eight years ago."

"What? Are you sure?" Cain spoke up, now joining their conversation.

"Yeah, I mean, you don't have him mixed up with . . ." Ray interrupted, almost as if the officer had spoiled their expected scenario of how the case should play itself out.

"Yeah, I'm sure. I went to the funeral. She was my aunt. Your victim's my cousin."

"I'm sorry," Ray said. "We didn't realize."

"Is his father alive?" Cain asked.

"Yeah."

"Can you tell us where his father lives?"

"I'll ride over there with you when you're finished here if you'd like."

Ray moved from the front of the car to the back and stood over the trunk of the vehicle where Chelsea had just finished taking photographs.

"What do you think? Not too bad, uh?" Chelsea said.

"Great blending of colors! I Love the red and yellow."

"Have you ever considered changing careers?" Ray looked at her, shaking his head.

Ray stood at the back of the car staring down at several words on its trunk. The writing appeared to be a continuation of the poem from the conductor's house, except this time meticulously detailed in what looked like the victim's blood and framed in with a neatly trailed out band of yellowish liquid.

"If you're wondering, it's brake fluid, the yellow stuff, that is. I think I'm going to have this guy frame my next piece of artwork. I love the way the lines of brake fluid spin through the blood in a candy-stripe pattern." She raised her eyebrows. "Don't know if I'd want him working with the family photos, though."

"You're sick, you know that?" Ray said.

Chelsea smiled her little fake grinny smile as Cain walked up behind the car.

"Great, he's an artist," Cain said.

"Aren't you guys going to read it? He did so well with the handwriting. Even took the time to put those little swirls on the ends of the capital letters," said Ana.

"You both really need some help!"

"I think they're making a point here, Cain," Greg said from the doorway of the mechanic's bay as he walked in.

"Oh, hey, Greg," Ray said.

"I don't think this guy has plans to stop any time soon, not if it's up to him. And the people in this city are beginning to get a little worried knowing there's somebody like him out here running around."

"So my point?" Ana said.

"Her point," Chelsea interrupted, "is that this guy is so precisely detailed about what he's doing that he took the time to cross his 't's" and dot his "i's", all in brake fluid, which wasn't easy. He's passionate about his message. He wants it to be seen very clearly. He's not messing around. He's going to keep killing, to keep making his statement, whatever that is."

"Souls of children scream in his head?" Ray read part of the poem.

Cain read the next line. "Beckoning, calling, from the dead."

"It just keeps sounding more and more like our killer's lost a child," Ray said. "Something along those lines."

The officer in the doorway spoke up. "Or he's got a bunch of children laying around dead somewhere."

"I really hope that's not the case," said Greg, bringing a more serious tone to the conversation.

"Look what it says next." Ana pointed to the third line.

"He's gone too far, he's crossed the line, the darkness fell, the light must shine."

"Well, we're stating the obvious now," Cain said.

"No," Ana spoke. "Our killer is talking about someone. '*He's* gone too far, *he's* crossed the line.'"

"Or he's talking about himself," Greg said.

Cain read the rest of the poem out loud.

"He commands the moment, he holds the key, only he can stop this killing spree.

Will he trade a heart of flesh for his heart of stone, as he lay in darkness all alone."

"He holds the key," Greg repeated. "The killer's talking about himself or someone else doing the killing and saying that he is the one that can stop it."

"If he's talking about himself, it looks like he recognizes that the killing is wrong," Cain said.

"Yeah," said Chelsea. "*He* commands the moment. Only *he* can stop this killing spree."

"That last verse references the statue you like, Cain," Ray said.

"I noticed that."

"Heart of flesh for a heart of stone? What's that mean?" asked Ana.

"It's a verse on the statue by the Lake Estates. The verse says, 'I will give you a heart of flesh for your heart of stone.' I think it's something religious," said Cain.

"It's talking about God taking an old, hardened heart full of sin and making it soft and pliable again," Chelsea said as she cupped her hands into a little chapel. "Learned that one in Sunday school."

"So is our killer talking about himself, or about someone else?"

"He lays in darkness…" Cain said. "He lays in darkness."

"I don't know," Greg said.

"Well, maybe we can find something out from this man's father," said Ray.

"I'll see you guys back at the division." Greg turned to leave.

Ana spoke from across the repair bay. "Hey, guys, you might want to see this."

She was pointing at a line of brake fluid she had just noticed near the vehicle.

"Right, so, some more brake fluid?"

"Exactly, but follow me."

Ana lead the group around a long trail of brake fluid that wound its way past the driver's side door of the vehicle and then turned left as it approached the wall at the head of the bay. The yellowish liquid zigzagged and danced about the floor in a continuous trail, appearing to abruptly stop at the exit door that led to the storage lot behind the shop.

As they approached the door Ana opened it, revealing a continuing trail of fluid. The trail became somewhat wider, passing by a water hose and several vehicles until it settled upon an older vehicle with its passenger side completely destroyed, part of its interior burned out. Cain stood at the front of the car. He couldn't believe what he was seeing. The grill, the fenders, the chrome, the cut line of the trim.

"You gotta be kidding me," said Cain. "A 1953."

"Well," Ray said. "That's one less out on the market when

you finally go shopping for it."

Cain ran his hand across the fender of the car.

At the front of the Corvette the fluid seemed to roll off into several separate streams, each turning inward and going underneath the vehicle at various entry points.

"No license plates!" said Ana. "I'll get the VIN number and pull the information on it, try to see what happened."

Greg spoke. "Ana, have your team work the two vehicles over. See if we can't come up with something from one of them. Chelsea, crack that trunk first, just in case he left us a surprise. Remember, we're still missing victim two."

Chelsea walked back toward the shop, then returned with a toolbox. After a few moments she lifted the trunk lid.

"Empty. Why does that not surprise me?" asked Ray.

"Doesn't look or smell like anything's ever been in this trunk," said Chelsea. "Couple of old stains. That's about it. I'll scan it for blood."

They pulled away from the curb and drove several blocks into the neighborhood of small houses. Kids rode their bikes on the sidewalk. A middle aged man pushed a lawn mower.

"This one changes our case, huh? Ray said

"Some, but not much."

"So much for your conspiracy theory ideas."

"Yeah, well, it's obvious now that the killer doesn't care if his victims are on the brink of some great discovery or have changed the world."

The officer interjected from the back seat. "Hey guys, I'm not real familiar with your case, but I've heard some of the details about it. My cousin may not have been like those other people, famous and all, but he changed people's lives every day. He made a difference for regular people on this side of town who just needed a hand. He was the kind of guy we all need a whole lot more of. He changed this little world, here in the neighborhood, for a lot of people."

"Well, on all of the previous murders he contacted the mothers of the victims before he killed them, some crazy part of his ritual. Now, he either contacted your uncle or he's changed his own rules entirely."

"We'll see. Turn right at the end of this block. It's about ten houses down on the left hand side of the street."

They couldn't pull up to the house. The drive was full of cars. The street was lined with cars.

"You'd better just stop over here. We'll have to walk a little. Oh, hey, wait. Pull into this driveway here. It's my aunt's house. She won't care. She's probably across the street anyhow."

They parked the car, then made the short walk down and across the street to the house. Several people stood on the grass and in the driveway. The officer gave an older woman a hug, then shook the hand of a man his own age. There were a lot of people at the house. It was obvious that many of the extended family lived in the neighborhood.

"Hey," Cain said to the officer, concerned about intruding. "One question, that's all that matters right now. We can talk to him again later, maybe tomorrow morning."

The officer pushed ahead of them through the crowded doorway and into the equally crowded living room.

"Uncle Joe, I got a couple of guys here who need to ask you a quick question. It's really important."

The expression on the man's face as they asked him their question showed Ray and Cain that he knew what they were talking about.

"About seven, eight-o-clock last night. I mean, everybody knows everybody in this area, so I thought it was a little weird, strange. We usually only have local customers and most of them know my wife is gone. I was sitting here watching the news. A phone call rang in on the second line. We put it in as a business line here at the house years ago. There were too many calls on the house phone before that. Most of our regular customers know the phone number, but it's also up on a sign in the window at the station. Anyhow, this guy asks if the lady of the house is home. I said I wished she was, kind of jokingly, then told him she died years ago. He asked if I was the owner of the shop. I told him no, my son was. He said he was interested in having some work done on his vehicle. I told him my son had gone to an eastside warehouse to pick up a part and should be back around eight-thirty."

"That's all you heard from him?" Cain asked.

"Why the woman of the house? Seemed odd. But yeah, you know, there is one more thing. When I told him my wife was dead, he didn't say the usual condolences someone would say. He just said, 'That's okay, if she's not available, you'll do' You'll do? What does that have to do with him getting work done? And he said, 'sometimes the father just has to be the strong one. A mother can be reluctant."

"Thanks for your time, sir," Ray said.

"Sure."

"I'll just be staying here, the young officer said. Can you let me know as soon as you come up with anything?

"Yeah, yeah, we'll keep you posted."

Cain and Ray stopped at the curb, waiting for a car to pass.

"I didn't like what he had to say," said Ray.

"Yeah, this guys connecting both parents to the victims."

"Not just the moms. The dads are an acceptable path to the victims as well."

Ray hung up his desk phone. "That was Chelsea. We've got a perfect DNA match on our locks of hair!"

"Why is that not a shocker?" Greg said from his doorway.

"Well, obviously the murderer is the same," said Cain.

"So the trooper and the mechanic are directly linked," said Ray.

"Or the killer is linking them mentally," said Greg. "If they're actually physically related in some way, I'd almost have to settle on the idea that a child died. Other than that, it really doesn't seem to have any relationship to the other clues."

"Except for the pictures," said Cain. "Maybe the locks of hair are from the girl in our pictures."

"No, they're more delicate, like that of a young child. Besides, Chelsea said they were most likely from someone between five to ten years of age," said Ray.

Greg spoke. "Well, now that we have a match, let's try to do some cross referencing, cars in accidents in let's say, the last six months for starters, anything involving a child fatality, especially a younger child. We might find the perfect scenario to connect with this. Maybe we'll find a survivor that has a reason. Cross reference the vehicles involved with anything worked on in that auto shop and the wreck on the lot. I'm guessing we're gonna have something involving that vehicle."

15

The killer held the child down, pressing her hard against the stainless table. The girl pushed her little head against its surface, to the left, to the right, in an effort to get away from him. He grabbed her head, clawing into her neck with his fingers. Fear encompassed her little soul, her mind. There was no breath to be inhaled. Her chest felt the pressure of his grasp. She urinated in fear.

"Aahhhh, God!" Cain yelled as he awoke. "Oh, my God! You sick . . .!" His breathing was heavy and labored. "I need, I need air."

Cain stepped out onto his patio and gazed down at the courtyard.

I'm so tired. I can't do this anymore.

There was a faint knock at his door, then quiet.

Little Elsie appeared in the courtyard below, looking up at his apartment.

"There you are!" she said. "Come on! We're gonna be late. It starts at seven o'clock."

Cain looked down at her. "Okay, baby. I'll be right down. You just wait by your apartment for me."

"Hurry up!"

"Hey! You two need to slow down," Ray said. "Somebody's going to bounce their head off something."

Kenny and Elsie slowed to a trot, then turned down another row of tables and chairs, zigzagging back and forth between the people sitting at them.

"Kenny, Elsie, get up there! They're starting to hand out the prizes," said Holly.

Kenny and Elsie turned their attention to the long table full of prizes at the front of the banquet hall, everything ranging from squirt guns to the grand prize of a shiny red bicycle. Si began to rattle off names of the children attending the event.

Washington walked up and took a seat at the edge of the table near Ray and Holly, facing the prize table.

"What's the matter, Ralph, a little wore out?" asked Holly.

"You try keeping up with thirty kids in a sack race! And they didn't tell me I wouldn't have an air tank for all those balloons. If I hadn't gotten my kids involved, I'd still be out there huffing and puffing."

"Yeah," said Ray. "I did the balloon stomp last year. They don't tell you about having to blow them all up yourself."

"Well, I'm ready for a sit down. I'm kinda glad they started doing the prizes."

"Hey Ralph," Kenny said as he and Elsie ran up to the table. "Look what I got!"

Kenny held up an oversized squirt gun.

"That's pretty cool. Shoots fifty feet? Should be fun!"

"And I got a art set!" said Elsie.

"That's a nice art set."

"Yeah, it is," said Holly.

"Look dad, a ginormous squirt gun!"

"I feel sorry for all the birds and cats in the neighborhood. At least it's not a BB gun."

"Kenny, who's your little friend," Ralph asked, motioning toward Elsie, who was now sitting with Holly and pulling out pieces of her new art set.

"Elsie."

"Oh, this is Elsie! I've heard a lot about that little girl."

Elsie looked up at him, and then went back to pulling apart the art set.

"Come on, Elsie!"

Elsie gave Kenny a flustered look, then got up from the table. They both ran off together toward the snacks.

"So, that's Elsie, uh?" said Ralph. "From what I hear, she's got you guys wrapped around her fingers. I think Cain's already saving for her college education or something."

"Hmm, maybe a little bit," said Ray. "Kenny adores her. They've really become best friends."

"Cain told me mom's addicted to drugs," said Ralph.

"Alcohol, mainly. Elsie's pretty much a loaner half the time. She bounces around the neighbor's houses. She'll eat lunch at one house and dinner at another. Everybody watches out for her, especially the families," said Holly.

"Her mom's a mess," said Ray.

"I wish I could adopt her or something," said Holly. "I'd scoop that little girl up and love her as my own! She really is precious. But we just want her mom to get better."

Ralph's son walked up. "Hey, dad. I'm gonna take off, okay?"

"You guys remember my little boy, don't you?"

"Yes. Wow! I missed last year's banquet and it looks like you shot up four feet," said Ray.

"His football team's going to state next week," said Ralph.

"That's awesome!" said Ray. "There were a couple tough teams this year."

"It's been a lot of fun though. I'm going over to Caleb's house to hang out. I'll be home around eleven or twelve. Is that okay?"

"Just call us when you're on your way home."

Cain walked up to the tables looking exhausted.

"Well, baked enough lasagna and cooked enough spaghetti to last a lifetime," he said. "Thanks for volunteering me, Ray."

"Another hour or so and you can get some beauty rest," said Holly.

"I don't think that's going to help him," said Ralph.

"I must not be too bad!"

"Yeah," said Holly. "I noticed you got a couple dances out of the gals."

"Sympathy dances," said Ray.

"Okay, Ray," said Cain.

"No, no, I'm pretty sure they like you," said Holly.

"Ana's half your age," said Ralph.

"I know, I know. It's all just for fun."

Rays cell phone vibrated in his pocket. He pulled it out and looked at the screen. He held it up to Cain.

"Great!"

Ray looked at Holly and then Ralph. Ralph knew the look.

"I gotta go, hun."

Greg stepped through the side door from the parking area.

"You guys get that?" he yelled across the room.

"Yeah," Cain and Ray said as they got up from their seats.

"I'm sorry," Ray said to Holly. "God, it's only been a few days . . ."

"It's okay, babe. I can get the kids home. Cain, I'll take Elsie to her mom's. Don't worry about that."

Greg walked over closer to them.

"Ralph, I'll need you on this one. Karen's there, but we're

gonna need more support. Kollasch was first on scene. She's saying it's heavy bio. Ana's here somewhere. Let her know to get a van ready. They'll need to suit up and be first in. Kayla's over by the stage. I'll let her know on the way out."

Ralph waved across the room to Si, giving a rallying signal.

"Great," Si said as he set down the bucket with the prize tickets in it and motioned for his wife to take over for him.

Ana walked up to Ray. "It's a bad one," said Ray. "Greg said you'll be suiting up."

"Fabulous! Great way to finish out the night!"

Cain and Ray hurried past Greg, who had already made his way back outside, then watched as he tossed the keys for his car to his son.

"AJ…" Greg began to speak.

"I know dad. I'll be careful. I've driven it before," Alek said back.

Greg cringed a little as he glanced back over at his son and watched him slide into the driver's seat of his Camaro. He let out a deep breath and jumped into the back of Cain's car.

"Hand him the keys, he's ready to leave the party! I'd rather drive around town in the Camaro too," said Ray.

Cain turned toward Greg in the back seat. "I heard it's really hard to insure those classics."

"Yeah, Cain, but it's insured. Thanks for caring," Greg said sarcastically.

"We got an address?" asked Ray.

"Yeah. Miller's Court at 29 Hanbury Street. I just talked to Karen. She said it's the worst one so far."

"That's wonderful!" Ray said.

It had been four days since the murder and their first response to the house. Shrubs lined the sidewalk just past the wooden gate they walked through at 29 Hanbury Street. A small tree grew in the middle of the backyard. Children's toys lay scattered about the grass and six bicycles of varying sizes stood on their kickstands in a neat row at the end of a concrete slab porch under a corrugated metal awning. The victim's husband sat where he had told them to meet him at an outdoor table on the porch. A small, hard liquor bottle sat on the table, along with a set of keys and some papers.

"The kids are at my parents. I came back to get a few things from the garage. I don't know that we could ever come back here. It's hard enough just sitting here. I don't understand. My wife was the sweetest woman anybody could ever know. She was so involved in our children's lives." He hesitated." You know, as men we don't like to admit how much we need our wives…" He started to tear up and hung his head. "But this woman, I just don't know how I can ever do this without her. She was my best friend. I feel like my world's collapsing around me. My children, there's nothing I can say to them. I can't explain this. I can't fix it. I can't bring her back," He sobbed, catching his breath.

"I lost my wife to cancer and I'm still not over it. I can't imagine what it would be like to have to deal with what's happened to your family."

"We're so sorry for you. I know this is difficult, but we've gone over all of our initial information we were able to gather. There are a few important details only you can provide. We know you were busy with the children that day."

"Can you tell us if your wife received any kind of phone call in the last couple of weeks or so that may not have seemed right, or an attempt from somebody in person who may have first contacted her mother, trying to locate your wife?"

"What? Why? I don't understand."

"Your wife's not the first victim of this killer."

"We think your wife was the victim of a specific person we're tracking. In each case they contacted the victim's mother first, trying to find them, trying to get to them. All of the calls have come from pay phones in secluded urban areas of the city and we haven't been able to find anybody else who has seen this person."

"Anybody else? What do you mean, anybody else? Somebody saw this guy and you haven't caught him yet." He was becoming angry.

"No! An Elderly woman had a person come to her house at night, but it was too dark for her to tell what he looked like. She couldn't give a good description," Ray said.

"I don't know. Her mom lives out of state. I don't talk very often with her parents. They usually come during the holidays. My wife's mother and father had just left for vacation in Europe this week. They do a lot of traveling. They're arriving back this afternoon. I called them right away, but haven't given them any details yet. Her father is a retired deputy, so this is going to hit him pretty hard. I told them there was an accident."

"Can you ask your mother-in-law if she received any kind of contact like that and have her call us immediately if she did. If you'd like, you could just give us a number to contact her. That would work."

"I'll ask her when I talk to them."

"We'd like to take another look at things inside and we'll be out of your way," Ray said.

"Oh, don't worry about me. I'm not going back in there."

They had been in the house four days earlier and understood why the husband didn't want to be there. From any position as you made your way through the house you could still see the stains in the carpets in the middle of the living room and blood on the walls. The carpet would have to be torn out, along with several pieces of furniture. Plastic sheeting had been laid over the floor to help cover it. Ray and Cain stepped back into the house to re-examine the scene in hopes of finding some simple thing they may have overlooked.

Cain thought of the scene once again. As with the last murder, the killer had stepped outside of his original thinking. He'd chosen another ordinary person, which made it seem even more urgent he be caught. This time he had struck at the heart of a home. A stay-at-home mom, a wife, a mother of four children, thirty-seven years old. He had used all of the same methods. A sharp instrument was inserted into the back of her head and her brains had been scrambled and pulled out. Except now he had added something new. Her head was torn from her body and was attached by only a string of flesh and tissue. Massive arterial bleeding from her neck had shot outward and sprayed the furniture, splattering the couch, the coffee table, the love seat and wall. Bits and pieces of flesh and brain lay scattered on the floor around her severed head, some floating in the thick coagulated blood. Her left arm was torn clear off her body. Bleeding from that wound had hit other areas of the living room. There didn't seem to be a single piece of furniture or carpet area that hadn't been touched. Family pictures were pulled from the walls, their glass shattered, some torn to pieces. One family photo lay on the coffee table, a hole burned through it at the place where the mother had stood, and a dark line drawn through each family member's face. It was as if the killer had tried to dismantle any resemblance of the family as a unit. The very life of this woman had been dispersed around the living room. And in her hand, in clenched fist, was another picture, another high school picture, wallet size. From initial viewing it appeared to be a copy of the same one found in the hand of the high school math teacher.

And there was the list . . .

It was one of the most disturbing items they'd found. A

handwritten list nearly fifty pages in length, neatly numbered, of people's occupations or stations in life. There were no names. The first eight people on the list matched those of the first victims: The first one said: one who feeds many. The second was conveniently smeared with drops of blood, the killer still holding control over who the victim was: Number three, one who cures: Number four, one who protects: Number five, a musician: Number six, one who gives knowledge: Number seven, one who serves others: Number eight, a matriarch. The list went on and on, naming occupations and stations in life: Author, detective, fireman, minister, grocer, janitor, college student, cashier, military man or woman, dancer, actor, convict, farmer, pilot, retiree, bus driver, secretary, drunk driver, doctor, statesman or President of the United States, accountant, woman and man from nursing home, mother, father, son, daughter, grandparent . . .

They had all chuckled as they read detective, looking at each other as if to say, "not gonna be me." The next group on the list, separated onto its own page, disturbed them the most. It was as if the killer had gotten his mind on them and just kept writing, some descriptive of who seemed to be actual people.

Small child who smiled at me at the park and made me laugh, teenage girl, toddler, infant, my neighbor's son, a sick child, child from the playground, a baby in blue, a baby in a stroller, the little girl at the store with ice cream on her face, a child with a dirty face, somebody's grandchild, boy riding bike, high school boy, little girl with curly hair...

There were at least fifty different descriptions of children. Different ages, different locations, different sizes, different reasons. When they came to that part of the list, the room fell silent, a sudden seriousness pulling back their attention and focus.

Cain remembered what Greg had said.

"We stop this killer now! Every resource. I don't care if we have to work double shifts for six months straight. We're gonna find this idiot before he even thinks of getting that far on the list. It's bad enough he's picked our current victims, but not this. We can't allow this to happen, especially if he decides to deviate from this order because of opportunity, though I don't think he needs any help. He seems to make easy access of his victims."

At the end of the list, after almost a hundred numbers, were blank numbers that didn't have occupations or stations added to them yet, as though the list was to grow later. And written along the side, vertically, "The possibilities are endless!"

Cain pictured the mother with her children: a younger one laughing as she tickled him; an older daughter snuggling up next to her mom, knowing she had a close friend to storm the trials of life with; a husband smiling proudly as he watched his wife hug a daughter in a military uniform; an older son thanking his mom as family and friends gathered after a graduation.

As Cain looked at the pictures of the children on the wall, their images, as he was seeing them, began to fade in and out. What looked like pictures of the children when they were much younger began to sink in and out of the wall, their smiling faces blending into the warm peach colored paint on its surface. A picture of a bright, energetic looking teen in a volleyball outfit blurred in his vision and then suddenly she was gone. A young man in a graduation gown wearing a valedictorian medal slipped in and out of his vision. Another picture of a small boy faded in and out and then melted into the wall. Cain squinted his eyes. He felt like he was hallucinating, yet knew where he was. A small flame started in the middle of a wedding picture and burned through the image, blackening the bride and groom as it went. A picture of the family became distorted; the husband and wife fading into the back of the picture as though they were never there, then one by one from oldest to youngest the images of the children in the same picture faded and disappeared. A young woman in an ROTC dress uniform broke away into a thousand pieces and floated away into the air around him.

"Cain?" Ray said.

"Cain!" Ray nearly shouted, shaking him from his trance.

"Sorry, I was . . . just thinking."

"Ready to go?"

"Yeah, sure."

Cain and Ray started for the back door to leave, wanting to say goodbye to the husband and not seem uncaring. As they were leaving the living room one picture stood out to Cain more than any other. It appeared to be a picture of the victim's daughter when she was younger along with another young girl. Cain recognized the other girl. He had no idea why, but her face seemed to pierce deep into his thoughts, like he knew her. Maybe a niece or someone from his wife's family, he thought. The picture was that familiar to him. The picture bothered him.

Ray looked at him inquisitively as he reached up and pulled the picture from its hook and stood there staring at it more closely. He ran his finger across the picture, looking at the young teen.

"What is it?" Ray asked.

"I know this girl."

"Okay, yeah, she looks a little familiar, but this isn't the biggest city around. Maybe it's someone you've seen somewhere. She probably works at a store or something."

"No, it's something else."

"Like what?"

"Well, I don't know. Maybe you're right."

Cain looked past the patio door and saw the husband still sitting there going over some papers. *Everything else in my life is crazy. I'll just go out on a limb with this one.*

"Come on, Ray, let's go."

Ray got a sick feeling in his gut as he noticed that Cain had not put the picture back in its place on the wall, but was still holding it with two hands as he walked toward the patio.

"Sir, I just have one more question for you," Cain said.

Ray looked on and listened, his eyebrows lifted up in an "oh, great, here we go!" expression, mentally biting his tongue and trying to give Cain respectful investigative space as his partner.

"This is your daughter, right?" Cain asked.

"Yeah, when she was about ten," the husband said a bit reluctantly, turning his head sideways with a puzzled look on his face and wondering where Cain was going with the question.

"So, who is this girl next to her?"

Ray was a little agitated, feeling like Cain was asking questions for no good reason and thinking their victim's husband may consider the question a little intrusive.

"That's Kelly, Kelly Daniels, my daughter's best friend. It's kind of an old picture. They met at dance class when they were little. They're pretty much inseparable. She goes to Crossroads High with her."

"Does she have any siblings?"

"I don't think she has any sisters. She lost a brother recently in the military. The family was in the news about a year ago. Her brother was killed in combat somewhere, I think Africa. He received a Medal of Honor for saving some men from his team. Her dad's a doctor or something. He was just in a serious accident. He's in the hospital right now. Her mom died a couple years ago."

"So that's the only brother Kelly has?"

"I really don't know the family very well. I think so," the man answered.

"What kind of car does your daughter drive?"

That's too much fishing, Ray thought.

"I don't really understand. What are you getting at? She drives an older Chevy."

Cain remembered.

"Your daughter! That was your daughter who answered the door at the estate."

210

"Yeah, Kelly lives at the Lake Estates. Kind of outside the normal group of people I would hang around so I've never really gotten to know them. She's been up there a lot more since Kelly's dad got in the accident."

"Your daughter answered the door. The victim's, well, his sister, didn't want to talk at the time."

"Victim? What do you mean, victim?"

"There was information that Kelly's family was kin to another victim in these cases, someone who would've been her brother. That ended up being incorrect." Cain felt like he may have already let out too much information.

"No, I'm pretty sure she only had one brother, that's the one who died in Africa. I met the family a couple of times at school events. Besides, Kelly never mentioned another brother and I remember at least on one occasion asking her how many siblings she had. I think she only had the one brother. You know, don't start thinking Kelly has anything to do with this, not a chance! She's a good girl. My daughter and her just started a peer group at the high school to help kids with teen issues. She's got a full scholarship to college in the fall. My wife and her were really close, especially after she lost her mom to cancer. I'm not sure what you're thinking, but I can tell you one thing. She would've never harmed my wife."

"Thanks for your time," Ray said, puzzled, yet still wanting to move Cain along and leave. Ray was feeling as though Cain had crossed some invisible line.

Cain set the picture on the small table. So now he knew who the mysterious girl in the picture was. They hadn't seen her that day at the estate, and yet her face seemed to jump off of the page and scream at him. He kept the image of the girl in the back of his mind, hoping to see her again. Maybe he would go to the estate and try to find out more. *Hopefully we'll get a search warrant and be able to question her father when he comes out of whatever he's in*, Cain thought.

"What was that?" Ray asked as they walked down the drive.

"You get some funky feeling and you think that you can just ask the guy some question that doesn't seem to apply to anything? You need to stop letting your weird feelings drive you." Ray held up his hands and made quotation mark symbols as he said the word 'feelings.' "We need to be concentrating on the real, the tangible stuff, so we don't miss something important. Like whether the killer contacted the victim's mother!"

"You realize this information puts that Kelly girl directly in the lives of two of the victims? And she goes to Crossroads High, which puts her near our math teacher, making it three victims."

"I'll give you that much, but you didn't even know who she was until you asked a question based on one of your feelings and I don't think that's good investigating. If it turns out to be anything, you got lucky, that's all! Besides, now, according to the records, our conductor wasn't related to her. He never existed. God, this is crazy!"

"And that was an older picture, but she looked like our street runner we've caught buying drugs. It's got to be the same Kelly Daniels!"

"Your stretching it, Cain. That picture's gotta be ten years old. You can't make that comparison."

"That's ridiculous. There's a connection here!"

"There could be two people by that name."

"Yeah? I'd bet a paycheck its her."

"So what if it was! No, I don't think so. If that's the case, it's like two totally separate people; one's a druggy and one's a perfect child. Which one is it? It probably a different girl."

"Listen to me. I don't understand everything I've been dealing with, but I know it's for a reason. Maybe some of these feelings are off base. Maybe some of them seem absolutely insane. But there's something deep inside of me that makes me feel like I'm...."

"Like you're what, Cain?"

"Well, like, maybe this stuff is connected. Do you realize

that in at least a couple of my dreams the victims had the same numbers as the victims we found later. Later! Not before. The numbers were not in my head yet. I haven't told you all the details."

"You could have been anticipating the numbers because you knew what number the last victim had. You need to keep this scientific. We need to stick to the facts, period! Not feelings, not dreams, none of that. Wake up! Get the dreams and feelings out of your head. They're affecting your investigating."

"Do you realize that the day this woman was found I had another dream? The killer in the dream grabbed a little girl . . ."

"I don't want to hear this!"

"I think he was going to tear her head off! Not one of our victims has had that happen until this one! I have an uneasy feeling here. Something *is* connected! I don't know what. I'm not some psychic or something, but maybe the gods are throwing something our way. Maybe we're actually getting some help for some reason. Maybe this guy is so conscienceless that he flat out needs to be stopped. Somebody, something, wants me to stop this man and I feel like I need to listen to what I'm hearing."

"Maybe you're slowly becoming some nut case that doesn't need to be doing your line of work anymore." Cain had finally gotten on Ray's nerves. "It's stuff like this that causes killers to walk out of courtrooms as free men. One mistake, one blunder, one mismanaged crime scene, and a person can be acquitted so fast that months of investigating can mean nothing. A lot of hard work straight down the drain because of something stupid!"

The ride back to the division was quiet. There was no talking, no discussing the case. Cain stared out the passenger window into the distance. It had been a long day. The sun had already set and hues of orange, red and blue mixed on the horizon with the darkened outlines of trees in the foreground. The city's downtown silhouette rose into the darkening sky to their right. Cain's eyes wandered from the sunset to the car next to them and then to the pavement below. He watched its tires roll to a stop and then start turning as the car slowed, stopped, and accelerated again in the late afternoon traffic. One long white line, two, three, a reflector, a hubcap laying against the middle divider wall, the sound of the tires rolling over the pavement, a horn honking. Cain fell asleep.

"Hey, wake up," Ray said as they pulled into the division parking lot. "Cain, wake up, we're here . . . Cain!"

Cain stirred awake.

"Listen man, you've got me worried. You've been at this for a lot of years. We grew up together. I don't want to see you lose everything that matters to you over something you could sort out on your own. You can always make adjustments to how you approach your work, what you choose to do, or whether you continue to do it. I don't really know what's going on with you, but you need to take a good hard look at it. Maybe you should think about early retirement. I'd never lie to you. You're wigging me out! Try to sort out your thoughts a little better. If there's anything to it, you'll get it figured out. But until you have something concrete I really want you to think a little more before mixing what we know is reality with things that are in dreams or feelings. Maybe you should sit down with somebody. Tell them what's been bothering you. Maybe a priest or pastor, someone who's not gonna judge you."

"We'll see, huh?" Cain still remembered what Ray had said thirty minutes earlier.

Cain pulled off the winding road and brought the car to a stop, its front end facing the river and the wide field of prairie grasses. The lake shimmered through the trees behind them. He rolled up the driver's side window and stepped onto the asphalt. He walked toward the front of the car and leaned against the hood, sitting partly on the car and standing at the same time. His eyes took in the scene. Little rolling hills of tall grass were in front of him and a small dirt path cut its way through the fields of grass and down to the trees by the river and lake. The small stand of pine trees stood to the right near a pond, rising upward and casting their shadows over the small bench they encircled. The sun was shining down on the fields and there was a stillness in the air that kept anything from moving. It was like a photograph. He looked down at the ground, lost in thought and pushed around a few small rocks with his foot and then returned his eyes to the scene in front of him.

The first time he had walked past the split wood fence and onto the path was as a child with his father, the last with Ray just a few years ago. This was his dad's favorite fishing spot: down the trail around a little hill at the bottom, navigate a small ravine drop off and then up against the side of an old oak tree by the river. A short distance from there, the river spilled into the lake. There was plenty of shade at the right time of the day. Many times he had walked the short trail, bounding along behind his father carrying a fishing pole that was too big for him and thinking about the fish they would catch and the ones they would say got away.

At the time Cain had truly thought it was about fishing. It was on the day of his father's funeral that he understood. After the graveside service, during the reception, he had broken free of everybody and wandered down the trail to this spot. Torn inside, he had screamed at the top of his lungs toward the river and the lake. He'd had stood there, feeling a deep emptiness in his heart as he told his father he missed him. It was in that moment he understood. That day he realized it wasn't about fishing at all, but just about being together and enjoying the simple things in life.

He pictured his father, head leaning against the trunk of the old tree, a splattered mixture of sunshine and shade across his face as he spoke. His father's words reverberated in his mind. They were clear. "Son, nothing in life matters as much as life itself. No matter what you lose, you always have your life. You can breath, you can feel, you can taste." His father took a deep breath of fresh air and looked at him. "And you have the others around you, that is truly all that matters, like I have you here. You're a precious gift from God. I thank Heaven for you every day of my life."

Tears rolled from Cain's eyes onto his cheek. He sobbed a deep sob. "I miss you so much, Dad," he said out loud. "I'm so confused. I need clarity. I just don't know about this anymore. I look back now, I realize maybe this wasn't the right path for me. I think Ray's right. I need to stop, change what I'm doing. It's ripping me apart inside."

A strong gust of wind shot across the little hills before him, shifting the grass back and forth in waves of colorful patterns and drying the tears on his face.

16

Cain's exhaustion had worn hard on him. He stared upward at the blank ceiling above his bed, letting out a short, quiet breath and feeling the weariness close in around him.

He fell asleep, and dreamt . . .

The flame re-lit itself as Cain turned to walk away. Out of the corner of his eye he could tell the faint flickering of a candle. He turned back, cupping the candle's flame in his hand, snuffing it out.

Another flame appeared, taking its place in the darkness. The flame was farther away. He moved toward it, staring at it. As he came upon it, he brushed the candle away. It fell into the darkness of the room and disappeared into the void.

Once again, he turned to walk away.

Another light, a candle, dimmer this time, starting to go out on its own, stood in the darkness in front of him.

He moved upon it slowly, then pushed his finger into the flame and hot wax, staring at it oddly, extinguishing the flame.

The darkness closed in around him. He saw nothing. He reached for his face, confused, anguished. A dull pain gripped his head. He looked into the darkness. Another flicker, bright, but distant, illuminated the darkness.

He backed away from it slowly until the darkness, the blackness, once again enveloped him, extinguishing the distant light from his vision.

The next day Greg called Ray and Cain into the operation's room. He motioned their attention to a city map on the wall.

"Look at the map. Do you see it?".

"Yeah, I see it," Ray said.

"Why haven't we noticed that before?" said Cain.

"The numbers weren't there yet. Now there's enough of them. We can finally see it. I started running the lines just for the heck of it really, number to number. The number two missing threw me off at first. Then I got our second set of connected lines. If there's a pattern here, he'll strike directly along this line next."

"And number two should be somewhere along this line!" Cain nearly shouted as he ran his hand across the map board in a straight direction.

"So the victim's number sets of three and four and five and six, when connected, run straight through this center point," Greg said.

"What's there?" asked Ray. "That's right next to the hospital."

"I don't know, I just noticed this. Let's try to find out the layout for those buildings. Call downstairs and see if we have a set of blueprints for that building in the SERT ready room," Greg said.

Ray picked up the phone and dialed downstairs. "Hey, this is Ray. Can you see if we have a schematic of Crossroads Hospital and Clinics?"

"I think that's a clinic across from the main hospital," said Cain.

"What kind of clinic is it?"

"It's a birthing clinic," said Ray.

"You do realize that's the clinic from the picture at our conductor's house, don't you?" asked Cain.

"No, I didn't."

"The lines intersect at the clinic," said Ray.

"No, no." Greg pointed at the map. "They don't. Look at this enlarged layout of the hospital grounds. They intersect within the clinic. Our killer has been very meticulous about what he's given us so far. If the killer was pinpointing the clinic itself, he would have run the lines through the middle of the clinic, which is right here."

"It appears to be off a little, at least an inch," said Ray.

Greg's extension rang for an inside call and Cain answered it.

"Great, can you bring them up? Thanks!"

"They've got the blueprints. They're bringing 'em up."

"Little pieces," Ray said. "Little pieces of what's in his head."

"Alright, let's put this all together," Greg said. "He's given us quite a lot."

"Okay, we've got key clues from every crime scene." Cain went down the list pinned next to the map, reading each clue aloud. "Medal of Honor, cancer bracelet."

Greg interrupted, "You can't leave out the second clue."

"There wasn't a second clue," said Cain.

"Exactly, there wasn't. And this killer has given us nothing but clues, so not giving us a clue is very likely in fact a clue," said Greg. "Maybe even the lack of a victim?"

"Okay, so here's what we have: a geneticist, number two and no clue, or no number two; number three, the biologist and cancer bracelet; number four, state trooper and a lock of hair; number five, a conductor, musician. That scene gave us multiple clues and our first piece of poetry. Medical tools used for abortions: a burned house, a lighter, a corner piece of paper with two finger prints matching nothing on file. We've got a possible link to the family at the Lake Estates and our doctor, an OB doctor at that, at the hospital in some kind of coma or something. And don't forget the erasure of data on our server."

Ray took over. "Victim six, a teacher, a picture; victim seven, a shop owner mechanic and another matching lock of hair, possibly a direct link to the trooper; victim eight, a stay-at-home mom, another picture and our kill list. Three poem pieces, different, one at the conductor's house, one at the school, one in the mechanic's shop, all seemingly pointing to the death of children."

"And now we've got the mapping clue. Seven known victims, two matching locks of hair and two possible matching photographs. And our killer is pointing to this clinic and whatever sits right here at the intersecting points of these lines. Our symphony conductor had a link there."

"Cain," an officer said. "You guys call for these?"

"Yeah, thanks," Cain said as he took the blueprints from the officer who'd stepped into the doorway.

"Alright, let's take a look at this," Greg said.

Cain popped the cap from the end of the blueprint tube and pulled out its contents, separating them on the small table.

"That one there!" Ray pointed to a detailed print of the clinic.

"Compare that to the larger map," Greg said.

"Spin it to the right a little," said Ray.

Cain moved the map. "Bingo! That spot."

"The lines intersect through this wing of the clinic here,

right on this room," Greg marked a small "x" on the schematic. "I'm pretty convinced that isn't an accident. Call the clinic. Find out what that room is used for!"

Ray fumbled through the phone book until he landed on a page and then dialed the number.

"Hello, Crossroad's Clinic," a voice said on the other end of the line.

"Hi, This is Detective Ray . . ."

"Could you please hold?"

"Sure." Ray looked at Greg. "I'm on hold."

Ray leaned back in the chair and stared at the ceiling, then across at the map, mentally connecting the lines for the victims.

"How may I help you?"

"This is the Crossroad's Police Department calling. I need some information about your clinic."

Ray spoke again after a pause. "No, I think you should be able to help us. Are you familiar with the rooms in the clinic and what they're used for? Oh, okay, thank you. She's getting me one of the nurses."

"Yes," Ray said. "Well, what we need to know are specifics about what a particular room is used for, um, let's see, room 3B. I don't know if they're numbered the same for you. It's toward the end of the hall, one of the last rooms. It looks like its directly across from a staff bathroom." Ray paused. "It is? Really? Okay, thank you. Thank you for your help. Could I get your name? Thanks."

"This is getting creepier. It's the body room, the cold morgue. It's where they store the aborted fetuses, babies, fetal tissue as she stated it, whatever, until they can send them to the crematorium across the street."

"It is now?" Cain asked.

"It always has been. That room's been used for the same thing ever since the clinic opened over forty years ago. At least it is according to this nurse, this Nurse Dyer, uh, Amelia Dyer."

"I think we've got one of two situations here," said Greg. "A botched abortion and an angry family member or an abortion foe making a statement."

"I think it's a statement," said Ray.

"Why do you choose that?" asked Greg.

"Because of the people he's killed. They're so random."

"What about retaliation for an accident or something, you know, the trooper, the mechanic, the matching locks of hair?" Cain said. "We can't discard that thought."

"The teacher, the conductor, the biologist, some of it fits and some of it just doesn't seem to go together at all," Greg said.

"The teacher and the mom had what appears to be the same pictures of a girl," Cain said. "And those were both involved with children or other people's children."

"Come on guys, this is crazy," Ray said. "You know, let's not forget the geneticist. We all just need to try to think this through and figure out the main point over the next few days. It's going to either come to us that way or, unfortunately, by more clues."

"If only we were on an uneven number," Cain said.

"Why's that?" asked Ray.

"Because then we would at least know the line he's going to strike on next," said Greg. "Maybe then we could match the line with people along it and their occupations and then notify people in those occupations to be cautious and report anything suspicious."

"Well, we can halfway do that," said Ray.

"You're right, we can," Greg grabbed his landline. "I'll call in Karen and have her put together a team to work on notifying anybody in our next occupation on that list. What was the next occupation?"

"Where's the list?" asked Ray.

"There's a copy here somewhere," said Cain. "Author, if he's following this list, his next victim should be an author of some sort."

"What if that's what he *wants* us to be concentrating on?" Ray pointed at the map.

"It's better than nothing. Either he's playing us on this one or we're going in the right direction," Greg said. "Somehow I think he'll actually follow that list, almost as if he's decided who it will be."

Ray and Cain were completely blown away by what the last victim's mother told them. They may have finally received the break they were looking for. He was there! The victim's mother had clearly seen his face. He had actually come to her house inquiring about her daughter before she and her husband had left for Europe. It was just before dusk, but she remembered his clothing, his shoes, every detail. It was at the end of the conversation that she had given them the information that intrigued them the most, and the reason she was so willing to disclose her daughter's location. He had shown her the badge of a City of Crossroad's Police Officer.

"I really want to help you, but I have a daughter to bury. I'm trying to deal with this myself and I need to be there for my son-in-law and my grandkids. There's a lot of arrangements to be made. I know how important it is for you to have this information. I'll come down Sunday afternoon if you can't wait till Monday, but we have a meeting at the funeral home on Saturday morning and, well, I don't think I'll be up to that sort of thing on Saturday."

"No Ma'am, that's fine, we understand," said Ray. "What's a good time on Monday morning for you?"

"It doesn't really matter."

"How about 10:00?"

"Okay. That's fine."

"We'll have it set up with the artist. You can just come in and take your time. Hopefully with the information you give us and a drawing, we'll be able to take this guy down for what he did to your daughter."

Ray hung up the phone and turned towards Cain, "I think this is it. I think we're gonna get him."

"Yeah, I feel like we're getting close to finishing this. That it's almost over."

"Let's just hope we get through the weekend without another killing."

"Alright, this changes things. I'm gonna skip cutting out early. We need to be on this as we get the information."

"She's not gonna make it in until Monday. It's not very often you get a couple extra hours. Take advantage of it. Besides, you need the rest," Ray said. "I'll let Greg know about this development. He's probably going to want to release this to the public. Get outta here. I'll handle it. It's just a couple hours. Anything important happens, I'll call you."

"You're right. I need a little mind break from this."

Cain slipped his jacket off the back of the chair, looked over his desk area, then turned and walked toward the front door.

"Hey," Ana yelled to Cain from the top of the stairs as he opened the door to leave. "Check this out. You were right. They look like a perfect match. Whoever this girl is, she's definitely connected to at least two victims."

"I knew something was up with that girl!" Cain said. "That's our little socialite druggy I keep running into. Let me see those. I want to show them to Ray."

"Weren't you just leaving?" Ana asked.

"Yeah, but…"

"I'm on my way up to Greg's office. I'll show them to Ray."

"Alright," said Cain. "Tell him to call me if he's able to get a warrant for that doctor's house."

Cain sat in his car letting it warm up, relishing the idea of just relaxing for the evening. He looked forward to a few hours off, an early start for his weekend, some reading, a nice dinner, maybe work on the Corvette. He couldn't help but think about this new piece of information from the mother of the last victim. What would she know? Did she really remember him? Would she remember his face clearly enough? Would they catch him? Cain couldn't help but think he should still be there with Ray.

Ray's phone rang.

"Hello, this is Ray."

"Hi. We just talked a while ago. My husband told me it's best that I give you the description tonight. It's as fresh as it's ever going to be in my mind, though I can't imagine ever forgetting his face now. He changed our life forever."

"Are you sure? It can wait till Monday," Ray said, not really meaning it.

"I'm positive. I want to do this as soon as possible, right now, this evening. We want him caught."

"Okay, if you want to head this way, I'll set you up with an artist. Do you know where we're located?"

"You're still near downtown, right?"

"Yep. Same building we've been in for years."

"Alright, we're on our way, probably take us about fifteen minutes."

Ray thought about calling Cain. *No, I'm going to let him get the rest he needs. A few extra hours should really help him. He needs to detach a little bit right now. I can give him the details on Monday or give him a call if we ID this guy.* He looked at his sandwich, which he had only managed to take one bite of, and proceeded to attempt another bite.

"Ray?" Karen yelled from her office as she stood up. "You'll want to see this. Tell Greg to come here also."

Ray flopped his sandwich back down on his desk and he and Greg walked into Karen's office. Karen had already sat down in front of her computer and was scrolling down a list. Her printer was rapidly spewing out page after page of the list she had just sent it.

"We only put out an inquiry for the four surrounding states. Apparently we weren't the only ones keeping this quiet to begin with. There's agencies in cities from every surrounding state that have been dealing with the same type of killings."

"I wonder if the mapping patterns are the same," Ray said.

"I just submitted an inquiry for a broader area."

"Crossroads? I don't get it. How could our little town be part of something so big?"

"I don't think this could be just one killer, but I suppose if they kept busy they could pull it off. Unless it's some weird sect or group? A Cult? Maybe Satanic? Shoot, most of the kills look more like the work of the devil than the work of a man."

Ana stepped around the corner of the office door. "Guys, we reworked the pictures from the crime scenes."

"I'll get with you in a minute on them," Greg said.

"Okay, but you might want to know, they're a match!"

Ana held two printouts side by side.

Ray stood in shock looking down at the pictures.

"Cain was right. There is something to that girl!" Ray said. "There's a connection."

"Yeah, I just showed him on his way out."

"This is the girl who lives at the estate, Kelly Daniels. The supposed sister of our dead conductor. There was a picture of her with the daughter of our last victim at the woman's house.

We've dealt with this girl in person. Cain stopped her on the street in his neighborhood and took pills from her that she'd just bought from a dealer. A while back, we brought her in for public intox. We had her call her father to come pick her up at the station. Well, if it's the same girl. She looks a lot younger in the other pictures we saw. The clerk handled the paperwork, so we never met the parents or saw the address."

"By the way," Ana said. "Cain wants you to call him. Especially if you get that warrant."

"This gives us what we need for a search warrant on that house. There's no way the judge won't work with us now," Greg said.

"Somebody at the Lake Estates is closer to these murders than we know."

The smell of Italian Sausage and fresh chopped garlic filled the air in Cain's small apartment. Other than burning his finger on the saucepan it was turning out to be a restful evening. He needed the break.

He finished his meal and sat on the couch, taking in an old western, then looked down at his cell phone. He decided that no matter what happened, he just wanted rest. He grabbed his phone and set it to vibrate. *I'll be back there Monday. It can all wait until then. Ray will get with me if he needs me.*

As he sat watching the show he started to slip in and out of sleep. A switch to a commercial awakened him. His vision blurred as he looked at the TV's screen, attempting to focus. *The estate. Cain was right!* Cain thought he heard Rays voice. He rubbed his eyes. He pointed the remote at the TV, turned it off, and fell asleep on the couch.

Searing pain, his face was being pulled on, tugged on. There was a ripping sensation. He couldn't see anything, but felt as though somebody, something, was peeling back the skin on his face and pulling it away, a deep, stinging pain elevating some crazy threshold of insanity. *Oh God, I can't stand it. Help me! It's too much!* Bright light, flashes, fire. Cain's breathing was shallow, yet his mind was racing. He heard voices . . . *We'll be back next week, okay.* He couldn't understand what he was feeling. There was more searing pain, a stinging, burning sensation.

Cain awoke. He was breathing heavy, burdened breaths. His hands went to his face, feeling it, touching it. It felt spongy, different. He stood up from the chair, walked to the kitchen, and splashed water on his face. It felt cool, better. It was soothing.

Just set it on the chair in the corner. Again, Cain thought he heard Ray's voice.

What? Do what? Cain wondered.

Cain walked over and poured himself a glass of wine, setting it on the end table before he flopped himself back down on the couch, resting his head sideways against a pillow and closing his eyes. He dosed in and out of sleep.

"Got another bingo!" Karen said as she walked up. "Oh, hey, where's Cain? He had my guys checking on something."

"He went to get some rest," said Ray. "What do you have?"

"Well, I don't have all of the details yet, but several weeks back we had a deadly accident near Old Town, a drunk driver. He'd just left a local tavern. He came up on a red light doing seventy miles an hour, brakes failed and he t-boned another car. The passenger fatality in the car that got hit was a little girl. I've put a medical records request in on the girl. Soon as we get them we'll see if we can get a match with the hair DNA and the records."

"Good! If it's a match, it'll be some much needed progress."

"Oh, I think it'll be a match.

"Why's that?"

"That's not all I have for you.

"What else?"

"The drunk driver is across the street in county. We transferred him there a couple of weeks ago."

"What's the relevance?"

"Days before the accident he'd had his car in a shop to get the brakes fixed. He decided he couldn't afford it, so he drove off before they got him in. He'd scheduled an appointment with our mechanic in old town, who'd offered to do it for the cost of the parts."

"Really? But that car wasn't wrecked. That would be like two different scenarios. And the brakes never got done."

"Yeah still trying to sort some of this insanity out. But that's not all. There's another connection and it's the one that brings the whole thing together."

"What's that?"

"Your doctor from the Lake Estates, the one at Crossroad's Hospital."

"Yeah?"

"He was driving the car with the fatality. It was his granddaughter who was killed. It's his Corvette that's sitting demolished behind the shop."

"Oh! Now, that is very relevant! That's what, a possible three victim connection, plus the connection between his daughter and the last victim?"

Ray noticed an officer on the other end of the room pointing at him, directing a man and woman to his location.

"Alright, Karen, can you let me know as soon as you have anything on the locks of hair?"

"Yeah, I will."

"And try to find our wrecked car. It's out there hiding in the fog somewhere, VIN switched maybe, shoot, I don't know."

17

"Where's Ray? I've got a call on line three for a detective. Some gal. She says it's urgent," Chris held up the phone.

"He took that lady and her husband downstairs to the artist. Oh, hey," an officer said as he motioned toward Ray, who had just re-entered the room. "Phone call."

"Take a number. Tell them I'll call back. I'm busy." Ray gave him a frustrated look and ran his finger across his neck in a 'get rid of the call' fashion as he walked up to his desk and took a bite of his pastrami sandwich. He sat down to finish the last of the documentation on the call he had received from the victim's mother. He watched as Chris continued to talk to the lady on the phone.

"Yeah, yeah, okay. I got it. Hold on ma'am. I'll get someone."

Ray gave him a dirty, angered look and started to tell him "no".

"No, Ray, you need to take this call," he motioned him to

pick up the phone. "I think this lady has seen your killer! She's saying somebody is trying to get her son. She's pretty upset. Sounds like the real deal."

"Alright, I got it. Ray finger-punched the line for the call. This is Detective . . ."

"Listen!" She interrupted him. "My son lives on your side of town. I think he's in danger. He's not answering his phone. He lives at 512 10th Street NW in River Bend. Send an officer to his address. Something is terribly wrong. I can feel it!"

"Whoa, wait a minute, can you tell me . . ." Ray tried to interrupt. He looked through the door of the operations room and tried to pinpoint the street on the map.

"I'm on my way there, but I've got a twenty minute drive in traffic. He's just a few blocks from you," she said. "There's only been one time in my life that I've felt my son was in this kind of danger and I was able to protect him myself. I know this feeling. You've got to get somebody to his house. A man came to my door."

Ray's ears perked up. He could almost tell what was coming next. Now he wished Cain was there with him and hadn't left early for the weekend. "And?"

"This man came to my house claiming he needed to talk to my son. He said it was important; that it was part of a plan for the City of Crossroads. That he really needed to speak with him. I knew my son would be home, so I gave him the address. Then as he walked away, he said something really strange. It didn't make any sense. He said, 'Thank you, I couldn't have done this without your permission.' Permission, I mean, something just wasn't right about it."

Rays mind was spinning.

"Why in God's name would you give out that kind of information?"

"He showed me a badge, a City of Crossroad's Police Badge. He said it was important. At first, I trusted him. But now I don't feel right about it. I started to feel there was something wrong. Right after he left I saw your press release on the news. I know this feeling. You've got to get to my son! This man is going to hurt him!"

"What's your son's occupation?"

"He's an author, a well known author."

"Okay, we're sending officers right now! 512 10th Street NW, down by the river! I want patrols moving on that address, ASAP!" Ray shouted across the room. "You come here to the station. Don't go to his house. Yes, I believe you. I'm leaving right now!"

Ray slammed his chair backward as he stood up. "Somebody put out the call on this. Possible murder suspect going to that address."

He pulled out his cell phone as he ran down the ramp from the office area and out the front door. He punched the number three. The call went straight to Cain's voicemail. Cain's cell phone sat on the little end table by the couch, vibrating, moving toward its edge.

Ray flung open the car door and jumped into his vehicle and started the motor, then left a cloud of vaporized rubber and a long tire streak across the lot. His car bounced and scraped bottom as he left the driveway.

Si and Chris followed pursuit in a marked vehicle. Ray heard another patrol for that area say that they had an ETA of about ten minutes.

The River Bend Neighborhood was about seven minutes north of the division in an upscale neighborhood close to the Civic Center and some other community venues. Most of the people who lived in the area were usually very affluent. Ray realized that the neighborhood matched the status of some of the original victims. *This has to be him*, he thought.

He anxiously hit the speed dial number again for Cain. No answer. "Man, of all the freaking times for you to turn off your phone!" He dialed Holly's number.

"Hello?" Holly answered.

"Holly, listen, keep dialing Cain's cell. If he picks up, have him call the station, it's important!"

"Alright!" Holly said as she hung up.

Ray was about three blocks from the street he needed when the cars in front of him came to a grinding, painful halt and blocked him in at a traffic light.

He honked steady on his horn and put the vehicle in reverse, nudging it toward the vehicles behind him.

"Come on, come on, move!"

Ray clipped one of the cars as he backed his way out of the gridlock. Si and Chris were stuck in another lane. They jumped from their vehicle and left it sitting in traffic and ran north toward the neighborhood. Ray made his way the opposite direction where the street was open, crossing a corner curb and driving partially on the sidewalk for half a block, knocking over trash cans as he went.

Once again, Cain's cell phone vibrated across the end table, then fell to the floor, the carpet muffling the sound. Cain was still dreaming. He stood just inside the front door in the entryway of a dimly lit house. It felt late in his dream. Only a few lights were on. There was a small lamp in a living room to his right and he could see a kitchen light shining through glass inserts on the doors of cabinets that hung closer to the room.

Wood spindles ran upward to the ceiling from a short wall to the right of the entryway. Cain reached out and grabbed the inside front door handle. The metal handle felt cold.

He was aware of everything around him. He felt the warmth of the house, even its comfort. He slowly pushed the door shut, twisting the handle for the plunger to stay in the open position, then he turned the handle and let the plunger set in the lock.

He made sure that he was quiet. He felt a need to be quiet. *My God, he thought. Is this his house? Am I finally going to figure this thing out? Will I finally stop this murderer? Is this the final clue, the answer? Is that why I'm here?*

Ray circled the block and headed back north. The River Bend area consisted of a square mile area of mostly large estates on acreage plots. The house was near the river. Ray passed a hundred feet of black wrought iron fencing and stone pillars as he approached the entrance to the drive. He could see Si and Chris running up the street from behind him.

He pulled into the drive, turned off his car's headlights and allowed it to come to a quiet stop. He got out of his car and headed toward the house, motioning the others toward the front door and signaling them to cover both sides of the house.

He moved to the left and slowly went around to that side of the house, picking out the most brightly lit room just off a large deck. The expansive yard with all of its trees and hiding places made him feel vulnerable. *Always better to have someone covering on this stuff,* he thought. *I wish Cain was here.* He hoped Holly had managed to contact him.

Leaning against the wall, he slowly and quietly moved toward the doors off the deck where the light shone through from the house. His breathing was quick, his nerves frayed.

Cain stood in the entryway. A long hallway stretched out in front of him. There was a decorative table to his left against the wall. It held a vase with fresh flowers which permeated the air with their fragrance and two picture frames with pictures that were not visible in the dimly lit house. Light shone softly from a room through glass paneled double doors and onto the floor at the end of the hallway. Cain could feel his heartbeat. It screamed at him from inside his chest. He felt sweat on his eyebrows and the side of his face.

He looked forward at the light coming from the room. He slowly moved toward the light. As he came upon the edge of the doorway, he leaned forward to view the inside of the room. A man sat at a desk, his silhouette illuminated by a computer screen as he pounded away at a keyboard.

The door was open, but not enough for Cain to move

through. He feared the door creaking and the man becoming aware of his presence. His face and head hurt. He felt pressure inside it, pain, and a brief but bright burst of light jolted across his eyes.

He slowly pushed the door open and gently stepped into the room, relieved at the feel of carpet under his feet. The man sitting at the desk was totally unaware of his presence, or so he thought. Cain edged his way across the room.

He now stood directly behind the man at the computer. The man was typing feverishly, as if he felt the same urgency Cain was feeling. Cain's breathing was heavy now, almost labored. His pulse was violently pronounced. Sweat ran down his face and dripped off his chin and fell to the floor. A fearful adrenaline coursed through his body.

I'm going to get him! He's not getting away, Cain thought. Cain slowly moved his hand toward his coat and reached inside it.

Suddenly there was a flash of light across his mind. He felt faint, dizzy. He was no longer in the house.

He was now standing in a small room, a different place entirely. *Oh God, what's real?* He stood over a young girl sitting on a chair in front of him. She was possibly a teen, maybe in her early twenties. She was cradling a little boy, an infant, in her arms, looking down at him with wonder and awe, her hand gently brushing the side of his face. He wore a tiny blue and white outfit. The little boy looked back up at her with innocent eyes. Then the child faded away, seemingly melting into her and disappearing. Her hands rested on her belly. She was pregnant, six to eight months along. She looked at Cain and stood up.

The young girl followed him through a solid red door and down a long aesthetic hallway. They came to a door near the end of the hallway. As Cain opened the door to the room, the girl by his side, he had a strong feeling that he was making a horrible mistake.

The door swung open and hit against the inner wall of the room. The girl gasped, grabbing her face and chest in horror, crying out and sobbing hysterically. She put her hand on her rounded belly, looked at Cain, then ran down the hallway and out the door to the little waiting area Cain had led her from, then to the parking lot. Cain looked into the room behind the door he had opened. A stainless steel table sat in the middle of the room. The table was lined with the bodies of the babies from the dreams: little girls, little boys, their arms torn off, their eyes sunken in, fluids draining from their bodies across the cold metal surface and pooling at the edge of the table. Tags with numbers hung from their ankles. *The cold storage, the morgue*, Cain thought. He watched as a single drop of blood broke free from the end of a little girl's tiny fingers and fell to a glistening pool of red on the tiled floor.

Flash!

Standing behind the man in the house again, Cain's vision blurred and then re-focused. His hand in his pocket, he felt the coldness of steel. He pulled from his coat a long pair of scissors that came to a sharp point. An evidence tag dangled from them. He brought them upward, slowly moving them to the back of the man's head. He moved the scissors back and forth in his hand. They looked, felt, foreign to him. *I have to stop him*, Cain thought. He examined the scissors, gripped them tightly in his hand, then reached to grab the man's head with his other hand. A numbing deadness in Cain's psyche blocked out even the minutest feelings of human empathy. A darkness swooned over him, invading the inner cavities of his conscience and, like a cold sun setting over some distant arctic region, slowly dimmed any light that remained in his mind. The coldness, the darkness, the process, won. And then there was blackness, no anger, no rage, just methodic motion, that of a machine, running through a preset program, a routine, just another part of his day.

Ray rested his head against the wall near the doors. He felt Greg's hand touch his shoulder, signaling him he was there. He turned his head slightly so he could see in the house. They watched through the patio doors as someone's stretched-out shadow moved slowly across the room. The shadow stopped moving and stood still. Ray followed the long shadow across the floor to someone and then up their legs to assess the situation. He would have to act fast. "Go!" Yelled Greg.

The sound of the patio door crashing open pulled Cain from his trance.

"Cain!" Ray yelled. "Put it down, now! Now! Put it down!

Ray had his revolver pointed at Cain and was shaking from shock. Terror filled his eyes, his heart. Cain was very aware of him being there. Cain's hand started to tremble, losing grip of the scissors.

"Come on brother. You need to let go of those." Ray could hardly speak, could not believe what he was seeing. *This isn't real.* Ray was confused. He thought of the call.

Cain was alert. He felt awake. He was dizzy. He saw Greg with Ray and then Si approaching him from his right side. He looked down at the scissors in his hand and felt their coldness. His hand opened, his fingers contorting like they were touching something foreign to him, and he let go of the scissors.

Si grabbed Cain's right arm tightly and squeezed. Ray reached into Cain's coat and pulled his revolver from its holster, handing it to Greg.

Greg handed the revolver to Chris. Si turned Cain's coat pockets inside out as he searched him. "Just stay still, alright." he said.

Ray's shock was compounded as Si emptied Cain's pockets. The Medal of Honor, the bracelet, two locks of hair, all in their evidence bags.

Ray felt sick as Si pulled a meticulously painted 1953 Corvette model from Cain's left blazer pocket.

What? Ray thought.

"Those are mine," Cain said. "They mean everything. I need them. I need them to remember."

The man at the desk turned to look at Cain. Cain returned his gaze. He then continued to bang away on his keyboard, splattering words across the screen with a fervor and seemingly oblivious to their existence. *My God, what's happening,* Cain thought.

Cain stared down at the words on the monitor as the man typed them, and as he typed them, Cain read them. His eyes blurred as he tried to understand. He saw his own name, Ray's and Greg's. He saw the word Corvette, and revolver. The words continued being typed onto the computer screen and Cain kept reading, feeling as though he was caught in some kind of trance, his mind meshing and blending with the words on the screen. And as the man kept typing, he typed the following words . . .

. . . Greg cuffed him and led him out of the room and toward the front door. The lights in the house were bright, several of them having been turned on by the officers who had now converged on the scene. As Cain was led out the door, he turned and looked down at the two pictures on the table in the entryway. He could see the people now. One was of a young woman holding a little boy in a blue and white outfit, the young woman in his dream he'd led through the red door and down the hallway. The other was of the same woman, older now, standing with a smiling young man who held a novel in his hand. They were in Pellili's bookstore with a poster behind them. Near them on a table sat more copies of the same book. The man was the same person Cain had almost just killed. Cain just shook his head, perplexed.

Greg and Si led Cain out of the house and onto the porch, then past the faces of other officers, their eyes serious, confused. Cain saw several police cars in the driveway and on the street below, their lights flashing and dancing across the wrought iron fencing and the grass.

Cain felt the air around his body. He felt his footsteps. He heard the voices of those around him. He felt the cushion of the seat in the police cruiser as his body flopped down in the caged area of the vehicle. He looked forward, seeing Ray at the front of the vehicle shaking his head and hanging it low as Greg spoke to him. Cain rubbed one finger against the finger he had burned while cooking, feeling a tinge of pain course through his hand. He felt lost, numb. An officer's flashlight splattered it's beam across his eyes. He closed them, irritated by the brightness.

This wasn't a drive he was accustomed to experiencing, watching cars pass by and looking at people from the back seat of a police cruiser. He tried to sort his thoughts, but he was having too many odd feelings to pull himself together. *This is what it feels like to get arrested. Am I awake? I've been arrested. My finger hurts from that burn. I don't even know what cop is driving me to the station.* He realized it was Washington. *I wonder if I could break free. I've never thought about how to escape from one of these cages. What am I doing here? What just happened? Is this real? Who was the man in the house? Why am I not at home?* On and on his mind raced. He closed his eyes and tried to relax. He desperately wanted to fall asleep and wake up in his apartment.

They pulled into the drive and parked near the front door of the building. Cain could see that a lot of officers had made their way outside and onto the landing of the stairs. He didn't want to feel what he was about to experience. He knew their eyes would be on him. People shrugged and shook their heads, some said comments, eyes wide open in shock. At least one person told him not to worry, that it would all get sorted out.

It was more difficult inside the building. This sanctuary of understanding and shelter from the criminal element was the place where Cain and Ray would sit every day working against the people who did evil, and surviving the mental stress of the job was often a good reason for the levity everybody brought into the room each day.

Cain felt no levity. He was now the evil imposing his

presence upon the sanctuary. Every person in the room seemed to stop what they were doing to pay attention to them and watch. Officers at desks, secretaries, people waiting to be seen. As they walked down the ramp to the lower level of the building, he looked into the main division room as Karen uncrossed her arms holding her hands in an upward gesture, silently voicing, "What's going on?"

The lower level contained interrogation rooms, holding cells, officer locker areas and several work areas. Beyond those was a booking area and then a large steel gated door that led to the main holding area with several rows of cells and a drunk tank. Farther yet was a hallway that was actually a tunnel that allowed easy access across the street to the basement of the city's fifteen story jail and the courthouse next door.

In the hallway were large windows to the right on one of the rooms. Cain turned his head and looked into the room, not really thinking about what he was doing. As he did he saw a middle-aged man and woman sitting to the left of another person at a table with a computer on it. Several pieces of paper lay across the table. Behind the computer screen sat the department's sketch artist. The woman was shaking her head yes to something she was viewing on the screen.

As Cain stared at her, she looked up at him and her eyes widened. Her face went flush. She had a look of fear, shock. Her facial muscles tightened. She grabbed the table, steadying herself. Her mouth moved, saying something, and the artist looked up at Cain. Cain could tell the artist was asking the woman if she was sure. He saw him lip the words. The artist immediately picked up the telephone and put it to his ear, dialing a short number and at the same time yelling out of the room for Ray to come to him. Ray stopped, leaving the police officer to finish escorting Cain to the holding cell and walked into the room.

"She just gave me a positive ID on Cain as he walked by. And look at this. We just finished it a few minutes ago."

Ray couldn't believe his eyes. Looking at the computer screen on the table he saw a nearly perfect image of Cain.

Cain lay in his holding cell. *The dreams were a warning*, he thought. *Or were they what made this happen? Yes, the dreams were real*, he concluded, *dreams I must have lived out in reality?* He remembered waking up in his car on the street in front of his apartment. His keys being locked in his car, not knowing how he got into his house that night. *Did I pick my lock? I must have broken in.* He could hear Ray and Greg down the hallway.

"Would you have pegged this on Cain?" Ray asked Greg. "I didn't even give it a second thought at the time."

"If you had a handprint on a windowsill at a crime scene that brought you to question something, you should have talked to me," Greg said.

Cain's mind raced. *The handprint from the school! It all makes sense. I never remembered going near that windowsill.*

"I wasn't positive, Greg!"

"You just said you didn't see him go to that side of the room the whole time."

"I thought maybe I missed something, got busy, just didn't see him over there. I put it out of my mind as soon as I thought it."

"That was how many victims ago, Ray? Is it his fingerprint on the paper from the fire too? Maybe at that point you should have considered a cross reference on the two sets of prints."

"I didn't think of that. I wasn't even going to consider Cain unless something else came into play. It all seems to fit now though. I should have seen it. It was like he was becoming a different person. He isn't who he was when we were growing up. He's changed a lot over the last several years. I think his job has been eating on him. It's got him all screwed up. Besides, just because Cain may have snapped and gone into some kind of crazy mode here doesn't mean he committed a single murder. We don't know that he's killed anybody. He had evidence items, and he went to someone's house. Maybe he had a break, then started to act out what we've been dealing with. I hate to say it, but he's been acting odd lately and I've never seen his work bother him this much before."

Cain listened to them.

Is the conductor's DNA on my shoes? My dreams matched the killings, the numbers. I killed on my days off? I wasn't getting any sleep. I was always so stinking exhausted! Am I a psychotic killer? No! No! I can't be.

"Well, I need every detail you can think of that might apply here," said Greg. "Because if he didn't do this, we're gonna have a heck of a time proving his innocence."

"I just want to go home and sort this out. I've got a family at home that's going to be crushed by this news. Can we talk tomorrow? I'm exhausted. I'll be far more useful with this mess if I can get some rest."

"Yeah, we'll talk tomorrow, fine. First thing in the morning."

Ray turned to leave, glanced down the hall toward Cain's holding cell, hesitated, and walked out. *I warned him . . . I told him to get help.*

Cain lay on his cell bunk, alone with his thoughts, considering what Ray had said. The cold feel of the inadequately thin mattress penetrating his clothing kept him awake. If he changed his position, the torn parts of the mattress cover would scratch against him, making him ever aware of this new reality. He looked at the door and remembered how many times he had led suspects in and out of the cell he was now trapped in, no longer having the option to walk back out. He had been led in. He would be led out. He was being dragged along against his own will. The reality of being caught in the act was sinking in, the craziness of the nightmares. He wondered again if he had killed them all, or were just some of the later ones his? *Mine . . . Mine,* Cain thought. It made him cringe inside as he thought about it. Was he awake when he killed? *Did I kill at all?*

Rays words reverberated in his head, "You had to have been fully conscious of what you were doing, Cain, fully conscious! There's no way that deep down inside you weren't ignoring everything you know about life, everything he ever taught us. You can't tell me you don't know you're ripping human beings apart. For what? Why? Tearing them up and discarding their bodies like trash. You could choose any other path! This is what I fight against every day. You took an oath to preserve, to protect life. How could you do this? It's the exact opposite!"

"When did he say that to me? When? What did it mean? Why is that so familiar to me? Cain felt dizzy in his thoughts and tried to push back the feeling of confusion, dread, and an incomprehensible guilt that he couldn't seem to detach himself from. *Maybe the judge will see that I'm crazy, that I lost it somehow. I was obviously in some trance. Who could kill another human being unless they weren't in reality? If I tore that woman's head off, how couldn't I have been absolutely insane? No! I couldn't have done that. What kind of maniac, what*

demented, twisted mind can do that to another life? Nobody could do this to another human being unless there was something wrong with them. I'm ill, that's it. No, no. I've never allowed that excuse for others. Murderers, they take someone's life, something that's not theirs to do! They extinguish life, that's what it is, nothing less. I didn't do this. I would never hold the destiny of another life in that kind of disregard. Something's not right!

Cain realized the utter helplessness of the isolation cell. He had no control over what would come next. His eyes traced a line up the wall by the bunk. Marks were scratched into the cinder block like somebody was counting their days of captivity in this darkened place. He rolled onto his side and stared at the wall. Etched into the wall directly in front of him, were five simple words.

I make all things new.   Revelations 21:5

He stared at the wall and the words burned themselves into his mind as he fell asleep.

Kevin Patrick Smith

18

"What's happening? I don't understand. I don't get it." Cain's thoughts were sporadic, confused.

"Let's go with another 2.5 milligrams. Cain? Cain? What do we have for a BP, nurse? Nurse? Nurse? Doctor. Cain. Cain!"

"We've got some strong eye movement. Turn down the overhead lights more, please. Cathy, please."

"Yes, Doctor." Beep . . . beep . . . beep . . . "I have an increase . . . I have an increase . . ."

"Cathy, can you hold this? BP is rising."

"Who is that?" Cain thought.

Then, rolling, spinning, across his mind in unison, children's voices, began reciting the poem.

"You drew down the hammer . . ."

"Crushed and tangled bodies weaved, Innocent, Guilty, Your mind deceived."

"Doctor, I have a rapid increase in vitals . . ."

"Drowned their voices in gurgling blood, you can't deny, you can't deny. Your own flesh you chose, tormented now your little . . ."

What?

"Let's increase that drip by .05 milligrams. Cathy, what did we have for vitals?"

"Vindicate, Vindicate . . . You had the final say, your seed to sow, seed to sow."

"I don't, I can't breath, I can't . . . somebody help. What's happening?" Cain pushed outward against something. It was difficult to move.

Beep . . . beep . . . beep . . .

"Murderous killer, seed to sow . . . the hunted

"Souls of the lost scream . . . beckoning . . . Darkness, darkness . . . all alone . . . darkness"

"Cain? Cain, can you hear me? Can you hear. Cain?

Then, a still voice, strong, re-assuring, hopeful . . .

Will you trade your heart of stone? . . . I make all things new . . . I make all things new . . . I make all things new . . .

"Cain. Cain!"

"I think it worked."

"There was . . ."

"An increase in activity after the second dose."

"Yes, it's apparently worked."

Cain's arms and legs were restrained. He couldn't move. He heard voices, muffled, followed by footsteps. There were beeping sounds and then a buzzing sound followed by what felt like somebody grabbing his right arm and squeezing down hard. It felt like a vein in his arm was going to explode. He felt trapped. The voices became louder and clearer. His eyes opened, strained, bothered by the light that shone down from the ceiling above him. He was lying in bed in what appeared to be a hospital room. Surrounding his bed were doctors, obvious from their long white coats and stethoscopes and pockets full of pens.

"It looks as though the new method of treatment has worked somewhat."

They were leaning inward, peering down at him as if he had some answer they were awaiting. One of them had a quirky smile on his face, like he was nearly happy with Cain's apparent demise. Cain felt the urge to speak. His mind was unable to bring the word to his lips as he attempted to mumble the word.

"What?"

"Oh, thank God!" another doctor said. "I thought there might be some hope after his last MRI. Just take it easy, don't get too excited. You've done enough of that while you were out."

By 'out' he assumed he'd been asleep or something. He tried to gather his thoughts. *Did something happen to me while I was asleep in the cell? Why am I here now?*

"It's good to have you back, Cain. We've missed you," said the quirky, smiling one.

"Yes, we're not used to seeing you on this end of the spectrum. It's really quite a miracle you're still with us."

"How do you feel?"

"My head hurts bad, what happened?" Cain struggled with his words.

"He's speaking well," a doctor said.

A nurse spoke. "That's probably cause he was so vocal while he was under."

"You're at the Crossroads Medical Center," another said.

"Well, quite frankly, we just want you to stay with us. We'll talk later. You've had a very serious head injury. Right now no talking. Just keep your mind at rest. The nurses will be keeping an extra eye on you tonight, especially if your vitals rise while you're sleeping," the doctor said as he motioned to the nurses.

Another doctor turned and quietly talked to the other nurse, thinking Cain could not hear him. He was older than the rest. Cain figured him to be in his sixties.

"Let's keep the soft restraints on him until we know he's stabilized and has come completely out of this thing. We don't need him kicking someone again."

They continued to talk around him. He slipped in and out of consciousness. He focused on the clock. Two o'clock, two thirty. More nurses. Different doctors. A lifted eyelid, lights on his pupils, agitating. Three o'clock, four o'clock. Cain closed his eyes again, not wanting to think. He was tired and confused. He dosed off.

No dreams. No nightmares.

He awoke to the pressure cuff inflating on his arm and nurses moving about the room. He was more alert this time. His head hurt and his body ached. He felt something touching his face and lips. When he went to reach for it, he could only move his arm a few inches. He realized that he was restrained to the bed. It made him angry.

"What happened? Why am I here?" Cain asked anxiously.

"Well, doctor, you don't remember?"

"Doctor? What? I was, well, I was lying in the cell," Cain sighed, trying to think. "No, I don't, why don't you remind me," he said, a little irritated.

"It's been several weeks since your accident."

"Accident, what accident? And why did you call me doctor?"

"I'll tell you what, let me get Doctor Cornelder to come and talk to you. He asked that we call him if you had any questions when you woke up. He's your neurologist."

The nurse left and Cain turned his head sideways to look at the heart monitor and the light shining into the room from the window.

It looked sunny outside. *God, was I dreaming all of this,* he thought to himself. *No murders. I'm not a detective, not a cop. Not a killer. A doctor. A doctor! That's practically the opposite.* Cain breathed a sigh of relief. The hospital bed was far more comfortable then the holding cell. His face itched. He felt an awareness, alertness, that made this reality seem real. He just didn't remember much about who he was or why he was in the hospital. *Great, I'm a doctor with no memory whatsoever. That should be useful.*

The door slowly opened with a gentle knock and the doctor who had whispered to the nurse the day before walked in.

"Cain, how are you feeling?"

The man looked at him with a seemingly genuine concern, like somebody who cared about him.

"I'm sore all over. It hurts to talk."

"Do you know who I am?"

"No."

"Do you know what year it is?"

"No, no, actually, I don't."

"Do you know where you're at?"

"No, I don't," Cain was feeling irritated again.

The doctor noticed his frustration.

"I'm sorry, but it's important that we take this slowly so we can gauge if there was any permanent damage. I need to know what you can remember so we can note any type of memory loss you may be dealing with. Just a few more questions for now, okay?"

Cain hesitated. "Sure. I mean, you could just tell me everything. That would be easier."

"Do you know how old you are? Do you know your last name?"

"No, I don't."

"I'm Doctor Cornelder. I'm a neurologist here at the medical center. I've been here at the hospital for many years now working in different departments. We've actually worked together quite a bit throughout the years. You are a doctor yourself. You're very well known. You have an office on the east side of town and practice here at the hospital clinic. You've been a doctor for over forty years. You're sixty five years old. Your name is Cain. Cain Daniels." Do you remember any of that?"

"Just my first name."

"Several weeks ago you were in an accident. You were hit by a drunk driver. He was going over seventy miles an hour and his brakes went out on him as you left a stoplight. He was unable to stop and hit the passenger side of your car. Do you remember that?"

Vague thoughts came to him. He wanted to remember, to make sense of it all. He couldn't. It was all fuzzy, blurred, indistinguishable.

"You've spent most of your time since then slipping in and out of consciousness. You've been in what we call an MCS, or a Minimally Conscious State. It's similar to a coma but not quite as deep. This was brought on by Subarachnoid Hemorrhaging caused by the head injury you received in your accident. I must say, you've taken us all here at the hospital for quite a ride. An average patient, honestly, would probably have been transferred to a different type of facility. Though we couldn't awaken you, you had an incredible amount of brain activity going on. You got pretty intense a few times, actually. There were several times we had to forcibly hold you down to keep you from hurting yourself. It was after you injured one of our nurses that we decided the soft restraints would be a good idea. Even with those restraints you would just, well, start swinging at the air at times. It was almost as if you were fighting someone."

Cain couldn't speak the words. He gave the doctor a tired look.

"Let's try again tomorrow. I'll come back and we'll talk. It will all come back to you eventually."

The doctor walked out of the room and Cain was left with his thoughts. *"Well,"* he thought. *"I've woke up two times in this place. I think this is real. I don't think I'm going back to the world of detectives and the murders. I don't remember this, but I'm beginning to believe I'm here to stay. We'll get this figured out. It's definitely a better place, a better situation, well, maybe. God, hmm. I actually feel rested."* Cain felt a little psychotic, crazy. He thought of Ray, Holly and the kids and was saddened. *Where are they?* He wondered.

He dozed off to sleep . . .

There was laughter in the small space of the car's interior. Her beautiful, childish eyes were bright and full of life. Her curly hair bounced around on her forehead as she giggled. It was just them now, he and his granddaughter, since her mother had died. They'd be alright. It would be okay. It felt good. They were sitting at a traffic signal. Rain danced on the windshield. He reached over and playfully tickled her pudgy little belly. He turned and looked into the most angelic face he had ever seen.

"Do you know what my mommy told me once?" the little girl said.

"No honey, what's that?" asked Cain.

"She said you told her I should have been taken care of before I was born. What's that mean? How can somebody be taken care of before they're born? Even I know you can't take care of a baby before it's born. You have to wait till after."

Cain's eyes swelled with tears. "It doesn't mean anything,

baby. It doesn't mean a single thing, not now, not since the day I first saw your face. I love you, Elsie. Grandpa really loves you."

Cain pulled away from the traffic light.

The car's headlights flashed into the scene so fast. There were no screeching brakes, just an ear-shattering explosive impact that consumed the car at the very place where his little granddaughter sat.

He awoke, thrashing about in his hospital bed, still restrained. The monitors were flashing and beeping, alerting the nurses to the intense increase in his blood pressure. He was wide awake. Thoughts of the little girl in his dream, his nightmare, her bright eyes still shining up at him, her angelic face, flashed across his mind. And then the glass shattered! Then fire. Then darkness. His Elsie, his beautiful little Elsie, his granddaughter! Now he remembered her! Now the pieces were coming to him in a torrential flood of thought. "Where is she?" he yelled. "Where is sheeeeeeeeeeeeee?"

"Doctor, you need to calm down," a nurse said.

Cain pushed hard against the restraints that held him to the bed.

"No, no, no, I don't need to do anything! Noooooooooooooo!"

Cain pushed his body, his chest, upwards against the restraining arms of the hospital staff that now filled the room and attempted to hold him still. He could smell, taste, the narcotic in the back of his throat as he went under.

Cain awoke hours later. Dr. Cornelder was in his room at his bedside as he came to.

"Thank you, Cathy," he said to the nurse working with Cain's IV pump. "Could you give us some time alone?"

The nurse nodded and left the room.

"You've taken quite a hit. We've all been pulling for you. It's been hard the last few years."

The doctor paused before asking his next question.

"Do you remember Elsie now?"

"Yes," Cain said, now knowing that this was his true reality because of the pain he felt in his heart for his little granddaughter.

"Elsie was Kelly's daughter. Kelly was your youngest. You had adopted Elsie as your own. Do you want to keep talking about this?"

The memories flooded back into his mind. He saw Kelly's face. He remembered how tired she had been the last time he had seen her at the apartment. Kelly had gotten wrapped up with the wrong crowd at school and continued a terrible drug addiction into her twenties. At eighteen years old, she had become pregnant with Elsie. He had advised her to not have the baby, but she did. Their relationship became strained and she moved out on her own. As Elsie grew older, she had allowed him to be a part of her life. She knew Elsie needed him. Kelly never quite recovered from her drug problems. A year later, she overdosed on prescription painkillers. *Kelly, it was you. It was you at the apartments in my dreams. It was you and Elsie.*

"Where's my Elsie?

"I'm sorry, Cain, but Elsie was killed instantly in the accident. She was a precious little girl. I promise you she didn't feel anything. She didn't suffer in any way.

Cain's heart sank. He was sobbing, but inside with faint

breaths coming from deep within. He couldn't speak. He remained silent for several minutes. His eyes swelled with tears. Her face wouldn't leave his mind. His sorrow turned to anger.

"Who did it? Who hit us?"

"I don't remember his name. Some guy coming up the street out of old town. The newspaper article made its way around the staff here for a week or so."

"Do you still have it here, the article?"

"I could check, but it's doubtful. That was several weeks ago."

"How did he hit us?" Cain was angry.

"Are you ready for that?"

"I wanna know."

"You pulled away from a traffic light. It was starting to rain and the roads were slick. He'd just left a tavern in the area. Apparently he lived near there and was a regular. He was speeding. He tried to stop, but his brakes completely failed. The idiot told the police he'd only had a few drinks. He had a BAC of point two-one. He said he knew his brakes were bad. He just couldn't afford to get them fixed."

"What happened to him?"

"He's sitting in jail on vehicular homicide charges. We can talk again later." Doctor Cornelder felt he was pushing Cain too hard.

"Wait. Why are there bandages on my face?"

"When he hit you, your car's gas tank ruptured and there was a fire. The driver of the car next to you pulled you and Elsie from the wreckage. Otherwise, you would've died. You suffered some minor burns and had a slight grafting to repair some areas on your face. It was successful. It was done within a couple days of your accident. There was some bone structure damage that needed to be dealt with, so the grafting was done at the same time. Your rescuer didn't fare so well."

"How could they do that? Didn't somebody have to allow that? Who authorized my surgeries?"

"Well, that would be your brother, Ray. He felt it's what you would've wanted."

Cain thought of Ray, the detective, Holly, Kenny and the baby. *Wow, I must've really been hit hard.*

"Is Ray married? Does he have children?" Cain asked, hoping for at least something good to come of all the insanity, something to slice through the numbness he was feeling."

"You don't remember if he's married or has children?"

"Is he?"

"He is. He has a precious little daughter about eight months old and a little boy that likes to talk and apparently thinks a lot of you. Little Kenny kept asking why you wouldn't wake up and told you it's too bad about Elsie but that she's with angels now and that you guys, well, you won't be able to ride in the Corvette any, uh, well, any more. They've been up to see you quite a bit. Every visit that little boy jumped onto the bed next to you and would tap on your chest. 'Come back, Cain, come back,' he'd whisper in your ear. They stopped bringing the children for a while after we had to restrain you. I've got a call into them. When you awoke they were out of state dealing with a situation with Holly's mother."

Cain was confused, but realized that he wouldn't get it all figured out right away. *Corvette?* he thought to himself.

"Do you want to take a break till tomorrow?"

"Yeah, my head hurts. I just want to close my eyes. Will you come back?"

"I'll be here."

Doctor Cornelder walked out of the room, leaving Cain with his thoughts. He thought of Elsie and Kelly. *The apartments, my apartment in my dreams, the courtyard, the fountain - those were my daughter Kelly's! My daughter! Kelly and Elsie's apartments in real life. She was my little Elsie.* He remembered her calling him Grandpa in his dreams. He wished he had said, "Yes, I am your grandpa," even to a dream child. *The restaurant . . . that was right before Kelly died.* Cain realized that parts of reality had slipped into his mind and must have affected his thoughts while he was unconscious. Doctor Cornelder stepped back through the door.

"Oh, one more thing. Ray and Holly left you something they said was very special. It's on the chair in the corner. They thought it might help you if you awoke. I don't think they intended for you to open it alone. Your brother said it was important you read the note first."

Doctor Cornelder walked out and Cain looked at the chair in the corner of the room. On it sat a box, wrapped like a gift, except with the top wrapped separate so it could be easily lifted off. Cain wanted to look in it, but he was tired. Exhaustion won. He laid his head back and rested it on his pillow. Closing his eyes, he drifted just barely across the threshold between slumber and awake.

A voice cried out in his head, Elsie's voice.

"Grandpa, you have to stop the killer!"

Cain sat up in his bed and let out a deep sigh, feeling sorrow that he couldn't bring Elsie's voice back again.

The killer? The killer's gone. There is no killer.

Cain fell back to sleep with his thoughts, and he dreamt . . .

He stood in a field, staring forward. Tall prairie grass blew in the wind. He felt the touch of a small hand slip into his. He turned and looked down at the face of his granddaughter. She walked forward, slightly tugging on his hand. He let her lead him, across an acreage, down a hill of wavy grass, past a small grove of pine trees, along the edge of a pond. They turned toward an orchard of fruit trees that backed up against a large greenhouse. He hesitated.

Elsie stopped and reassuringly squeezed his hand.

"Come on, Grandpa. It's what's best."

She pulled at his hand as she lead him past the trees to the side of the greenhouse. They stood there, facing an old weather worn door with a rusted handle.

A shadow fluttered across the sun above them, and Cain could just barely hear the clanging of metal as the great bird alighted on the pinnacle of the structure.

Elsie took his hand and placed it on the doorknob.

"You'll stop him. I love you Grandpa."

Cain looked down as her hand slipped from his and she faded into the air, her face seared in his memory. He turned the knob.

Kevin Patrick Smith

19

The killer's blank stare reflected back at himself from the mirror. The small white sink, with its outdated, roundly bulbous faucet handles and rusted spigot, collected droplets that fell from his sweat covered face as he leaned forward peering into his own eyes, his face just inches from the mirror's surface. Where he leaned upon the sink with his hands, smears of blood mixed with water droplets and ran down into the sink. He lifted a hand to his cheek, pinching at his skin near his eye and pulling at it. Blood streaked across his face where his fingers had touched. He grabbed at his face harder, tugging, pulling, at the skin and flesh on his cheek bone. He brought his other hand up, grabbing at the other cheek, squeezing, scratching, digging. His movement became more rapid. What appeared to be flesh began to pull away from around his eye, papery, spongy, breaking, yet still connected in spots. With both hands, he reached up and grabbed bigger pieces near the top of his forehead and hairline and scratched downward, his face peeling away like dry flaking mud and cloth, revealing the face of an older man.

Cain awakened, the images from the dreams still etched into his mind as the dietary lady set his food tray on the little table by his bed. He was numbed by his thoughts of Elsie.

He's hiding his identity, Cain thought. *He's not who we think he was. The washroom. The greenhouse washroom. What was that place? Why am I even thinking this? That's all gone now. That was my dream world. Time to move past all the insanity.*

They had initially started him on softer foods, but today's tray held more of a regular breakfast.

"Whoa, that's a lot more food than I've been getting."

Cain looked at the spread in front of him. It included scrambled eggs that were just a little softer than usual, cottage cheese, sliced peaches and a single serve apple juice in one of those little disposable plastic cups with a foil seal.

"I hope you enjoy it," the lady said.

"I'll try. Oh, hey, um, miss, could you do me a favor?"

"What's that?"

"Could you hand me the box that's on the chair in the corner there?"

"Sure."

"Thanks."

"You're welcome."

He pulled the box onto his lap from where the lady had set it on the bed next to him and rested his arms around it, almost hugging it. It was a piece of reality. It was a connection to his life: to Ray, Holly, Kenny, and baby Ranae.

"Well, I don't know what you hold, but I'm very interested in finding out."

As Cain started to lift the box lid, he noticed a small note attached to the wrapping paper.

We know this will be tough for you. We all love you very much. Kenny misses spending time with you. Ranae has grown a lot. Holly sends her love. We weren't sure whether to do this or not. It was Kenny's idea. It should help you remember some things. If you want to wait until I'm there with you, we can go through the box together. If you have not remembered the things in this box it's going to be very hard for you.

PS. I'm sure this is what you would want. Love Ray

Cain gazed at the box one final time.

I'm not waiting! How much worse could this get?

He thought once again of what Ray had written in the card.

It's going to be very hard for you . . .

He reached into the box and pulled out the first item. It was an eight-by-ten photograph of a young girl in her teens. He stared at the picture, and as he stared at it, his memories immediately surfaced, his mind snapped open, commanding his every thought, grabbing hold of darkened chambers of his consciousness. Suddenly, he was awake and aware, acutely aware. It was like a switch had been tripped inside his head, a physical switch. He felt the change.

"My God, it's my Kelly."

This was the picture he had chosen to be placed next to his daughter's casket, centered in a ring of fresh roses and vases with dozens of lilies. He could almost smell the roses mixed with the musky smell of the funeral home, a stench he hated. He felt like he should be sad or hurt inside, but he didn't feel anything. His relationship with his daughter had just begun to mend. His feelings had been expended at the time of the funeral, harsh, angry emotions toward a death that shouldn't have been.

The picture from the crime scenes; the ones Ana showed me that matched in my dream world.

The mysterious girl from the photographs, the matriarch murder scene, the estate. This was Kelly, his daughter, just at different ages in her life. She was the street girl. She had called him 'dad' in his dream state on the street that day. When she was in highschool she'd come home drunk, high, several times, been in trouble with the police. He began to understand.

Wow, my dream state was so backwards.

Ray's words resounded in his mind.

This will be hard for you...

There was something going on inside him, a remembrance, moving from deep within his being. Thoughts began to flow freely. He was seeing them now. There was no doctor reminding him of people or places or accidents. These were his own thoughts, his own memories. His loved ones, his family, began to emerge onto the surface of his mind.

People from his dream state were now crowding into his thoughts, claiming the places they held in real life. The thoughts were mixed though, with voices that spoke into his psyche, demanding his attention.

A still, calm, heavenly voice spoke to his heart.

"They're interlocked. The murder victims, the children, your family. They're connected."

What? Cain questioned this thought, shaking his head, then looked down at the photograph of Kelly. He remembered finding alcohol and drugs in her car after he'd been called down

264

to pick her up from the police station.

What does it matter? She'd told him that night. *It's only high school. So what if we party! Can I go now, Dad?* She could barely make it to her bedroom from the front door. Cain remembered her words clearly, then thought to himself. *The girl from the street, the girl buying drugs in my dreams, that was Kelly, my youngest! How do these things belong together? I just don't understand.*

Again, the voice spoke to him.

He would have given her hope, Cain. Your daughter would still be alive.

Cain's vision blurred. The pain centered in his head increased. A bloodied image of the math teacher flashed across his mind, the photograph in his clenched hand. The teacher slowly opened his hand and the small picture of Kelly fell from it.

His mind was spinning.

What the . . .? Am I losing it? This is crazy. My dreams weren't real. This teacher wasn't real. Kelly never had this teacher!

He knew the people from his dreams weren't real. They couldn't be. They were part of some altered state while he was unconscious.

Now I'm awake. I'm past all of that! Could these people really exist? Why would it matter if they did?

Cain reached inside the box, fear, apprehension, now gripping him. He felt something square with his hand and pulled it out. It was a beautifully decorated wooden box. It had a closeable lid with tiny brass hinges and a hasp on the front.

He went to open the box, not sure if he wanted to know what was in it. He grabbed the hasp between his thumb and forefinger and unsnapped it. He lifted the lid. Covering the inside was a flat layer of cotton. Whatever was in the little box was hidden under it.

Cain lifted the top layer of cotton. Immediately, his eyes filled with tears. A flood of sorrow mixed with a tinge of joy that made him feel alive. She was real again now. Nobody could take that from him, even though she was gone. In the box lay a delicately curled, shiny lock of hair. *My precious angel, my precious little angel.* He remembered her curly, bouncy hair. He saw her innocent, bright eyes looking up at him. He held the box close to his chest and sobbed. *I love you, Elsie. I miss you. I can't believe I'll never see you again, never hear your little voice. I can't believe you're gone.*

He sat in silence for several minutes, holding the box in his hand and running a finger across the tiny lock of hair.

I don't think I can do any more of this. It's too hard, like Ray said.

He pondered the thought of the little lock of hair and what it meant. In his dream world the trooper and the mechanic had held locks of hair.

He remembered the mechanics bay in the gas station, the old brakes lying on the floor near the car. He remembered the wrecked vehicle, the trail of brake fluid.

My God, that was the car that hit us!

Cain thought of the lock of hair in the mechanics hand. He saw the mechanic's face clearly in his mind. The mechanics eyes opened.

Vindicate me!

He heard Elsie whisper into his mind.

You have to stop him, Grandpa.

Elsie's little voice made him go flush. Her image in his mind faded away.

"I'm losing my freaking mind!" Cain said aloud. "I've had enough of this!"

Cain grabbed the lid and placed it back on top of the box.

"Later, I'll look at you later. I'm done for now."

He took me from you . . .

"Now I am going crazy! No, I can't do this. I can't handle this."

The sweetness of the voice was undeniable. It had strength in it, a firmness, yet was gentle and soft. It was as if Cain was suddenly aware of a void in his soul, an emptiness he'd forgotten about. He saw his wife lying in her hospital bed close to death. *Oh, God, no.* The pain he felt, the sorrow, was intense. It was like losing her all over again. It was as though he'd forgotten so much that now he had to feel it for the first time.

His wife was so beautiful. Cain had found Delores irresistible, strong, brilliant. She had always taken such good care of herself. She had worn her gray hair proudly, as if it were a crowning glory to the years of her life. But her vitality wasn't enough in her battle against cancer. It hit hard, fast, and crushed her. By the time it was discovered it had already wrapped itself around her esophagus and into several of her organs. They tried to eradicate it, but were unable. After several months and weakened by treatments, her body couldn't pull through the disease. It was his wife's death that had taken the final toll on his daughter Kelly's emotions. She and Delores had begun to mend their relationship. Just four months after Delores' death, distraught, Kelly overdosed and killed herself.

Now Cain was angry, driven along by his emotions. He grabbed the box again and opened the lid. He had watched his beloved die of cancer. *If somebody took her from me, I am going to do something about it!* He reached into the box and felt around. He found two more boxes similar to the one that held Elsie's lock of hair. Cain set the two boxes in front of him. He unlatched both lids. *This is it! I'm finishing this!*

He opened the little boxes, but this time was not shocked by what he saw. One held a beautiful bracelet, its pink diamonds

267

wrapped and interwoven within a platinum chain. A single, blazing pink sapphire sparkled with fire in a mount at the center.

This was the bracelet Delores had custom made the week she was diagnosed with cancer. A small platelet on the bracelet was inscribed with the words, "This will not conquer me."

His eyes shifted toward the other box and as they did, almost immediately, a man's voice spoke into his mind. It was a voice of strength and authority. He loved the voice. He missed its strength.

"Be strong, Father. Only you can fix this. You have to do the right thing. Too many people, he's changing too much.

Cain looked down into the box at a Medal of Honor, its ribbon carefully folded and laying under the medallion. "I get it," Cain said aloud.

Cain's mind was coming back to him. *How could I forget these things? Things in my dream state were so out of place.*

He thought about Nick, his oldest child. They'd grown cold toward each other during Nick's college years. Nick joined the military after college and commanded a unit in the US Army. During a food relief mission into Southern Africa, he was killed. There was civil unrest there due to an extended drought. What few crops were produced had been lost and thousands of civilians were starving to death and were in desperate need of food and medical supplies. His son was one of the commanding officers on a mission to bring the supplies to the area. Their convoy came under attack by militant factions. Nick, along with several other soldiers, was killed in the firefight that ensued.

"Kelly's brother was killed in the military. He received a medal of honor for it." Cain thought about his dream world and what Kelly's friend had said at the estate. *"Kelly, Elsie, Nick, Delores. Each one so real, yet displaced in my dream world. But why the murder victims? How could they possibly be linked to my family? This is my third*

day waking up in the hospital. I'm not going to prison for killing anybody. Life is real. I'm awake. I've got to have some answers!"

Cain was greatly bothered by some of his thoughts, and rightly so. *"If Ray is real, could the victims be real? Could I still save them? Is Ray even a cop? I haven't had another dream about the babies. Why the babies? Why any dreams at all? Were they even dreams? Dreams inside my coma, my sleep. I just don't get it. I'm so confused."*

Again, Cain was feeling as though somebody was trying to give him a message, to make him understand something. *"I'm not crazy,"* he thought. *"There has to be something to this!"*

Two nurses stood just outside the door to his room near a computer cart talking and working on charts, then one walked into the room.

"Doctor Daniels, I'm Cathy and I'll be your nurse again this morning. Is there anything I can get for you? Would you like to watch some TV?"

"No, thank you."

How about some music? We have a nice selection of CDs you can choose from. Would you like me to bring you a list and we can order something up to the room?"

"Do they have any classical?"

"Do you like classical music?"

"Oh yeah, it's my favorite. I tried to talk my kids into going that direction for a career, but they just weren't interested in music or the arts."

"I'll get you a list."

"Thanks."

"No problem."

Wow, I actually remembered something.

The nurse turned to leave the room.

"Oh, hey, nurse? When will I be able to get these bandages off my face?"

"It shouldn't be much longer. Most of the healing is done. There were just a few areas that were sensitive and were taking a little longer, but they've improved quite a bit."

"How bad was it?"

"Your face really is healing nicely. I don't think you'll even be able to tell. There were only some smaller burns. That's why they felt they could take care of them right away. I'll check with the doctor."

"That would be great."

The nurse left the room.

Cain sat thinking. *"Well, when you have questions, it's time to find answers!* He pressed the call button on his remote. A few moments later a beep sounded and a voice spoke from the little speaker on the remote.

"Can I help you?"

"I hope so. I really need a phone book. Can you get me a phone book?

"Give me just a second. We'll try to find one."

Cain thumbed through the phone book the nurse's aide had brought him. *If I can just find the victims, if they're real, maybe, just maybe, there's something to this whole thing. If there's one simple clue, anything, I need to find it.*

"Cross . . . Cross Cleaners . . . Crossroad's Plumbing . . . wait, no, I need the public section. Okay, City of Crossroads, County, City, Schools, Crossroad's University…bingo!"

Cain dialed the general information number for the university and anxiously tapped his fingers on the phone as he listened to it ring several times.

"Hello, Crossroad's University, how may I direct your call?"

"Yes, I need to know if . . . well, I need to know if you have someone on your staff."

"That shouldn't be a problem, let me pull up that screen.

What was the name?"

"Name? Well, uh, her name is . . ." Cain stopped himself.

Oh my God, I don't know her name. I wasn't given that in my dreams. He thought of the other victims. *I don't have any names at all. I wasn't given any names in my dreams. They didn't have names! None of the victims had names! Cain felt perplexed, trapped.*

"Um, well, I'm sorry…but I don't actually have a name. She's involved in cellular biology research dealing with cancer."

"We have lots of people here at the university who are involved in different types of research. I really have no way of helping you without a name."

It was a crazy question, but Cain threw it out there just in case.

"Have you ever had a professor murdered on your campus?"

"I'm sorry, what was that?"

"Has anybody ever been killed at Virchow Lecture Hall, near the Karkinos Research Center?"

"Well, first of all, I have no idea what you mean. I've never heard of either one of those places. And though that's a very strange question, I've been here at the university for nearly thirty years and no, not that I'm aware of. At least not in that timeframe."

"What do you mean by you've never heard of either of those places?"

"Well, exactly what I said. There isn't a lecture hall or a cancer research center on this campus by those names. Are you sure you have the right university?"

"Maybe I'm mistaken. Thank you for your help."

Nothing! The lecture hall and the research institute don't exist. I don't get it.

Once again, Cain quickly flipped through the pages of the phone book, desperately trying to find a number for the cities philharmonic orchestra or the civic center.

"Crossroad's Civic Center," Cain read.

He called the number.

"Hello, you have reached the general offices of the Crossroad's Civic Center, if you know your party's extension please dial . . ."

Cain was frustrated. He dialed "0". It rang several times.

"Civic Center, how may I help you?"

"Yes, I'm looking for a conductor. I'm a detective with the Crossroad's Police Department and I need to speak with him concerning a case I'm involved with."

Okay, now you're going crazy. Cain thought to himself. *You're not a cop and this is impersonating a police officer!*

"Hello?" an older gentleman answered on the other end of the line. "Can I help you with something?"

Cain immediately recognized from the man's voice that he was much older than the victim in his dreams.

"Yes, I just need to ask you a few questions pertaining to a case I'm working on."

"I'm not aware of any investigation involving the Civic Center. Usually the city is fairly forthcoming with us when it has to do with things like that."

"Oh no, it doesn't involve you directly, sir." Cain was trying hard to think of a way he could ask a question that when answered would give him the most information. "Do you have a younger conductor who works with the philharmonic who happens to live out near the lake in the canyons area?"

"We don't have any other conductors on staff here. I've been here for almost forty years. Occasionally we'll have a guest conductor come in and work with our group. Other than that, no, there's never been any other conductors who've worked here. It would've been nice, because I've wanted to mentor someone for years. Apparently, the City of Crossroads never saw that as a priority. Now, where did you say this person lived? I've never even heard of a place called 'The Canyons'."

Cain bypassed the man's question. "He would have probably been in his late thirties."

"Oh, absolutely not. The youngest conductor we've ever had visit us was well into his fifties."

Cain felt insane asking the next question.

"Have . . . well . . . have any of them ever been murdered?"

The man on the other end of the line had a slightly irritated tone in his voice as he answered the question. "I would think that as a City of Crossroads detective you wouldn't need me to answer that question for you, so I'm not so sure I believe you're being truthful with me, but the answer is no. Now if you'll excuse me, whoever you are, I really don't have time for this."

The line went dead on the other end. *Ticked him off,* Cain thought. *Okay, Strike two! I'm never going to find these people. This is insane. What am I thinking? I don't even know who they are. Maybe Ray can help me with it.*

Cain pressed the call button for the nurse.

"Can I help you?" a voice asked.

"Can you send my nurse in, please?"

"I'll tell her you need her."

He sat in his bed staring around the room. He felt like he was trapped. There was so much going on inside his head. He thought about the past, his wife, his children and Elsie. He just wanted answers, anything that would help him find the truth or the reason behind the things he was feeling. There had to be something.

The light was bothering him. He closed his eyes and dozed off to sleep.

The door thudding against the wall awakened him. It was his nurse, Cathy. "Can I get something for you?"

"I need something for this headache?"

"There's an order for that. I'll get it. Is that all you need?"

"One more thing. Do you know when Ray is supposed to be here?"

I'm not sure. We talked to him the day you came to and they had some loose ends to take care of with his wife's mom. They were driving back as soon as that was done. I'll try to put a call in to him to see if they've left yet."

Cathy returned with a syringe and attached it to his IV and pushed in a small amount of liquid.

"Thank you."

"Let me know if you need anything else."

The events of the day coupled with the emotions Cain had experienced had worn hard on his strength, exhausting him. He drank some ice water from the cup on his tray, shuffled around his sheets and blanket until he found the remote, then turned off the remaining lights that were bothering his eyes. It was dark, quiet and peaceful and the medication was starting to take affect. Cain fell into a deep sleep.

Nothing could have prepared him for what that sleep held for him.

Cain was dreaming…

He and Delores stood on a long, paved driveway. Delores cradled a small child in her arms. The child was an infant boy. The little boy was naked and covered with fluids like he had just been born. Cain didn't recognize the little boy. He didn't understand.

Ahead of them in the distance was a house, which sat on a beautiful acreage. In front of the house was a Jaguar and a 1969 Mustang. Sitting to the far side by itself was a mint condition 1953 Corvette that Cain insisted on purchasing and restoring on the anniversary of his twenty-fifth year of practice.

They walked toward the house. Beautiful trees and hedges shot upward at the front of the residence. Rose bushes lined a garden area near a circular brick drive with a large stone fountain in the middle. They came to the front door, its crystal glass inserts shining like bright diamonds and sparkling in the sunlight. They opened the door and walked into the house.

Just inside the front door was a beautiful marble entryway. A chandelier hung above their heads, glistening, and splattering its prisms of light across the wall and onto the marble floor. An arched staircase ascending to the second level spun across in front of them from the left to the right.

There was laughter and classical music coming from another area of the house. They turned to the right into an expansive living room with leather couches and a polished mahogany coffee and end table set. An oil painting decorated the wall near a marble fireplace and a large Asian vase sat on plush white carpet. They walked through the living room into a kitchen filled with stainless appliances, cherry cabinets and marble countertops.

The laughter was coming from a dining room off the kitchen. There were four people lounging at a small table covered with a white tablecloth. It looked like two couples gathered together for dinner and some drinks. The couples were misted in a shadowy shroud. One woman was visibly pregnant. She spoke into the mist. Her voice was distinguishable, clear. It was Delores. Cain heard his own voice coming from the shadowy figure next to her. Two tall candles were burning. There were white roses in a vase on the table, and next to the roses a bottle of wine with a rustic off-white label with the date barely visible. Cain and Delores stood watching the scene. It was as if they were experiencing something that had happened at a different time, viewing it now from another dimension.

The couples in the room laughed as they toasted each other with their wine glasses. The red wine sparkled. Against the wall stood a hutch full of fine china and serving dishes.

Cain recognized the older man and woman, but wasn't really sure who they were. The air of their conversation seemed to switch to a more serious subject. The older woman spoke.

"You know, we didn't let something like this slow us down when Moran first started his practice. It's far too inconvenient. There's too much to do. You're just getting going. You've only been at this a few years now. You need more time. You really don't need to have yourself tied down like that. There are relationships to build. There's business to tend to. I mean, we made the same move and we don't regret it. We took care of it a little sooner when it happened to us. You know, sometimes little things pop up in life and you just have to make them go away. Now's just not the best time, is it dear? Not this early in Cain's practice."

The older man spoke. "Oh, I agree. Even later on it seems like it's impossible to juggle a practice and activities and everything that comes with that. I really need you to be committed right now, Cain. You and Delores can come by on Sunday. With the new laws in place we can perform the procedure so much farther along now. I'll have one of the nurses scheduled in and we'll take care of it. Amelia is usually available on Sundays. That way nobody else is there. The young couple at the table both looked at each other.

"We've actually discussed this quite a bit already. We'll be there," the younger Cain said as he looked at his young wife. Delores gave him an apprehensive look.

Cain and his wife lingered at the side of the room, listening to the four talk, watching themselves curiously. They both looked down at the little infant boy in her arms. They looked at each other, eye to eye, contemplating. The room went silent but for the sound of the symphony music. The four were gone, leaving the room and the empty table with no settings or decorations, the two lifeless candles standing sentry.

Just off the dining area was a set of French Doors that led to the patio at the back of the house. Cain and his wife opened one of the doors and stepped onto the patio. Its area was expansive, running the distance of one side of the house, then around the entire length to the other side. Mixes of beautiful colored stone blended together with flowers that cascaded out of large planters. To one side of the patio was an outdoor eating area with a stone fireplace and a slate kitchen. To the other side was more sitting area surrounding a crystal blue infinity pool that disappeared into the landscape.

From the middle of the patio, wide stone steps led to formal garden areas. Both large and small trees of different sizes and shapes rose up from the groomed acreage. Trees surrounded the border of the yard and flowering trees sprinkled their blossoms on the green lawns below. To the right side of the property was a small planting of rose bushes. Just in front of the rose bushes was a sitting bench, and several pine trees rose up around the bench. Directly in front of the bench and roses was an acre pond. Ducks swam near its shoreline.

Beyond that toward the left side of the sprawling estate a rectangular patch of tall grasses and weeds grew upwards. It was surrounded by an old broken fence, it's posts having been hand cut from twisted wood branches. A small gate with worn swirled circular patterns of willow sat in a permanent open position, stuck in the tall grasses. Rabbits ran in and out.

Not far from the fenced in area, another patch of weeds about fifteen feet across stood blowing in the breeze and just beyond that several rows of fruit trees stood. Some fruit hung from the branches but most lay coloring the ground beneath the trees and rotting.

Rising up from the weeds that surrounded it, almost as if it didn't belong, a rustic looking greenhouse stood, sections of its glass looking faded and worn from dirt, the wood weathered to a light gray. Small chips of white paint peeled back, curled, holding onto the wood in a defiant stance of victory against the elements. A brick foundation wall rose up from the weeds, barely visible, to meet the lowest section of glass.

On the top of the greenhouse were two pinnacles, their weathervane arrows pointing in different directions. Atop one of the pinnacles, a large hawk perched, fat from the abundance of prey from the yard and pecking and tearing at what looked like the flesh of a small animal.

My father's acreage . . . my estate . . . this is my estate!

Cain and his wife stopped in the middle of the patio overlooking the grounds of the estate. They looked down at the child in their arms and thought of the older couple at the table inside the house. Cain took the child in his hands. They knelt down and placed the little boy on the stone patio in front of them.

Delores lifted her head up, a saddened look on her face. His eyes met hers. With a sudden thrust of his arm he drove something into the back of the child's head. Cain took a deep breath. Something inside of him started to close off, to shut down. Wrong, his mind thought. He displaced the thought. A numbing deadness came over his psyche, blocking out even the minutest feeling of human empathy. Something inside of him tried to push upward, through the numbness.

A light. A burst of light. "Cain . . . no," he heard his father's voice. "You'll regret this the rest of your life."

Cain pushed the instrument farther into the child's head. The light darkened, but once again tried to surface. The darkness swooned over him, spinning around him. It shot inward, invading the recesses of his conscience. Another light tried to break through. *No!* Cain thought. The dimming light flickered. Then, like a cold sun setting over some distant arctic region, any light that remained slowly dimmed. The coldness, the darkness, had won. There was a void in Cain's mind. No anger, no rage, just emptiness.

A darkness fell over his soul.

The child's legs shot outward as his nerves responded to the pain. Cain twisted the implement in his hand, methodically scrambling the brains of the little boy, his arms and legs shaking.

Then, in a shocking flash of confusion and light, the child shifted in shape and became a full grown man. Cain gazed down into the eyes of the symphony conductor from his dream world. The man shook and trembled. He looked at Cain. Cain remembered Ray's question, *"Did you see who did this to you?"* The man convulsed again, his arms and legs shaking. He seemed to be almost whimpering. He attempted to speak, and what he said sent chills through Cain's body.

"Mmmm…Mother…Father…why?"

He looked at Cain and then at Delores and back at Cain again. Blood poured from his head onto the patio. The man again looked at both of them. His face was losing color. It turned pale, ashen. He started convulsing sharply. His eyes went straight forward into a blank stare. He stopped moving. Cain held his hands in front of him. His hands were twisted and covered in blood. The symphony music faded and then stopped. A little baby boy lay dead on the patio before him.

Cain awoke and lay there on his side staring at the reflection of himself in the shiny railing of his bed. *Who am I? Who was this man, this child? What does this mean, this little boy? Who . . .?*

Cain remembered.

He pushed his thoughts deep within.

I'm not ready to deal with that!

20

The nurse walked into his room and noticed his blank stare and a single tear that had formed at the edge of his eye. The tear rolled to the bandages and soaked in. She didn't know what to say.

"Doctor Daniels, is there anything I can get you?"

"No, thank you."

"Have you watched TV at all?"

"No."

"Do you like reading? I could get you something to read."

"No! I don't feel much like reading."

"Well, here's the remote in case you change your mind. I could find you a couple of things to read for later?"

She wasn't getting it.

"That's fine," Cain said.

Cain lay on his bed staring forward, lost in his thoughts as the nurse walked about the room checking the IV pump and the monitor he was tethered to. He was free from the soft restraints that had originally bound him to the bed. They were removed after his talk with Doctor Cornelder.

"I'd like to go for a walk."

"Let me check with the doctor. Even with the therapy your legs are probably still very weak."

He didn't wait for her to return. He gathered himself together and sat up on the edge of the bed. He had already done this a couple of times, sitting on his bed and standing for a short time, but had yet to walk any farther than the window in his room. His legs wobbled as he put the weight of his body on them. They did feel weak and were shaking. He began to get dizzy. He made himself stay standing, steadying himself with the pole his IV was attached to. The dizziness slowly subsided and he started to shuffle toward the door, not realizing the IV pump was plugged into the wall. He had to stop halfway to the door and yank the plug from the wall to release it. He was just about completely out the door when several of the nursing staff noticed him and jumped up from their station.

"Doctor Daniels, you need to get back to your room. That's not such a good idea . . ."

The nurses were interrupted by Doctor Cornelder.

"It's okay, let him be. I'll walk with him."

Doctor Cornelder walked up next to Cain and gripped the arm Cain wasn't using to hold onto the IV rack.

"You don't mind if I help you a little, do you?"

"No," Cain said, realizing that he didn't have as much strength as he had originally thought.

Cain slowly walked down the long hallway. After about twenty feet Doctor Cornelder became concerned about his shaky, wobbling legs.

"Are you alright? Do you want to go back?"

"I . . . I want to keep walking."

Doctor Cornelder seemed to give him more liberty than another patient might receive.

Cain was tired, but struggled and spoke. "I remember the hospital. I remember being here, not so much where my room is at, but when I looked out the window I knew the buildings, the drive. It's all very familiar. I could even remember the spot where I parked my car, the side entrance I used, a lot of it. Some stuff, it's fuzzy, but not everything. I worked in the building to the left just off the parking lot.

They walked for what seemed like a long time, leaving the wing where his room was and going into another hallway. A skywalk crossing from one building gave Cain a view of the driveway below and cars passing underneath. It made him think of the accident. He looked away, pushing the thought from his mind. They came to a lounge area with a grand piano. Couches filled the room. Magazines lay on coffee tables. Display cases held artwork, pottery and items people could purchase at the hospital's little gift shop. Along one of the walls were pictures of hospital CEOs and surgeons. There were pictures in color and black and white. Some of the men in the black and white photos wore out of date horned-rimmed glasses that seemed to now cry out for people to not look at their once dignified picture. Past all of the individual pictures were group photographs of people from different departments, each one portraying the uniform or style of dress from that era.

Cain's eyes looked over the pictures as he slowly walked down the long hallway. He came to a stop in front of an older color photograph. The group stood in front of the sign for the building across the drive from the main hospital. Crossroads Planned Parenting Clinic 924 North 25th Street.

Cain's vision blurred as he stared at the picture. An uneasy feeling struck him. He felt as though he was slipping between reality and his dream world again. There was something about the picture that resonated within his soul. Cain's eyes widened as he realized he was looking at the same picture he had seen in his dream world in the conductor's house, except now, it was different. Someone was missing. There was no young teen in the photograph. The conductor's childhood image was missing and the man that had stood out to Cain in his dream state now stood out to him as never before.

Cain stared at the man in the picture and began to feel sick. He was staring at the man from his nightmares. He was staring at the killer! *The killer is real.* This was the man whom he had watched kill the children. It was as if now, the killer had gutted Cain and was pulling out his entrails. Cain's insides hurt. His heart pounded in his chest. All of the insanity seemed to come back to him at once. He was reviled by the man's image, his soul, his spirit, grieved. *I know this man* . . . Cain thought. *Who are you?*

He remembered the man from his dreams, businesslike, as in the picture before him. He remembered the children again. He saw them struggling, their legs kicking, trying to get away from the man's grip. He saw their bodies go limp. He saw the room, the table, the man's face. The numbered tags dangled from their legs. Then, the numbers seemed to lift away and fly past Cain's face, larger, more clear to him. 1,4,6,7,5,3 disappearing into the air.

Cain tried desperately to focus on the picture, only to have the images of the little children and the killer play out again in his mind. Then it happened. It came together for him as never before.

As he thought of the murdered children, each of their faces overlapped with the face of one of the adult victims from his dream world. A child's face would fade, shift shape and grow older, toddler, adolescent, teen, and then the adult victim. The murder scenes streamed across his consciousness, lights fluttering, strobing. In each scene was the adult victim, and a ghostly image of the same person as an adolescent. Each were one in the same person!

It was like a movie reel had begun to play in his mind. He had gone totally tunnel vision. The hallway was now an empty backdrop void of anything real. He entered what seemed like another dimension, oblivious to anything around him. The darkness, the void, flickered with bursts of light.

The poem rolled across his mind, voices of small children in unison speaking aloud . . .

"Seed sown this reaper's slave, seed sown, your wife not saved."

A flash, a flickering of light in the darkness.

From out of the darkness Delores' sweet voice beckoned his attention. "If she had lived, Cain, I would be with you." The face of a little girl victim on the metal table flashed and faded and became the face of the cellular biologist from the university. He saw Delores in his mind. She held out her hand and opened it, revealing the beautiful sapphire bracelet. "She was bringing the cure. He stopped her."

"Seed sown from a reaper's slave . . ."

Nick stood before him in the void. "I didn't have to die in Africa. I wouldn't have been there. He was going to feed them, but the killer stopped him. As a child, he cut him down. Stay his hand, father. Quench the fire of his confused calling."

Cain's mind exploded into a flash of bright sunlit sky. He was flying now, high above a desert region, a dry and parched land beneath him, lines cracked across the face of the hardened sod, overlapping flakes of dried ground peeling up. He slowed, then descended, alighting upon the dusty ground. African children surrounded him, thronging about him, their arms, their hands, touching him.

In front of Cain and the children stood the geneticist, grain pouring off his hands and through his fingers. In a great, sweeping motion he threw the grain upward and across the land. As the grain hit the ground, greenery burst forth, new growth, crops in abundance. The children walked, then ran forward and dispersed across the sea of green, dancing through the crops, celebrating.

Cain's eyes turned downward, looking at the dirt beneath his feet. Near them lay his son's Medal of Honor. He lifted his eyes toward the geneticist, who was now looking directly at him and shaking his head back and forth in a "no" motion, a sense of depression across his face. The man's eyes went downcast, distraught, saddened.

The new growth around him began to wither, shrivel up, and die. The children went silent from their celebration, struggling forward now as they walked. They dropped to their knees, to their hands, clutching at what was once again dry, hardened soil. Their skin stretched across malnourished, skeletal bodies, ribs pronounced as they heaved in deep breaths, struggling for life. They stopped moving and slumped over into the ground. A vulture landed nearby.

There was a flash and fluttering lights. Dust and smoke swirled up from the ground around him. In his mind he spun in a circle, a new vision appearing, a village, a violent firefight ensuing about him, an explosion to his far left. He watched as Nicholas pulled a man into the cover of a military vehicle. Then, as his son stood again and turned to fight, took a round in the chest, then the face, falling backward, his body landing near the wheel of the vehicle. Grain from the truck poured from damaged bags onto the ground.

Again, children's voices in unison . . .

"Seed sown, your son not saved."

Cain shook his head, attempting to clear his thoughts. For a moment he regained his awareness, his eyes focusing on the tightly looped carpet at his feet. Yet once again, his vision blurred, consumed by the images of more victims. Out of the darkness, the void, appeared the murdered mechanic, haunting, and the trooper, his body torn. There were flashes of light around him, circular spinning motions, a loss of focus. Suddenly, he was there again, in the bay of the old auto shop. There was a smell of gas, oil and brake fluid.

Cain focused on the mechanic and his cold, dead stare. Blood oozed from the number seven carved in his chest and brake fluid dripped from his fingers. The mechanics dead, sunken eyes came alive and he looked at Cain.

"His brakes . . . I would've fixed."

"I would have arrested him," the trooper spoke. "But I was never there to stop him."

The faces of two infant boys spun across Cain's mind.

"We never were," the mechanic spoke. "He killed us as children."

Like animated ghosts they crouched forward toward Cain, holding out their hands and opening them. Two tiny locks of Elsie's hair fell from their hands and floated to the floor as the men faded into the air.

Instantly, Cain was re-living it all again. Elsie's giggle echoed through his mind as he saw the light flash across the passenger window of the car, the glass shattering as the drunk driver crashed into him and his little granddaughter, killing her.

Children's voices, again, called out to him from the void.

"Seed sown, Elsie . . . Elsie . . ."

Her name echoed. Cain's mind spun. His dream world was colliding with his real world. *Am I supposed to stop a real killer? Did he kill children who would have brought hope into this world? People who as adults would've saved my family? No! This man isn't real. He's from some netherworld. He doesn't exist. He can't possibly be real.*

A heavenly voice whispered across his mind . . .

"Your family didn't have to die."

In his mind Cain was trying to bring himself back into reality. Anxiety gripped him. He couldn't seem to pull himself from his thoughts. What were only seconds seemed like an eternity.

Dr. Cornelder spoke. "Cain, are you all right?"

"I . . . I don't know."

"Would you like to go back?"

Doctor Cornelder's voice was interrupted by another flash of light, his voice becoming muffled and inaudible for Cain, distant. Cain bowed his head down, placing his hand on the side of his face over his eye. It hurt.

Again, a voice, Kelly's tired voice, spoke into the void around him.

"I needed their love, father, their encouragement. My teacher would've given me hope. My best friend and her mom, I would've never used drugs if they had been in my life. If only we'd met in dance class when I was little, how different it would have been."

Cain remembered the words of the girl's father.

"That's Kelly Daniels, my daughter's best friend. They're pretty much inseparable. They met in dance class when they were little."

But Kelly never knew this girl, Cain thought.

From the darkness appeared the matriarch who had been so brutally murdered in her living room. She held out her hand and opened it, a bloodied photograph of Kelly falling away.

"He killed me as a little girl. My daughter was never conceived. Kelly never knew our love."

Her image faded into the void.

There were flashes of light. In the flashes Cain saw the woman and the teacher standing near a stainless steel table, then darkness. The scene returned again. their infant bodies laying on the table. The numbers eight and six floated away from them, spinning past Cain's head in the darkness.

Then, suddenly, he was there again, in the woman's living room, facing the wall of photographs, watching as the pictures of the family splintered into a thousand pieces and dissolved into the air around him, a blank, empty wall remaining. *Kelly would've had a different life if she'd known this girl. I would still have my Kelly.*

Cain thought of the husband's words to him . . .

"My wife and her were really close. My daughter and Kelly started a peer group at the high school to help kids deal with teen issues. Kelly's got a full scholarship to college in the fall.

And the daughter's words . . .

"Her dad's in the hospital. He was in an accident. I'm Kelly's best friend."

Children's voices, again, rang out . . .

"Seed sown, your daughter lost."

Cain's mind was reeling. *Delores, Nick, Kelly, Elsie. The people who would've saved them, this man killed them when they were just little children. He took their lives before they could fulfill their destinies!*

He drowned their voices...

"He stopped them from doing what they would have done!"

Each child fought to get away...

Cain understood. *He killed them as children! These people were real, their lives cut short by this vicious killer.*

Vindicate, the souls of the children scream.

They want me to vindicate them! Cain had finally figured out the mystery. His dreams did have a message. The message was to find this man, this child killer. *He's real!* Cain knew he had to stop him. *I've been sent a message from beyond the grave. The children, my family, they want me to stop him before he kills again. Not one more child will be murdered at the hands of this man. I'm going to find out who he is and stop him!*

"*Only you can stop him, Grandpa!*" Cain remembered Elsie's little voice in the hospital room.

He tried to think if he knew him. His mind was still foggy, confused, from tiredness and his injury.

He's standing in front of that clinic. I've got to be able to figure this out. But I just can't seem to remember these people clearly. My head, it hurts so much.

"This man right here, he..." Cain started to speak.

"Do you recognize him, Cain?" Doctor Cornelder asked.

"Yes, but I can't quite place him. I can't remember who he is. I can't remember any of these people. It's important that I remember who he is," Cain said. *You have no idea what he's done. I've seen it. I know things about him.* Cain thought.

"Cain, that picture's over thirty years old. That man is much older now. He looks different today. You may not recognize him, even if he was standing . . . right next to you. I know this has been stressful for you. You've probably walked too far. Why don't we go back now?"

"No, I have to know who he is! I have to find him."

Cain thought to himself. *You really have no idea how much he's changed things.*

Doctor Cornelder just stood there behind Cain, watching him stare at the picture. His lips contorted into a strange grin and a twinkle came to his eyes, as though he held some piece of information that Cain desperately needed to have.

He reached forward, toward Cain, and rested his hand on Cain's shoulder.

"If you don't really know who he is, I'll tell you," he said, nearly cynically.

"Yes, tell me. *For when I know, I will do everything within me to stop his rampage. He will never lay hands on an innocent child ever again!*

"That man is standing right here in this hallway."

Cain's heart raced violently within him. He went flush, his body trying desperately to pull strength from his last breath of air. He turned hard and fast, gazing upon the elderly man standing before him.

"Cain . . . that man is you."

That man is you…that man is you…that man is you…

The words echoed through Cain's mind like they were shouted into an empty void. The void soon filled with emotion and confusion. Cain felt dizzy. He reached up and touched the bandages on his face. *No.*

He looked back at the picture. A flood of thoughts rushed into his mind. He began to fully remember the building behind the group of people. He thought of the dream about his estate, the two couples, and remembered who the little boy was. He thought of Delores. *No!* Cain thought. *Not that. I don't want to remember that.* In his mind he watched as he walked up to the building with the older man, Moran, from the dream about his estate. Delores, visibly pregnant, walked with them. The older man unlocked the door to the building. A young woman met them inside the door. "Good morning Amelia," his mentor had said. "It's a beautiful Sunday, isn't it?" They walked into the lobby area. It was the lobby that the young girl from his dreams had been sitting in. They went through a door and into a hallway that had rooms on both sides. It was the hallway from his dreams. He pictured the girl screaming and crying uncontrollably while running down the hallway and out the front door. He remembered thinking he would never see her again. She was real! He remembered it happening. He remembered the hallway, opening the wrong door; the smell, the tears, the fear in her eyes. He had shaken his head after she ran off. Amelia had said, "That's okay, Doctor Daniels, she'll be back. They always come back. Oh well, not the number we'd planned on. What's that, seven, eight for the day? Maybe we can all make it home early, huh?"

The older doctor walked through one of the doors off the same hallway and invited Cain and his wife in.

"I'll get Amelia to prep you, Delores. This shouldn't take

more than an hour or so. Cain, if you'll come with me, I'll go over the new procedure with you before you do it."

Cain kept looking at the picture in the hallway. He felt nauseous.

"Are you alright?"

"I'd like to go back to my room now."

"Okay."

As they walked, Cain thought about his visit to the building with Delores. He remembered it all. The nurse, Amelia, coming to the office where he and the older doctor sat, telling them Delores was prepped for the procedure. He remembered walking into the room and seeing his wife in a hospital gown with her knees up. He thought of the equipment tables, the cannula, the forceps . . .

Implements of destruction . . .

From the safety of the sanctum womb . . .

His own flesh he chose to destroy, tormented now, his little boy.

He remembered as Moran, his mentor, took him step by step through the new medical procedure. He remembered the child's head on the ultrasound screen. The arms. The legs. As the little body twisted in the ultrasound image, it became obvious that the child was a boy. He remembered pulling the little boy's body from Delores' birth canal, leaving only the head inside, then the quick yet simple thrust of the instrument into the child's head at the base of its skull. He remembered the sound of the suction tubes and the older doctor placing a tag with the number five on the leg of the little boy that had been ripped from his wife's womb. A familiar rhyme danced through Cain's mind.

"5, 4, 7, 6, 3, 2, 1, can't turn back time, you killed your son."

Cain had felt a deep, intense feeling inside as the machine went silent and he looked at Delores. Tears streamed down her cheeks. Her strength, her confidence, all he knew her to be, wasn't there. Her eyes looked empty. They had killed a son. He undeniably stared down at the lifeless body of a little boy.

The walk back to the room seemed to take an eternity. Cain walked into his room and went straight to the bathroom.

"Cain, will you be alright by yourself?"

"Yeah."

"Just pull on the cord if you need us."

Doctor Cornelder walked out of the room, shaking his head in bewilderment, shrugging off Cain's odd behavior and silence, feeling Cain should've been glad to have fully remembered who he was.

Cain pulled the bathroom door shut behind him. He reached up to his face and began to peel away the bandages. He closed his eyes as he did it, as though he was hiding from whatever he may find, bowing his head. Bits of old flesh came away with the bandages and fell into the sink, but the pain was minimal. His face didn't hurt. He had healed completely. He thought of the dream, of Elsie, leading him across his estate to the greenhouse washroom. He lifted his head and opened his eyes to see the murderous face of the killer from his dreamworld, the man from the photograph of the clinic, just older now. He knew who he was. *I killed those children. Me. I did. I killed the people who would've saved my family. I killed them as children. I aborted them, all in one day, over thirty years ago.*

Cain had taken just about all he could handle. He punched the mirror with all the might he could muster, splintering it, breaking open the skin on his knuckles. He grabbed the towels and the towel rack like he was going to tear the rack out of the wall but couldn't. He kicked the trashcan and threw the towels and the washcloths, knocking over everything from the sink. He collapsed against the wall and slowly slid to the floor sobbing. He was exhausted, but his memory would not be shut off. As he sat on the bathroom floor, one final haunting memory came to him.

Sitting in his office at the birthing clinic, he had held medical release of liability papers in his hand. These were the papers from the procedure he and his mentor had performed on Delores. It had been several years since that day. Delores was pregnant again with what would be their first, born son, Nicholas. Now, he sat staring at the papers. On the day of the procedure he had set them in the top left drawer of his desk, closed the drawer, and locked it.

Until that day, the drawer had never been opened. In the bottom right corner of the paper was Delores' signature. At the bottom left corner, under the title 'attending physician', was his. He had slid open the right drawer of the desk and moved a box of cigars to one side, looking around in the drawer. He lifted the cigar box lid and pulled from the box a shiny chrome plated flip top lighter he had bought while in medical school, its Asclepius symbol faded and worn. "My children will not know of this," Cain had said out loud as he held the paper in front of himself and lit the bottom right corner, letting it burn for as long as he could hold it before dropping it in the metal waste basket. There was nothing left of the paper except the small upper left corner, just big enough for his thumb and forefinger to hold it. He had held the corner so tightly that his fingerprint had been impressed upon the paper and the carbon sheet below. He peeled his finger away, revealing a perfect impression of his fingerprint. *Guilty*, he had thought at the time. He opened the lighter top, pushed the little piece of paper into its flip top lid, then closed it. He thought of Delores' tears that day, the emptiness in her eyes. *Somehow, though, I know I should never forget."*

Cain awoke the next day feeling tired, kind of in a sleepy slumber, but still rested compared to the day before. He had spent the night in and out of sleep, thinking continually in his waking moments of the little boy he had aborted that day at the clinic and the conductor from his dream world. He thought of his wife, son, daughter and granddaughter. He thought of the murder victims, that if they were truly real, if everything he now knew and felt was true, then he had in fact stopped them from fulfilling their destinies. He had stopped the very people from ever living their lives who would have saved his family from dying.

Did I really take those adult victims from this world when they were little children? Did I abort them in the first years of my practice, thirty-seven years ago, children who would have eventually saved Delores, Nicholas, Kelly and Elsie by simply living out their lives and becoming who they were meant to be? If so, then by default, I killed my own family.

There seemed to be a reality here that he didn't want to accept. Was this some crazy coma induced menagerie of confused thought, or reality? Had he not taken those people from this world when they were children, would they have become what they were in his dream world and saved his loved ones? They all would have been in their late thirties now, living out their careers, having families. A geneticist, biologist, a trooper, the others. Their children? What has the world lost? He would never know, because they were gone either way.

Cain sat in silence, thinking about it.

Then he got a crazy thought.

One survived!

He thought of the young woman from the clinic in his dream world and of the little boy in her arms. He remembered the picture on the table inside the house where he had tried to take his final victim before being stopped, his final dream while in his dream world, the dream where he was caught by Ray and Greg and arrested. This victim, this man, this little child, had survived. "Is that little boy alive?" He pondered aloud. "He would be grown now! He'd be almost forty."

I can know! I can know if this is all real. I just have to find the one who survived! But I don't know who he is. I have no way of finding him. No! As soon as I get out of here I'll go to the house in the River Bend District. I'll see if its there. I'll see if he's there!

Cain searched the room for the little remote call box for the nurse. He pushed aside a couple CDs and thought of what he had told the nurse about wishing one of his children would've become interested in classical music. He thought of the child, the man, who may have become that son. He couldn't think about it anymore. It hurt too much. He finally found the callbox up against his side. He looked around the room, then at the window. He could see it was dark outside. He tapped the light symbol on the remote, shutting off the main lights in the room. He was tired, exhausted. He fell asleep.

21

"Cain, Cain, wake up Uncle Cain!"

Cain could feel Kenny pushing on his arm. At first it was unreal. He was half asleep, exhausted from the mental roller coaster he'd been riding and the intensity of the day before.

"Caaaaiiinnnn," Kenny said again, dragging out Cain's name and smacking him on the chest. "Hey! Wake up!"

Cain stirred awake. Kenny sat on the edge of the bed with a frustrated look on his face, one foot dangling above the floor and one folded underneath him. Cain realized who Kenny was and instantly grabbed him and pulled him into himself in a huge bear hug.

"Kenny, oh man, I missed you!" Cain felt odd saying it because he couldn't really remember much about Ray and his family in real life. He began to tear up.

"I missed you, too, Cain. Where'd you go? Uh, you're smashing me!"

"I'm not really sure, Kenny, I'm not sure." Cain let up his

grip.

Ray had tears in his eyes. He reached past Kenny and grabbed Cain's shoulder and squeezed it.

"It's about time you came back. I was beginning to think you never would. Man, it's great to see you alert and awake for once."

Holly was crying, "And this little baby missed her Cain time like crazy."

Little Ranae, Kenny, Ray and Holly were just like Cain remembered them, or at least like he remembered them from his dreamworld. Cain knew one thing. He wanted to hold little Ranae.

"Can I hold her?"

"Of course you can hold her. She's your god-daughter."

"She is?"

"You were there the day she was born," Holly said.

"I was?"

"Yeah," Holly said, looking at him strangely and smiling. "Ray was upstate and we had to call you. Don't you remember? She came early after I fell. You came in from home and ended up assisting with the C-section because one of the doctors on the OB floor was busy with another one."

"I'm remembering different things, a little bit at a time, here and there. Some of it's really confusing. Trust me, when I tell you what I've been through, well, anyhow."

"How're you feeling?" Holly asked. "I see they took your bandages off."

"Yeah, your face looks really good. You can hardly tell you were in an acci . . ." Ray stopped himself, biting his tongue and becoming more serious. "Did you get the things we left you?"

Cain thought of Elsie, then slowly answered. He just wanted to sit there and bask in the presence of this little family.

"Yeah, I did. It really helped me put things together, you know, in my head."

"It was my idea." Kenny leaned toward him.

"Really? That was very smart! You have no idea how much it helped me remember, maybe a bit too much!"

Ranae was bouncing now, kind of jumping up and down as Cain held her sides. "Wow, she's gotten big, and strong."

"She's chunked up quite a bit," Holly said. "You're not so tiny anymore, are you baby?"

Ranae pushed her cheek into Cains. Cain felt ultra-aware of everything, all these little pieces of truth seemingly popping out in front of him as they became real, something tangible, something that was really happening.

"Where's Elsie?"

"She's next to Del, Kelly and Nick. Well, right next to Kelly. We waited as long as we could. We felt it best to lay her to rest. I haven't added anything to the bench, just her name. I . . . well, I thought maybe you'd want to do more, to add something special. Just wasn't sure if you'd ever come back."

Cain thought of the graveyard. He couldn't imagine his family there, all together. He started to wish he was there with them, that it was all just over.

"I really missed you, Cain," Kenny said.

"I missed you, Kenny." Tears swelled in his eyes.

"I've been watching your place," Ray said. "Everything's just fine. I get over there a couple times a week to make sure the cleaning company is doing what they need to. Haven't gotten the cars pulled into the garage yet. The Mustang's looking pretty dirty. I've just been too busy at work."

What Ray said triggered something in Cain's mind, yet he felt stupid not being fully aware of what Ray's work was.

"So, how is work?"

"Good, the usual," Ray said, not clarifying the information Cain was looking for.

"Anything new or exciting?"

"No, same old stuff. I don't know why I ever thought transferring to homicide in this little town was going to make my life more exciting."

"So, any new cases? Any murders?"

Ray let out a small laugh. "This city hasn't seen a murder for sixty years! Murders don't happen in Crossroads. Closest I've gotten to a murder is that book series about crime scene investigating you bought me for Christmas. You and I were reading them together for fun."

"I bought you those?"

"Yeah, you ordered it from one of those upstate bookstores because you couldn't find it locally. You thought I'd enjoy 'em. I let you hold onto one and you got hooked on the series. You've read most of them. I've only managed to read one."

"Oh, brother."

"What?"

"Forget it. Hey, I need you to look some things up for me, okay?" Cain said.

"I can try. What do you want me to do?"

"I'm not sure if it's even possible. I just . . ." Cain was hesitant to ask, figuring Ray would think he was crazy or something. "Okay, I need you to check the Canyons and see if there's a symphony conductor who lives there. I don't think he will, but . . ."

Ray looked at him oddly. "Wow, you wake up from a near coma and you're thinking about that crazy music of yours already. Yeah, I can do that. So where are these Canyons at?"

"On the north side of town, just off the bypass at Canyon's road. Past the main business district there's a little strip mall. You turn that hard left and head back north into the Canyons development. This guy's house is . . ."

"Cain," Ray interrupted, shaking his head. "I have no idea what you're talking about. I've never heard of a Canyons Road or the Canyons or a strip mall anywhere on that side of the city. That's all just fields. Can't see that ever getting developed. And God knows this city could use a bypass. You've been complaining about that ever since you built your place on the acreage and had to commute on all those old back roads. With all the ancients we've got on the county board, we'll probably never see that. We need some new blood, some younger people who want some development in town."

Great! Why would these places exist in my dream world but not in reality? Cain thought. *Crazy, absolutely crazy. The Civic Center is real. Crossroads University is real. Why not The Canyons? Why not the bypass? Oh my God . . .*

"Okay, Ray, I'm going to ask you some really crazy questions."

"Go ahead."

"What I really need is to take a spin around the city, but this will do for now. I'm going to name some places. Just bear with me. You tell me if they're real or not. There were all these crazy dreams I had while I was out."

"Fire away."

"Jack's Donuts?"

"Been going there for years. You've met me there a couple of times on the way to work in the morning. It's a favorite of the officers at my division."

"Have I met any of them?"

"You've been to some of our picnics and activities. You've met most of them, my bosses and superiors. You came to our family day at the division and toured the department. I locked you in a cell for fun. You've actually been dating one of our crime techs, Ana, pretty steady for a few months now, although I think she's a bit young for you. You met her at the department's family day, even danced with her. You and Elsie used to come to some of the events when it was just . . . just the two of you. You always brag about your cooking, so I volunteered you. You started spending a lot more time with us after Delores passed and Kenny got hit by that car the day he thought he could trek across town to your house on his own. He just had to see his Uncle Cain. It's a miracle he even made it that far. Holly was frantic. He'd gone missing for about three hours! You'd left work to help find him."

"Kenny got hit by a car?"

"Right out in front of your house. You went to check your place for him. They were loading him in the ambulance. It really freaked you out."

"I got my leg broke," Kenny said. "Don't you remember?"

"No, buddy, actually, I don't."

"I got to ride in the ambulance like my mom did."

"Was that fun?"

"A little, but it hurt. My dad said he thinks I learned my lesson the hard way or something like that."

Cain was getting tired. "Can I run a few more things past you, Ray?"

"Yeah, go ahead."

"There's a statue with its arms lifted up?"

"Don't worry, your statue is there. There you go again! What do you mean, arm's lifted up?" Ray asked.

"It stands there on the turn-around at the bottom of the hill with its arms lifted up. His chest is open and he's holding his heart of stone up toward the west, toward the sunset. It's called 'Heart of stone for a heart of flesh.' I think it's a bible scripture. The whole base is covered with trailing flowers every year that splash the hill with color and there's a beautiful Japanese Maple covering half the hill."

Ray looked at him with confusion. "Close, but not exact. There's never been flowers there, just grass, and no tree. His chest isn't open. He's just standing there with his arms up facing the sunrise. There's a bible verse, but not the one you said. It says, "I make all things new.""

Cain thought of the words etched into the cinderblock wall in the jail cell, in his dreamworld.

"What about the River Bend District? A bunch of older homes a few blocks from the river?"

"That was there when we were growing up. It still is."

"The Lake Estates?"

"Wow, you really did get hit hard! Sorry. . ." Ray shook his head, a little bewildered, but was now realizing he needed to give Cain plenty of patience. "We grew up there, Cain. It was developed years ago. Most of the houses have acreages. Now it's a mix of older and newer homes. That's the area where your house is, right there on the acreage we grew up on at mom and dad's property. You built your house there because you wanted to live in the country away from the city and I bought in town because of my work. I gave you my share of the property. You've kind of let most of it go back to the wild, not quite how dad kept things. It's been impossible to get down the trail to the river to fish, but I don't need to harp on you about it today. We've had that conversation enough times. "

"Is dad still around?"

Ray felt concern with Cain's question. "We lost dad ten years ago."

"Mom? I don't seem to have any memories of our mom."

"Well, Cain, you wouldn't. Dad raised us alone." Ray hesitated. "Mom died the day I was born."

Cain shook his head and sighed, then sat silent for a moment, his eyes closed. He thought of his father, the acreage.

He wanted more clues. "Old Town?"

"Yeah, there's an old town. It's on the west end of the city."

"Are you familiar with it?"

"I used to patrol there years ago."

"Is there an old ma and pa gas station on one of the corners, kind of toward the end of Main Street?"

"There was. That was a long time ago, though. It's been closed for years. The old man that ran it started having health problems, I think emphysema. After his wife passed away he kind of gave up on it."

"What about his kids? Did he have any kids? Didn't his son want to run it?

"He didn't have a son."

"Did he have children?"

"Four very beautiful daughters, none of who were interested

in running a garage or dating me. The place didn't sell, so they just shut it all down. It sits vacant to this day. I work with one of his nephews. He's a police officer. You've met him."

"Can we talk about something else?" Kenny said. "You guys are boring."

"Kenny, Uncle Cain needs to talk about this right now."

"So, Holly, how's your mom and dad?"

Holly got a puzzled look on her face. "Mom's doing okay, not great, but okay. She just moved out of state to be near my aunts. We had to get her into an assisted living apartment this week because they both still work and they're concerned about her walking away." Holly hesitated. "You went to dad's funeral with us last year."

"I'm so sorry, Holly. I'm really confused and not remembering things! I guess I know what your mom feels like now." Cain started to tear up, feeling frustrated. "A lot of its still just pieces."

Holly came close to Cain and gave him a big hug and kiss on the cheek. Ray sat down next to him on the opposite side of the bed and put his arm around him. Little Ranae was snuggled between them.

"I guess it's crush time!" Kenny said as he wrapped his arm around Cain's neck.

Holly spoke. "Don't worry. We'll make sure you come through this. We're here for you. We'll do this together."

"Man, I've missed you. I'm so glad you're real." Cain said.

"Real? What did you think? Did you think we were fake?" Kenny giggled and they all started laughing.

"You have no idea, Kenny. You have no idea!" Cain said, now struggling to keep his eyes open.

"I think Cain's getting a little tired. Why don't we give him a rest until tomorrow?" Ray said. "Maybe I'll come up during the afternoon or right after work."

"I wanna stay longer!" Kenny shouted.

"You'll get some more time with your Uncle Cain later,"

Holly said.

"I really love visiting, but I'm not gonna lie. My head hurts and I'm ready to drop again," Cain said. "I need you to come back though. You being here has lifted my spirits."

"We'll come back tomorrow," said Ray. "You guys go on out. I just need a minute with him alone, alright?"

"Come on buddy, get your jacket on." Holly handed Kenny his jacket.

Ray reached out to grab little Ranae and Cain pulled her in close and gave her one last big hug, stuffing his nose into her hair and breathing in deeply. "She still has that baby smell," Cain said.

"Holly." Ray handed Ranae off to her. "I'll be right out."

"Okay hun, we'll wait for you in the family area."

"See ya later, Cain," said Kenny. "Don't fall asleep for so long next time!"

Cain laughed inside.

"Oh, sleep's not my favorite place to be lately. I promise. Bye buddy, love you!"

Holly leaned over and gave Cain another kiss on the forehead and Cain pulled Ranae close and kissed her cheek.

"Come on, Kenny," said Holly.

Ray stood alone in the quiet room with Cain.

"You know, I hate to ask you, but it was such a big part of you before the accident. Cain, are you still being tormented by those dreams?" Ray asked.

"Dreams? What dreams? My whole life has been nothing but dreams for the last several, what, weeks probably. Ray, I don't know what you mean."

"Before your accident you were having dreams about a killer. Somebody was killing children in your dreams. I'm the only one you told about it. It had you to the point of near insanity. The killer would slowly turn around and it would be as though you were looking at yourself in a mirror. You were talking about retiring. You kept telling me that you couldn't get their voices out of your head. Dreams, nightmares, the poems."

"Poems?"

"You kept hearing voices in your head. You said you felt like the children were crying out to you from the dead. The children you had aborted during your years of practice."

"But you can't deny their resounding flood," Cain repeated the words aloud.

"What?"

"Nothing. Yeah. I was having those before my accident?"

"We talked about it a lot. When the hospital staff told me you had to be restrained so much, well, I thought maybe you were struggling with them again. They really messed with your mind and you'd lost a lot of sleep. I kept telling you to take some time off, to re-think some things, maybe look at retiring, being finished."

"Yeah, I had more dreams. But there was more, a lot more. Other people. Adult victims, not just children, one in the same, linked. Frankly, I don't even remember the dreams from before, and everything's just too much to go into right now, maybe tomorrow. I'd like you to help me sort something out. Some of the children I aborted in my practice, I think it changed some things. Things I wished it hadn't."

"What do you mean?"

"Life, Ray. It changed things in this life, in my life. If I had known then, in the beginning, what I know now, I would've done things differently."

"Alright, we'll talk about it later. It's probably not that big a deal anyhow. I love you, brother. I'll see you tomorrow. You try to get some rest, okay."

"Oh, I will, I'm pretty exhausted."

Man, Ray, you really have no idea. You have no idea where I've been and what I've been through. I won't have any trouble sleeping.

The TV remote cord had gotten tossed around in the shuffle of hugs. Cain finally found it again and after giving it a tug and releasing it from underneath his pillow and bedrail, he turned on the TV. He searched through the channels: cooking shows, home decorating, some reality show, an old movie, a sitcom, the news.

He settled on the news. The weather was followed by sports. There was a homicide in a big city across the state. *Hmm, no, not interested.* He bumped the channel up to the next news broadcast. The anchors small talked about the usual things: local happenings, the weather. The screen changed behind the anchors and a community story came on. One of the news anchors spoke.

"Tonight, we'll take you downtown to Pelili's where a local author is having a signing for his new book. The thirty-seven year old and a special guest, his mother, are at the bookstore this evening to sign copies of his first book. He says the book is dedicated to his mother, to her raising him as a single parent and to a man who . . . once tried to kill him."

The camera was zoomed in and focused on a man's hand signing a book. It spanned backward and away from the close-up to show the whole scene. Sitting at the table was the author Cain had nearly killed in his dream world and standing next to him was a middle-aged woman. It was the woman from the picture on the table in the man's house, an older version of the young woman from the clinic. *They're real!*

A nurse walked into Cain's room and checked his monitor and IV.

"Would you like the curtains closed?" the nurse said.

"No, you can leave them," said Cain, his mind alert from what he had just seen and his attention focused on the television.

"Do you like that author?

"I don't know who he is."

"He grew up in Crossroads and lives in River Bend. I donated his book to the wing when I finished it. I actually left it right here somewhere earlier. I got you that and some magazines to read. Let's see, it's should be right here." She shuffled through some books and magazines on the little shelf by the clock and handed a book to him. "Here it is. Maybe you should read it. Let me know if you need anything else. Dinner should be here soon." She left the room.

"When Blood Drops Fall."

Cain began to look over the cover. The book was a deep, blood red color. On the front was the title in white lettering. Across the rest of the cover was the gears of a timepiece, and imposed over them a single drop of blood. In the blood drop, nearly indistinguishable, upside down, was the body of a newborn child, his arms and hands curled as he came from the womb. On the back cover was a broken timepiece, its hands spinning away. The numbers, 5, 4, 7, 6, 3, 2, 1, floated through the air. The words, crushed and tangled bodies weave, under the numbers, and a summary:

Dear reader . . . suffer a thought . . . Is Cain losing his mind . . . nightmare . . .Crossroads . . . loved ones . . . destiny's clock . . . Victims . . .

Cain frantically opened the front of the book.

Redemption lies on many paths

He turned the pages.

Sometimes the blood of the innocent is shed to redeem the guilty.

To all who have ever felt they've gone too far.

And darkness fell . . .

And darkness fell?

Blood trickled down her tiny fingers . . .

Shadowy figure . . .

"What the . . . ?" Cain started to speak out loud. He quickly flipped through the pages from front to back.

He saw the last page of the chapter before the ending chapter. Cain looked to the right to read the final chapter of the book. The chapter heading stood out. It said, "The Final Chapter," but under the heading were no more words. There was no story. He flipped the page to see another blank page.

Blank? The final chapter had not been written!

"I will give you a heart of flesh for a heart of stone."

Cain thought of the statue.

I will give you a heart of . . .

Cain was frantic. *I don't understand. Am I even real? Am I just penned of some author's imagination? Am I insane? No. My family is gone. Ray and his family are real. Elsie was real. This author is real. I killed those people, those children. I aborted them. It changed my life, my family's lives, their destinies, forever. Too much of this is real for it not to be. I've found the one who survived. I've got to talk to him. I have to have answers. He . . . knows my beginning and . . . my end? I have to talk to him now!*

Cain tore his sheets off. He held the IV in place, turned off the drip dial and carefully pulled back on the tape, peeling it away from his arm. He held the IV needle with one finger on top and slid it out of his arm, wiping a drizzle of bloody saline solution on his gown's sleeve. He reached over and disconnected the monitor and shut it off completely. He looked around the room. He had a dilemma. There were no clothes. They had been cut from him after the accident. He looked in the closet for some reason, having a gambler's chance feeling that maybe he would get lucky and score some hidden stash wardrobe. He felt stupid, realizing the utter emptiness of the room.

He didn't care. He slid a second hospital gown over his back and buttoned it the best he could, tying the little fabric straps on his upper arms and down the front of his gown.

He had to know. He had to have the answers he was looking for. Now these two worlds had collided, and he was determined to figure it out.

He slowly cracked open the door to his room. The nursing station had only one nurse at it and she was facing the opposite direction. He felt like somebody trying to escape from a mental ward. He looked down the hallway toward the left side of the wing. No nurses. No doctors. Only a nursing assistant pushing a linen cart across the hallway and a man tying off a trash bag near a cleaning cart.

He darted the other way down the hallway and toward the exit of the hospital wing, hoping nobody would notice him in flight. At the end of the hallway he slid around the large doorframe near the elevators, out of sight of the hallway and the hospital wings staff. He pressed the down arrow.

Thoughts were running through his mind. *I'm not escaping; I should feel free to go. If I'm a doctor, then . . . Am I a doctor? Who am I? Is this real? Yes, it's real. Ray, Holly and the children were here just tonight!* He stood there in scattered thought waiting for the elevator to open. It was then that he noticed the elderly woman sitting on the small bench in the hallway outside of the elevator area. She was staring at him.

Was I just talking out loud? He nervously turned toward the elevator and watched as the numbers dropped from the 8th floor, 7th, 6th, 5th, ding. The elevator sounded its arrival and the doors slid open. He stood and waited as the elevator discharged it's cargo of people, leaving a younger woman and a little girl standing at the front and what appeared to be a family, parents and kids included, along with a couple of other people behind them, waiting for him to step into the elevator so they could continue to their destinations.

As he stepped into the elevator he realized the crazy appearance of the stealthy escape he had just made. *I'm not a mental patient. I can come and go as I please. Or can I?* He remembered the nurses injecting him with narcotics when he had awoken from his dream screaming. *Maybe they will come after me.*

I'm not crazy. He glanced back at the two people behind the family, relieved to see that they were wearing normal clothing and did not appear to be hospital staff.

He leaned against the wall of the elevator, looking forward at the young woman. She nervously looked back. The little girl holding her hand turned and looked at him.

"Hey mister, are you sick?"

"Maybe, a little," Cain said as he looked down at the hospital gown and the little slipper socks that had slid down to his ankles during his hurried escape. The draft of the elevator doors opening reminded him of his hairy legs, bare to the world. He anxiously double-checked the rest of his hospital gown, ensuring that it was secure, and gave a "please, you first" gesture to the woman and girl. The two hurried out of the elevator and into the busy lobby.

Now or never, Cain thought, then stepped out. He could see the main entrance and its turnstile doors through the crowded lobby. It seemed busy for that time of night. There was a

313

lounge area just to the left with couches and end tables and lamps. A man sat reading a newspaper, another a magazine. Two women stood talking. A young woman held a crying child and a small group of people of various sizes and shapes walked toward a sign that read "Emergency Room."

He walked toward the front door. He felt like he was being watched. He looked around. Nobody in particular was looking at him. *I am not dressed for the occasion; everybody here has probably looked at me already.* Once at the door, he waited for the big glass turnstile to flop past its point and stepped into the opening, walking around in a little half circle until he stood outside.

The air was warm. *At least it isn't winter. This could be cold.* He looked across the street at the clinic, which now seemed like some ominous beast laying in wait to devour the innocent. A still, calm voice spoke to his heart.

"Let their blood redeem you, let not their death be in vain. Listen to them, Cain."

He looked to the right and down the street to where he needed to go. It was about three city blocks. He wondered if the author would still be at the bookstore. It had been about fifteen minutes since he had seen the man on the news. He wanted to run but his legs were weak. He thought of flagging a taxi and then realized he had no clothes, let alone his wallet or money. He started down the street in the best walk-jog motion he could, past the main driveway areas of the hospital and onto the city sidewalk, catching a few odd glances from pedestrians and hospital staff as he passed. The hospital's parking ramp was on his right. Cars drove by on the street to his left. Trees along the sidewalk were in their full color, showing a fresh array of springtime blossoms. Their aroma filled his lungs as he ran by. A person walking toward him stopped in his tracks and stood and stared, then went back to walking as he ran past. A lady with a small poodle tugged on its leash as the dog moved toward him, horns honked in the traffic, and he vaguely thought he heard someone curse. *Life. Real life.* He began to gain some strength as he continued down the street, now breaking into a faster jog. *I'm outta shape. Just two more blocks.*

He jogged straight through a red light, looking both ways as he came upon it and staying in the crosswalk, which seemed to feel more legal to him.

Cars lined the street along the curb to his left, parking meters guarding their stay, timers running. *Tree in opening in the sidewalk. Another tree, same thing. Sidewalk square. Little green bush. Flower planter with flowers overgrown.*

Screeeeeeeeeech! A car slammed on its brakes as Cain ran into the street at the next intersection, not paying attention to the fact that he had jogged another block, his mind wrapped up in the aesthetics. Rrrrrrrrrrrrrrrrrrr. Another car barely missed him from the right. Several cars slowed down and some came to a stop, seemingly waiting for Cain to make the next move. He looked to his left and across the street. Down the next city block a row of shop and business facades and their different architectural styles stood out to him. About two hundred feet from the intersection he saw Pellili's Bookstore. Several cars honked their horns as Cain ran diagonally across the entire intersection. People on the street and in vehicles looked at him wildly as his hospital gowns flowed along behind him.

He graced the curb on the other side of the street just as a police cruiser pulled up hard behind him, facing the opposing traffic. One of the officers yelled, "Hey" out the window. He heard the driver say, "I'll call it in, Si," as the passenger side door swung open.

Cain glanced briefly at Si and then looked back toward the bookstore, increasing his pace. *"Si? Okay, this just got more weird."* He could see people walking out of the store as he ran up the street. Cain ran as fast as he could, reaching the store as the owner turned the key in the lock. The man looked at Cain strangely as he stood there in his hospital gowns. "I need in," Cain said. The owner looked him up and down and mouthed "Yeah, sure," and turned to walk toward the back of the store where the lights were still on and some people stood. Cain pounded on the front door as he saw the reflection of the police cruiser in the glass do a U-turn behind him on the street and come to a sudden stop. He could hear Si's approaching footsteps to his left.

He pounded again harder. The store owner kept walking toward the back of the store until one of the people at the table slowly stood up and looked inquisitively toward Cain and then motioned for the bookstore owner to open the door and let him in. "He's expected. Not this soon," the man said. "I wasn't sure when, but he's expected."

Now the second police officer was out of the vehicle and approaching Cain from behind. "Sir, you need to stop pounding on that glass," the officer said.

Cain wasn't sure what to do. *Should I bolt off and run.* He thought. He saw the storeowner turn back toward him as each police officer grabbed one of his arms.

"Si, you don't understand. I have to talk to . . ." Cain was interrupted by the door opening against him, pushing him backward. Si backed off some, confused.

"We're expecting him," the owner said, wondering himself what was going on as the police officers lessened their grip on Cain and let go of him.

"Well, I don't know what's happening here, but if you need us we'll be right here making calls to the hospital."

Cain slipped through the front door. He kept in step with the man who had opened the door until he came into the lighted area at the back of the store. There, sitting by a table with several copies of the book laying on it was the author from the house, from his dream world. The author's mother stood next to him. Cain looked into her face and saw the image of the young teenage girl from the clinic. The shape of her face was the same, just older. Her eyes looked deep into his. He remembered her like it was yesterday, opening the wrong door in the clinic, her clutching her belly, panicking, and running down the hallway and out the door. It was clear from her piercing eyes that she remembered him.

He turned to look at the young man in front of him, knowing full well now, that on that day thirty-seven years earlier he would have ended his life as an unborn child. He wasn't sure what to say. He was taken aback by the oddness of the man's face. Something was different, strange, bothersome, about his look. He wore something like stockings on his arms from his elbows to his wrists.

"I'm glad you came," the woman said.

The man spoke. "You don't remember me, do you?"

"What do you mean? From the dreams?" Cain asked.

"Dreams? What dreams?" asked the author.

"My dreams. You've been in my dreams."

"Interesting." The author looked at him puzzled. "No, not from some dream. From the street. From that day on the street."

"What? I don't understand."

"From the crash," the author said.

Cain looked strongly into the face of the man sitting in front of him, then he remembered.

The bright light, the shattering glass, the fire, the heat…

Cain saw him again, reaching into the darkness, the smoke surrounding him, the flames lighting his face, the smoke hiding it again. The man tugged and pulled desperately at Cain's seat belt as the car burned around them. Flames licked at the man's hands, his face, his flesh. His rescuer screamed in pain as the upper seatbelt, now melted from being on fire, snapped and landed against his neck and cheek, the burning nylon fusing with his skin. The fire flashed as the car's gas tank fully ignited. The man looked deep into Cain's eyes, determined, shielding him from the raging flames. The remaining seatbelt broke free and the man wrapped his arms around Cain's upper body and pulled him from the burning vehicle as Cain's mind went black, dark, and he lost consciousness.

Cain looked down at the man's scarred hands and arms, the skin twisted and damaged, some still healing. His neck had scar tissue and one side of his face from his chin to his forehead.

"You know, my mother was with me that day," the author said. "We were sitting there next to you at the traffic light, just a normal day. It was drizzling rain. I wasn't paying much attention to our light turning green. I was looking at your car, admiring it. I had just glanced upon the face of the little girl that was with you. She was laughing and had the most beautiful smile. You pulled away from the light first. The other car hit you so fast and hard. I couldn't just leave you there, trapped. In all the commotion after the accident, the fire, they ushered my mother into the wrong ambulance. By the time they realized they'd made a mistake, my ambulance had already left. Your burns weren't as bad as mine. At first, my mother asked them to stop, then chose to stay with you. Do you know that after all those years she recognized you from the clinic? She knew exactly who you were. She said she could never forget your face as long as she lived. She remembered you opening the door, the bodies of the babies, that your one single mistake saved my life that day. It was then, in that moment, in that hallway, my mother realized she wanted me to live. She chose to be my protector. She'd never tell you this, but she spent the ride to the hospital praying for you."

Cain felt humbled, but he needed to know. He still needed answers. He picked up a copy of the book.

"I don't understand the final chapter. There's nothing there! There are no words! How does this end? What are you trying to do? What happens from this point on?"

"Well, that's up to you, isn't it?"

"What? That's it?"

"It's up to you. You decide. You write the story. But

remember one very important thing."

"What's that?" Cain asked.

The author piercingly looked at Cain.

"It's not only *your* story that's being written."

Cain stood, silently, for a moment, looking at the scars on the man's face and hands. He thought of the little children he had aborted, the victims from his dream world, his family, their lives, their destinies, how all had changed. He understood.

"Thank you for saving me." Cain said.

He turned to walk away, feeling ashamed.

"Cain?" The Author held out his scarred hands. "I faced the fires of hell for you that day. I paid a painful price. Don't be a stranger. You know where you can find me."

"I know."

Cain shuffled his way down the aisle of the bookstore, away from the man and his mother and toward the front door, toward life. He pushed through the door and stepped onto the sidewalk. Si looked up at him from the squad car.

Cain stared forward at his world. Traffic was backed up from the light. Across the street, a young man in his twenties pushed himself along on a skateboard, weaving in and out of large square planters, a guitar strapped across his back and long brown shoulder-length hair flowing behind him. A short distance away another man in his fifties near a wrought iron fence snipped and groomed rose bushes planted in a row just off a sidewalk surrounding a beautiful white Victorian style house. A sign hung in front of it for a law office. A man dressed in similar clothing planted a young sapling nearby. An older, sophisticated gentleman wearing a tweed coat stood at the street corner to Cain's right. A little boy ran past giggling. A woman in her thirties hurried by, an armful of college study materials battling for the same attention given to the cup of latte she balanced with her car keys in her other hand. To his left a man leaned over the hood of a car as the motor cranked over and over without firing, a tow truck nearby. A couple down the sidewalk to his right threw harsh words at each other, then paused and hugged. The smell of the bakery next door blasted through Cain's senses. An older woman stepped away from the door as it swung shut, a bag in hand. The subtle sound of a passenger jet flying overhead whirred in Cain's ears. A young family passed by, speaking a different language. A man walked near him, bumping Cain with a blueprint he had tucked under his arm. The Author's words came back to him. *It's not only your story that's being written.*

A pregnant woman slowly waddled by in front of him, pulling a pudgy little girl at her side along by her hand as the girl turned her head, seemingly looking at every sight around her and taking it all in. The woman had a look on her face that said, 'Yeah, I'm ready, any day now, it won't be long.'

Cain looked up from the woman and then leaned back against the bookstore window, thinking of Holly and Ranae. Just to the right in front of him was a sheltered bus stop. On the side facing Cain was an advertisement. Its bold words beckoned his attention.

Abortion…it kills…Little People!

Cain pondered the thought, watching more people pass by. A man in his twenties hurried by in a delivery uniform followed by a teenage boy with freckles and red hair, blowing a bubble that popped and spread across his face. Again, Cain thought of the author's words. *It's not only your story that's being written.*

A city bus rolled to a stop directly in front of him, blocked from its destination at the bus stop by cars backed up in busy afternoon traffic.

Across the entire side of the bus was a large advertisement. It had a picture of a little baby boy, his face leaning forward, his tiny lips in a cute smile, his eyes bright and shining. Above the little boy's head in large letters read the word, 'Adoption', and along the bottom of the little boy's face read, 'Somebody little needs you!'

Cain immediately pictured the little baby boy from the NICU room in his dream world, all alone, the nurses covering his brother's tiny body.

*I wonder...*Cain thought.

Kevin Patrick Smith

22

To the left side of the yard stood a rectangular shaped garden, bean poles, corn and sunflowers rising up, surrounded by a short white fence. A small gate locked in the garden. Nearby, a smaller garden grew, about fifteen feet across and flush with the year's production of crops. Two young rabbits darted out from the garden and then back into its scattered multi colored patches of lettuce, mustards and other greens.

Kenny dropped a bag of bread crumbs to run after the two dogs that had given chase to a gaggle of ducklings further along the shoreline of the one acre pond. One of them yelped and barked as it ran by again, attempting a happy wag with its short, stubby tail.

"Come on stubby!" Kenny yelled at the dog.

"Kenny, wait!" little Ranae said as she ran after, struggling to catch up with him.

Under the shade of a small grove of pine trees planted fifty years earlier, Ray sat on a wooden bench overlooking the pond.

His eyes wandered across the acreage he grew up on, his arm resting across the back of the bench and fingers dangling down, touching the inscription on the metal plate dedicating the bench and grove to his mother.

Bright colors splashed themselves amongst the branches of a small, well groomed orchard of fruit trees. The fresh, clean white paint of the greenhouse reflected the bright summer's sun. Atop the greenhouse pinnacle the figure of a large hawk, dark against the midday sun, perched. Beyond the greenhouse, just past a small split wood fence line, little rolling hills partially concealed a small dirt path that cut its way through the tall grass to the trees by the river.

Down the trail and around a little hill at the bottom, a ravine dropped off toward the water's edge. The ancient tree stood in grandeur, its branches spread across the trail, the water, and the surrounding ground.

Branches of the old oak dispersed bright summer sunlight across the earth below it. A little boy reached backward, exerting all of his strength upon an old fishing pole and tracing a long arch through the afternoon air. The hook and sinker fell short of his great goal, flopping into the river's water near its bank, just a few feet from the shore."

"Dad, I can't do it. It's too far!"

Cain lifted his head from its resting place against the tree and smiled at the little boy he had grown so fond of.

"Come over here, *little guy*."

The little boy trotted over to Cain. Cain wrapped his arms around him, grabbing hold of the fishing pole along with the boy's tiny hands.

"Hey now," Cain said. "There's nothing . . . that's ever . . . too far."

The Final Chapter . . .

This book is dedicated to anybody who has ever felt they've gone too far.

No transgression, however great, can ever keep us from God's love.

"I will give you a heart of flesh for a heart of stone"

- God –

GUILTY

God **U**ltimately **I**ntends **L**ove **T**oward **Y**ou

THE AUTHOR

Kevin and his wife Karen and their six children live in Des Moines, Iowa.

To learn more about the author and upcoming works, visit his websites. For interesting facts about hidden meanings in the book, visit the website and . . .

Follow the Blood Drops

www.whenblooddropsfall.com

Watch for his next book, and meet some of the characters at the website.

In the Crosshairs of Hope

www.kevinpatricksmith.com

In the Crosshairs of Hope

If the bugs weren't there, it wouldn't have been so bad. The itching, her incessant scratching and digging at the bites exasperated the sores. The dirt, sweat, stung, causing infection. Her little hands were red, the left from irritation, the right from when mommy smashed two of her fingers in the screen door as she'd slammed it in anger.

The five-year-old was oddly comforted now by the silence as she played in the dirt just outside the back door. The itchiness of her sores and snot running from her nose negated the numbing feeling in her body from Danyelle nearly pulling out half her hair and shaking her around like a rag doll by her shirt.

Back to playing, she'd already forgotten the screaming, the spittle, the wide angry eyes. Things she never understood. At five years old you don't know why. Strong hands crunching your cheeks and mouth together, clutching your chest, tugging at your shirt, lifting you halfway off the ground.

Mommy was angry. But Terra Lynn didn't know what angry was, what it really meant. It was Danyelle's typical primal reaction. And this was a little girl's base survival response. She just didn't know it. For Terra Lynn, it was normal, her place, her existence.

Kevin Patrick Smith

www.ingramcontent.com/pod-product-compliance
Lightning Source LLC
Chambersburg PA
CBHW050921250626
47155CB00001B/323